A MILLION-DOLLAR VIEW

VIEW

HOWARD C. SANFORD

Cover design by Old Man Publishing, inspired by the art of Tyler Hays with images by Manuel-H and GDJ via Pixabay.

ISBN 979-8-9997241-0-6 Paperback

ISBN 979-8-9997241-1-3 eBook

For my mother, Frances Sanford,
and my mother-in-law, Jan Haselhuhn,
who told me I should write.

June 2019

I hadn't tasted dust for months. The winter snow had given way to relentless spring rain. Flooding had been awful in most parts of Nebraska and deadly in a few places. But here on my wife's family farm, we were all safe and sound. I didn't recognize the fancy SUV coming down the driveway, pulling a cloud of dust behind it. I know most of the cars in the area, and a Cadillac Escalade was somewhat out of place here in farm country. Then again, I'm a little out of place here, too. Now that the driveway had finally dried out, I wondered what it would cost to blacktop it.

"Hey, Sue. I think the Williams family is here," I shouted through our screen door. "Send out the bellhops."

A moment later, five kids came tumbling out the front door along with a big, friendly dog who ran up to the car barking and wagging his tail. As the family got out of the vehicle, I shouted, "Slobber! Slobber, don't eat those children."

A tall, slender man got out of the driver's seat. A well-dressed woman got out of the passenger side, and three girls streamed from the back. The oldest of the three girls, who was probably about thirteen, laughed as the dog ran in circles, stopped, leaned back, put his head down on his front paws with his rump in the air, and then sprang forward frenetically. The youngest girl was none too sure about this big mutt and stayed close to her mother.

"You must be Mr. Williams," I said.

"You call your dog 'Slobber'?" he asked.

"Yeah. The kids named him, but the name really does fit. My name's Bob." I stuck out my hand, and we shook. I looked over at the woman holding the girl. "You must be the missus."

"I'm Mrs. Williams, yes," she said stiffly. In the hospitality business, you get so you can read people fairly quickly. I'd made a mistake trying to be informal with her; my attempt at country charm doesn't always hit the mark. Trying to recover, I asked, "And who do we have here?"

The thirteen-year-old put out her hand and said, "I'm Sasha." I shook her hand. She had a good grip for a kid.

"Well, it's a pleasure to meet you. I'm Bob." I got down on one knee and looked at the youngest girl, who was doing her best to hide behind her mother. "And what's your name?" I asked in my gentlest voice. She buried her face in Mrs. Williams' pants leg.

"That's Alisha. She's a little shy," replied Mr. Williams.

"That's all right," I said. "We've got a whole week to get to know each other."

"And this is Leah," he nodded toward the middle child.

"Nice to meet you, Leah."

I turned to my kids. "Help the Williams' with their bags. They'll be in cabin one." Turning back to Mr. Williams, I said, "You don't have to tip them. They're slave labor." This was not my day. I'd just used the word *slave* while talking to a Black man about a group of children of various races.

I'm sure Mr. Williams saw the pained look on my face. "Your kids?" he asked, letting me off the hook.

"Our foster kids, yes, sir."

"Well, this looks like a fine place to raise them."

"Thank you. This really is a special place. I'm sure your family will enjoy being here."

"I'm sure we will." He turned toward the kids. "Let me get that." He took a couple of quick steps back over to the car and put his hand on a large case before any of the kids could touch it. "This is my telescope. It's quite sensitive."

"You're sensitive," teased Sasha.

"Your father doesn't want just anyone touching it," stated Mrs. Williams.

I wasn't sure if that was an insult or if it had just come out wrong, but I wasn't off to the best start myself. "Why don't you folks get settled in and then come into the house. I'm sure everyone could use a snack and something cool to drink after your long trip."

We got all their stuff from their car to the cabin. I showed them around inside, not that there was a lot to see. Our cabins are pretty basic: a queen-sized bed, a couch that folds out into another bed, a set of bunk beds, a small table, a desk, a small closet, and a large bathroom—at least, compared to the rest of the cabin. I built all four of our cabins myself, although I had professional help with the plumbing and electrical. "I get the top bunk," shouted Leah as she looked around the room.

On the way to our farmhouse, I noticed Sasha and my boy Charlie talking. "Bob and Jake and I are working on a tree house," said Charlie.

"Awesome. When can I see it?" responded Sasha.

Charlie loved talking about the place, and Sasha seemed ready to see and do everything. As we entered the house, my wife Sue greeted our guests with a warm hello and the smell of fresh-baked cookies.

"Come on into the kitchen," I said. "It's the best part of the house." I really meant it. The kitchen was huge, with a massive oak table some sixteen feet long. Sue's grandfather had made it from an enormous oak tree that had been hit by lightning. In fact, he had built most of this house himself, adding on to it over the years.

The kids all got cookies and a glass of milk. Mr. Williams and I skipped the cookies and had lemonade. "Would you care to do some porch sitting?" I asked.

"What else would a man do on a beautiful day while drinking lemonade?" he replied amiably.

We all walked out onto the porch, which ran the length of the front of the house, and plopped down on a rocker, swing, or wicker chair. "Can I show Sasha how Slobber can play Frisbee?" asked Charlie.

"It's OK with me if it's OK with her parents," I answered.

Without waiting for permission, Sasha went tearing off the porch. "Go ahead," said Mr. Williams after her. Charlie and the other kids followed, calling Slobber. They picked up a chewed-up Frisbee in the yard and tossed it. Slobber caught it, brought it back, gnawing on it all the while.

"Sasha, don't you touch that," shouted her mother. She turned to Sue. "That must be covered with germs."

"Now, Peg. The kids are having fun," said Mr. Williams.

I wasn't sure where this conversation was headed, so I was grateful when I saw the county sheriff's cruiser coming up the driveway. He stopped in the barnyard about halfway between our tractor shed and the front of the house and got out. I got another taste of dust in my mouth. I'd have to do something to knock the dust down or at least keep it under control. The kids shouted, "Hi, Uncle Marcus."

"Hi, kids. Bob, Sue, how are you?"

"Doing good. How about yourself?" I answered. "What brings you out this way?"

"Haven't been here in a couple weeks. Had to take care of something and found myself only a few miles away and knew I could get a cold drink here."

Sue was already up out of her chair, across the porch, and hugging the sheriff. "Well, you remember where we keep the lemonade, don't you?" Sue said, taking his arm and leading him into the house.

The Williamses exchanged a look. Perhaps they were startled that Sue was capable of speech. She didn't say much generally, except to me, Marcus, and the kids. "That's her brother," I explained.

"But he's—" Mrs. Williams stopped herself before she finished saying what was obvious: The sheriff is Black, and my wife and I are White.

Marcus saved us from another awkward moment when he walked back out and introduced himself to the Williamses. He sat down on a porch swing next to Sue. "I'm Marcus. Where're you folks from?"

"Lincoln," answered Mr. Williams. "This is my wife Peg, and I'm Henry."

"Glad to meet you. What brings you to our part of the world?"

"The night sky," said Mr. Williams.

"So that's why you've got a tele—" I started to say.

"Some men take their families on vacation to Paris. My husband brings me to the middle of nowhere, Nebraska." Mrs. Williams cut in. "Don't you get enough stargazing at work?"

"Now, Peg."

"Where do you work?" Marcus asked quickly.

"I teach astronomy at the university," answered Mr. Williams.

"I thought that they had a big ole telescope there," I said.

"Oh, they do, but there's nothing like a clear night in the country with your own telescope, showing the kids the night sky, and then zeroing in on the moon or even a planet. You can get a great view of the sky with the naked eye out here because there isn't much light pollution."

"That sounds great," I said.

"It does," Marcus agreed.

"Maybe your kids would like to have a peek at the night sky through my telescope," said Mr. Williams.

"They would absolutely love that. Thank you," I said.

"Well, it's settled then. I'll set up the telescope before it gets dark. With luck, it won't be too cloudy tonight."

Alisha had left her mother's side and was exploring the corner of the porch. She was watching the other kids play with the dog. Just then, Slobber ran around the children carrying the frisbee in his mouth. The kids chased him, shouting and generally just having a great time. I noticed Alisha looking around, so I asked her, "Have you ever sung campfire songs?"

She looked down and didn't say a word, but answered by shaking her head no.

"This won't do. It just won't do at all," I said, pulling my phone out of my pocket and making a big show of it. Usually, I use our landline in the kitchen or office, but I wanted this call to be public. I went through my contacts until I found the number I was looking for and gave it a call.

I could hear the phone ring, and then my friend Billy Joe answered. In a voice loud enough so everyone on the porch could hear, I said, "This is Bob, and it's an emergency.... No, not that.... No, I've got a little girl over here who has never sung campfire songs.... Yeah, just breaks your heart, don't it? ... Well, I was hoping you and the boys would be free tonight. I figured we'd roast some wieners.... Of course, we'll have s'mores, we're not barbarians, you know.... Alright.... No, whenever you can get here will be fine.... OK, see you later. Bye." I put my phone away. "Do we have enough hot dogs?" I asked Sue.

"Why do you always wait until after to ask?" Sue got up and walked into the house.

"Who were you talking to?" asked Marcus.

"Billy Joe."

"Is he going to that chuck wagon singing competition again this year?"

"I think so. He told me it's in Colorado."

"Who is Billy Joe?" asked Mr. Williams.

"Local farmer. Him and his boy, the high school music teacher, and the local mechanic have a band."

"Wonderful. Hillbilly music," Mrs. Williams said just loud enough to be heard.

"Oh, no, ma'am. Cowboy music."

"I only listen to opera," she replied.

"Really. What kind? Grand Ole Opry?" I asked and quickly ducked into the house.

"Do I need to get some hot dogs?" I asked Sue as I walked into the kitchen.

"No. I think we have enough for tonight."

"OK, good," I said.

I slipped out the back door and went the long way around the house to the side door of our tractor shed. No one had seen me. So far, so good. We have three gas cans of various sizes; I picked each up in turn to try to judge how much gas was in each. I went with

8

the can that felt as though it had between one and two gallons in it and made a mental note to fill the cans on my next trip into town. I opened the door just enough to see the front of the house. The kids were still frolicking, and the adults were still talking. I crept out and kept low as I left the cover of the shed. Making sure to keep the cars between me and the front porch, I snuck to the sheriff's cruiser and took off the gas cap as quietly as possible. After one more quick peek at the front porch, I poured the contents of the can into the sheriff's gas tank. As I replaced the gas cap, I wondered how I could explain this if I were caught. I made it back to the shed very stealthily, I thought. James Bond couldn't have done it better himself.

June 1970

The sheriff pulled up in front of the farmhouse. "Abe, you around here?" he shouted. He walked onto the porch and pounded on the door. "Sarah, you home?" No one answered. The sheriff walked across the barnyard and into the barn, calling, "Abe."

A very large man, just over six feet tall, with huge shoulders, close to 300 pounds, going a little soft around the middle, said, "Hey, Jeff, how are you?"

"Doing good, Abe. Is Sarah home?"

"Yeah, what's up?"

"I was hoping to talk with the both of you."

"Well, now you got me good and curious," Abe said.

Sarah walked into the barn. "Saw you coming up the drive. I was doing some weeding in the garden. What brings you to our corner of the county?"

"There was a bad car wreck out on the highway."

"Oh, no," Sarah put her hand to her mouth.

"Who was it?" Abe asked.

"No one you know," answered the sheriff.

"Dammit, Jeff, you could have said that first," said Abe.

"I suppose. Anyway, I came to ask a favor. Two adults were killed in the wreck, but their little boy came out of it with just a few broken bones. He's in the hospital now."

"So, what's the favor?" asked Abe.

"Abe!" Sarah glared at her husband. Turning to the sheriff, she said, "That poor boy. I can't imagine anything worse. How can we help?"

"So far, I haven't been able to find any next of kin to notify. That boy is all alone until I do. I was thinking, maybe you two might look after him once the doc says he can leave the hospital."

"Why us, Jeff?" asked Abe.

"Because I figure, the boy could use all the kindness he can get right about now."

"We ain't the only kind people in the county, you know," Abe said.

"Abe, be still now." Sarah turned to the sheriff. "You know we'll help any way we can."

"Thank you, Sarah."

"I still want to know, why us? Don't the county have a place for the boy?"

"Yeah, but I'm worried for the kid," the sheriff said.

"Why?" asked Abe.

"Now you hush, Abe," Sarah said.

"No, now, there is something, "said Jeff. "The kid's Black. I'm afraid if I put him in county care, he'll take a beating. The folks who take care of the kids do their best, but they don't have enough staff to watch all those kids all the time, and the Peterson boys are in again." The Peterson boys were two angry teenagers. The judge had removed them from a violent home, but no one could remove the damage that had been done to them. "Those boys beat up a Mexican kid pretty bad," the sheriff continued. "I'm as sure as I can be that they'll do the same to this boy. Their father is big on keeping the county White. I figure he beat that hate right into those boys."

"How come you don't put those boys in jail?"

"Because no one saw them do it, or at least won't say anything, and the Mexican kid won't talk." The sheriff paused. He looked at Sarah and then at Abe, "So I'm asking for you to take care of him until I can find some of his family."

Abe kicked at the dirt with the toe of his boot. "What would I know about taking care of a colored kid?"

The sheriff stepped over until he was standing very close to Abe. He looked up at the big man. "We have been friends for almost forty years, since we was little kids, I was best man at your wedding, and this is the first time I have ever felt like punching you."

"And if he don't, I will," said Sarah.

"I didn't say I won't do it," muttered Abe.

"You two are the best people I know. I figured you'd be more likely than anyone else to protect the boy."

"Of course, we will," said Sarah.

"So, what's his name?" asked Abe.

"Marcus."

JUNE 2019

I kept the kids busy by having them round up firewood. We've got a nice spot north of the barnyard set up for campfires; we use it every chance we get with our guests. I set up a small circle of rocks to contain the fire. All around the fire pit are benches that Sue's grandpa made. Big old logs split to form long benches, or "tree seats," as one of our kids called them years ago. I started a small fire as Sue put hot dogs on roasting sticks for the kids to hold over the fire.

"Now you all make sure you don't get too near the fire," I said for the benefit of our guests. My kids had done this many times and knew the rules. Mr. Williams, Leah, and Sasha were having a good time heating up their dogs, but Mrs. Williams seemed uncertain about the whole thing. It wasn't until Alisha looked up at her mother and pointed at the others that she relented and allowed her daughter to join the fun.

Marcus had said he couldn't stay. As he drove away, I saw him wave to an oncoming car with Billy Joe and his son Roy. They waved back as they turned into our dusty, tree-lined drive and headed our way.

"Thanks for coming out," I said as they got out of the car.

"Any excuse to play works for me."

"What you up to, now that school's out for the summer, Roy?" I asked.

"No plans, really."

"I think I can keep him busy on the farm," said Billy Joe.

I introduced them to the Williams family, got them a couple hot dogs, and began to help the kids pull the dogs off their roasting sticks with hot dog buns. Sue opened one of the two coolers we'd carried up from the house and got out ketchup and mustard. As people started eating their hot dogs, I got out a Ziploc bag of carrots and celery sticks and a bag of chips.

"Just help yourself to whatever you want," I said. "We've got bottled water and sodas in the other cooler."

A few minutes later, another car came up the driveway.

"Hey, Tom, Tim, glad you could join us."

"I was told there were to be s'mores," Tom said in mock seriousness.

"Not until you eat your chips," I said. "A man should eat a balanced diet. Folks," I said, turning towards the Williams family, "this is Tom and Tim, but we call them T'N'T. Tom, come shake hands with Mr. Williams here, he's a professor at the university. Tom here is our high school music teacher."

"Pleasure to meet you."

"I want to know who owns that good-looking Caddie," said Tim.

"Tim is our local mechanic," I explained to Mr. Williams.

"I've never had a chance to work on a machine like that before."

"I hope no one has to work on it for some time to come," laughed Mr. Williams.

"I was serious about those s'mores," said Tom.

"Oh, alright, you big baby." I looked through the cooler and pulled out chocolate bars and a box of graham crackers. "Sue, I can't find the marshmallows."

"We probably forgot them. Charlie, run to the house and get the marshmallows, would you please?" asked Sue.

Charlie took off running for the house with Sasha right behind him. A few minutes later, they were back with the bag. S'mores were made and happily consumed, and while I built up the fire, the T'N'T cowboy band got their instruments out of their cars. Billy Joe tuned up his guitar while Tim thumped on his standup bass. Roy applied rosin to his bow, and Tom pulled his accordion from a case bearing the bumper sticker, "Play the accordion, go to jail. It's the law."

While tuning his guitar, Billy Joe looked at the children and said, "Do you know why the French eat snails?" He waited a second and then said, "Because they don't like fast food."

The other members of the band pretended to dislike the joke, but Billy Joe continued, "Do you know what you use to fix a broken jack-o'-lantern? A pumpkin patch."

The band groaned, and then Mr. Williams spoke up. "I'm reading a book about anti-gravity. It's impossible to put down."

"Dad," Sasha sighed.

"Oh, so it's a dad joke throwdown, is it?" said Billy Joe.

Mr. Williams held up his hands, "No, that's the only one I know."

"The sheriff came to my house the other day and said, 'Your dog has been chasing a kid on a bicycle.' I said, Don't be silly. My dog doesn't even have a bicycle," Billy Joe said.

"Dad," sighed Roy.

"One more, one more," said Billy Joe. "I've got a dog with no nose."

The other three members of the band dutifully asked in unison, "How does he smell?"

"Awful."

"Can we play now?" Tom said, pretending to be mad, and the band broke into the song "Back in the Saddle Again." Then they worked their way through some more classic cowboy songs: "Cool Water," "Cattle Call," "Home on the Range," and several others. As it began to turn to dusk, they launched into "Tumbling Tumbleweeds." Alisha yawned and snuggled into her mother's lap. Billy Joe saw this and pointed to the sleepy girl. He held a finger to his lips in the universal signal to request quiet. Our band stopped playing their instruments but kept singing the last verse and chorus in very soft tones and wonderful harmony. "I know when night has gone, that a new world's born at dawn. I'll keep rolling along. Deep in my heart is a song. Here on the range I belong. Drifting along with the tumbling tumbleweeds." When the song was over, Alisha was asleep. Without another word, the T'N'T cowboy band waved their goodbye and headed for their cars. As we sat quietly in the firelight, I thought I noticed a softness come to the expression on Mrs. Williams' face.

July 1970

"Abe, I'm going into town. Can you watch Marcus until I get back?"

"Well, sure, uh, I can, but Sarah, that boy's afraid of me. Can't you take him with you?"

"No. I've got a week's worth of shopping to do, I've got to stop by the bank, and drop off some old clothes at church." Sarah walked into the next room, turned to Marcus, and said, "I have to go into town to run some errands. When I get back, I'll make the special hamburgers we talked about."

"I might not be here. Mr. Westerville might eat me," squeaked Marcus.

"He'll do nothing of the kind. Mr. Westerville enjoys having you here, don't you, Abe?"

Abe had followed Sarah into the room, picked up the newspaper, and sat in his favorite chair. "Sure do," he said from behind the paper.

"You boys behave. I'll be back after a while. Bye." She walked out to the car, got in, and drove away.

Marcus was standing at the window and watched her go. Abe folded his paper down and said in his deep voice, "Is she gone?"

Without turning around Marcus said, in a very small voice, "Uh-huh."

"Good! Let's get some cookies."

Marcus turned as Abe walked past him into the kitchen. Tentatively, he followed into the kitchen. This room made him nervous. It didn't fit the rest of the house. While most of the rooms were on the small side, the kitchen was huge. And the table was the biggest piece of furniture he'd ever seen.

Abe got out two glasses and filled them with milk. Then he brought down the cookie jar. "Oh, boy, chocolate chip. My favorite. What kind do you like?"

"All kinds."

"I guess I do, too, come to think of it. I don't get them very often, though. Mrs. Westerville won't let me have them. She beats me, you know."

"She does not either."

Four hours later, when Sarah returned, she found Abe and Marcus in the barn. Abe was shoveling out a stall into the manure spreader. Marcus was sitting on a rail eating an apple.

"Abe, it's too dusty for Marcus to be out here."

"How do you expect me to get all my work done without my right-hand man?"

"I'm helping," Marcus beamed.

JUNE 2019

"It got late on us last night," I said. "I'm sorry I didn't get a chance to show you around the place, but it looks like everyone found their way to breakfast." The smell of bacon filled the large kitchen. The table had plates of eggs, sausages, pancakes, and bacon, and everyone dug in. Our little girl Katie had cereal as she didn't like the other offerings.

"I'm sorry, too," said Mr. Williams. "I meant to get out my telescope and show the kids the night sky."

"Not to worry, we'll have plenty of time tonight," I said.

"Would you by any chance have a night light? Alisha woke up early and got a little bit scared being in an unfamiliar place."

"I think we can fix you up with something even better. How about a country night light?"

"What's that?"

"We'll get the kids to catch some lightning bugs tonight and put them in a Mason jar. We'll put a few drops of water in the bottom of the jar along with a big twig, some dirt and grass, poke a few air holes in the lid, and presto: a natural night light. I have to work tonight, but Sue will get you fixed up," I said.

"Sounds interesting."

I turned to Sue, "What time is the birthday party today?"

"They'll get here about eleven," said Sue.

"Whose birthday is it?" asked Sasha. She had appeared tired when she came into the kitchen for breakfast, but talk of a party perked her right up.

"A boy in town. We let people hold parties of all kinds out here. Weddings, class reunions, all kinds of stuff. We'll have twelve children and probably four of the parents out here today."

"I wondered how you made any money," said Mrs. Williams. "I mean, you're rather isolated out here."

"You're right. Tell you what, when you finish breakfast, I'll hook the wagon to the tractor and show you all around the property." That statement met with great excitement from the children until I added, "Jake and Charlie have to stay and help clean up."

"Oh, man."

"No way."

"It's your turn. You know how we do here." Jake was still mad, but Charlie cast a quick, disappointed glance at Sasha. It wasn't until that moment that I realized I was reentering the minefield of being the parent of a boy who was beginning to be interested in girls.

I hitched the wagon up to the tractor and helped everyone on board, except for Sue and her KP crew. I drove south of the house and around our little orchard. I'd planted a few dozen apple and pear trees years ago. They were maturing nicely and bearing fruit for us nearly every year. I swung back around the other side of the house, past our garden, and heard our kids telling the Williamses what they had helped plant, their favorite veggies, and how hard they'd worked. I couldn't hear all the conversation over the noise of the tractor, but I figured they were doing well enough that I wouldn't add any commentary of my own, even though I wanted to tell them about planting two rows of corn each week, so we'd have a fresh supply all summer long. I wondered what it would cost to build a greenhouse. Fresh veggies all winter would be quite a treat. I drove past the chicken coop and its fenced-in run and then headed northwest out of the barnyard. Sue's family farm was only 80 acres now. Her grandfather had started with a couple cows, some pigs, chickens, and 200 acres to plant. Once his son, Sue's father, was old enough to help, grandpa expanded it into a fair-sized dairy operation and more than doubled the acreage.

I drove around the big pond, now full to overflowing, thanks to the spring rains. Its surface area covered more than four acres. The kids talked of the year-round fun of fishing, swimming, and ice skating. Past the pond, beyond the next field, was a big stand of trees where we set up a place for paintball battles. I had thought that would be a moneymaker for us, but after building the structures and not having regularly scheduled competitions, we probably won't come out ahead on that deal. It was sort of like my bright idea to build a mini golf course. I won't go into how badly that turned out.

I turned the tractor back towards the barn. I drove past two acres planted with Christmas trees. I planted about a hundred trees two years ago and then a hundred more last year. I'm hoping they'll be big enough that we can actually start selling some by next Christmas. I haven't planted any more this year because cash has been a little tight and the foot-tall starts I buy from the nursery aren't cheap. Time will tell if this makes us money or is just another one of my follies.

I kept driving, continuing the big tour, and my kids pointed out where we planted our pumpkins. We have over six acres planted with pumpkins, because this is our cash crop. We make almost a third of our farm money for the year in October. The paintball area becomes our haunted village, and of course, everything else we do to make money the rest of the year—selling eggs, apples, pears, and pies along with games—we drag out to make what we can while the weather holds.

I stopped the tractor by the barn. "Do you want to see where the birthday party will be?" I asked. When they answered yes, I showed them into another of our small buildings—I'd also built this one myself—and dragged out the bounce house. I plugged in and turned on the small motor, and the bounce house began filling with air. "You can look around inside if you want to."

Inside the small building wasn't all that interesting, but it was where our kids came to play. On one wall was a "Pin the Tail on the Donkey" poster. On another were shelves covered with board games, toys, and art supplies. There was a table in the middle of the room, and two card tables folded up behind the door, and that was about it. If the weather was good, we'd have a wiener roast; if not, sandwiches inside. The parents supplied the cake.

A cat went tearing out from under the little building, around the corner, and was gone. "Looks like we startled Mr. Claws," I said.

"I like kitty cats," said Leah.

"You probably won't see much of this one. But if you do it'd be best if you didn't try to pet him."

"Dangerous?" asked Mr. Williams.

"Just not very social. He showed up here last November. Don't know where he came from. Jake bought a flea collar with his own money for that cat. The boy is tender- hearted and loves animals. When he tried to put it on Mr. Claws, the poor kid got all scratched up for his trouble."

"I assume Jake named him," said Mr. Williams.

"Yeah, when I first heard the name, I thought it was Mr. Claus, as in Santa. That, and it was just before Christmas. Not that you can tell now, but Mr. Claws is a white cat under all that dirt. It wasn't until Sue told me about patching Jake up that I understood."

"Do you think the kids will be safe around him?" asked Mr. Williams.

"Like I said, they probably won't see him again. He only hurt Jake when he tried to put the flea collar on. I did think about getting rid of Mr. Claws, but it turns out that he's a pretty good mouser. And there haven't been any more incidents since the first week he was here."

Sasha walked over to her father and me. "The little house is cute, and the bounce house is cool, but why do people come all the way out here for that?"

"Sasha. Have a look in the barn," I said, pointing at the big structure across the way.

Sasha walked around the tractor, opened the barn door, looked into the barn, and excitedly shouted, "They've got ponies!"

JULY 1970

A be had come into the house after finishing the morning milking. Sarah had breakfast ready. He sat down and sipped some coffee.

"You remember I went into town yesterday?"

"That long ago? How could I remember? Of course, I remember. What do you think, I'm senile?"

"I actually went over to Lowe," Sarah said.

"Why'd you go all the way to the county seat? I thought you were going to the bank in Crossroads."

"I went to see the doctor."

"You all right?" Abe asked, trying not to sound worried.

"I'm pregnant."

"You...wait, what?"

"That was pretty close to what I said."

"I thought we couldn't."

"I guess we can. We just had to practice for nearly two decades to get it right."

"What did the doctor say?"

"He said that sometimes it just works out like this."

"What did you say?"

"I didn't really know what to say. I told him I was too old, and then I just laughed," said Sarah.

JUNE 2019

"Did you boys finish helping Sue?" I asked as Charlie and Jake came running toward us.

"She sent us to help you set up for the party," said Charlie.

"Well then, saddle up the ponies."

I thought Charlie might burst with pride. He'd get to show off for Sasha. We walked into the barn, and I pointed to the two smallest ponies, "Let's use Trinket and Speck," I said.

Charlie pulled the saddle down from the rail and put it on Trinket's back. I turned to Jake, "Do you remember how to do it?" He nodded and wrestled the saddle up onto Speck's back. "Good job," I said. The saddle must be pretty heavy for an 11-year-old, but he seemed to manage. "Now remember, cinch it up tight. These ponies are smart, and they'll take a breath while you're pulling the strap. Then the saddle ends up loose. That's right, pull it tight. No, Charlie, we won't use the reins today, so you don't have to put the bit in their mouths. The kids are first graders, so I don't want them riding on their own. Just put the lead ropes around their necks. You and Jake are going to have to lead the ponies around. Now remember, the safety of these kids is your responsibility."

Each boy led a pony out of the barn and tied their lead rope to the hitching post. Charlie had helped me with the ponies for a couple of years now, but Jake had only done it a few times.

Two cars came down the driveway and parked in the barnyard. As the children piled out, Slobber came running up to greet them. "Slobber. Slobber," I shouted, "don't eat those children."

Melissa Grafton walked over to me, "Hi, Bob."

"Hello, Melissa. Where's the birthday boy?"

"He's the one in the red party hat. First thing Evan did this morning was put it on. I couldn't get him to wait for the party."

"Well, good heavens, how could a person wait until eleven in the morning on his birthday? Some things you just don't wait for."

Two more vehicles came down the drive into the barnyard.

"Is this everyone?" I asked.

Melissa did a quick head count. "Looks like it. Six kindergarten graduates and six extra brothers and sisters."

I was glad to see none of the extra kids were much older or bigger, so I wouldn't have to saddle one of the larger ponies. "Melissa, would it be okay if we did the pony ride first? I've got to leave in about an hour, and I want to supervise while the kids are with the animals." She was good with that, so I called out to the group, "Who's ready for a pony ride?" All the little hands shot into the air. Their teacher had taught them well. "Let's start with the birthday boy. Charlie, bring Trinket over here." I picked up Evan, red hat and all, and set him on Trinket. "Give him the grand tour, Charlie, and..."

"I know, I know, his safety comes first."

Melissa smiled as Charlie led Trinket on a slow walk around the barnyard.

"Who wants to go next?" I asked the group. Again, all the hands shot up. "Jake, bring Speck on over." I lifted another kid up onto the pony. "Now follow Charlie. Just a slow walk, remember it's all about safety." I turned back to the group as Jake led the pony away. "While you're waiting your turn, you can jump into the bounce house." The kids stampeded for the bounce house. "Take off your shoes," I shouted after them.

Melissa was holding the hand of a little boy. "Who are you?" I asked him.

"I'm this many," he said holding up three fingers.

"That's an odd name," I told him.

"This is Ben. He's three," said Melissa.

After all the kids had a ride on the ponies, I had Charlie and Jake put them back into the barn. I walked down to the house to check in with Sue. "How are the lunches coming?"

"PB&J for everyone," she said. "I'm glad Melissa decided against a wiener roast."

"Me, too. The idea of watching that many five-year-olds around a fire is more excitement than I care to have. Do you need anything before I go to work?"

"No. All good."

I ran upstairs, took a quick shower, and pulled on my khaki pants and polo shirt with the hotel chain logo on it. Usually, I worked a couple of overnights a week, but one of the afternoon people had called in sick, so I had a chance to pick up an extra shift. I kissed Sue goodbye, waved to the birthday party, got in my car, and started on the 30-minute trip to the hotel on the interstate.

July 1970

"I'm going to have a baby. That means you're going to be a big brother, and I'm going to need your help," Sarah told Marcus. "Today's job is to put away the grocery bags." She showed Marcus how to fold the paper bags and put them into another bag. "Now you try."

Marcus carefully folded the bag and ran his hands over the top to smooth it.

"Good. Very well done. Now you finish folding while I put the groceries away."

When Marcus finished with the bags, he said, "I should help Mr. Westerville with the firewood."

Sarah looked out the window and saw Abe walking across the barnyard. "Yes, you should," she said, trying to hide her growing grin behind her hand. Marcus ran toward the door. "Walk," she called after him.

June 2019

As I walked into the lobby, just before two, I was greeted by the manager. "Thanks for coming in, Bob."

"Not a problem Gene," We'd both majored in hotel management: he'd just graduated a couple of years ago; I'd graduated 30 years ago. He was a good kid, and this was his first time as a full-fledged manager, not just as an assistant. Whenever he had a problem, he knew he could count on me to help out. He didn't lord it over me about being my boss, and I showed him respect by never contradicting him in front of other employees. If I disagreed with him about something or thought he was making a mistake, I'd talk with him privately. To his credit, he always heard me out and then made the decision he thought was best for the business. In short, we worked well together. Most importantly, I picked up some extra cash.

"I've got to go deal with a supplier. We're booked for tonight, so you'll probably be busy all afternoon at the front desk. If you get a chance, we've still got some towels and sheets in the laundry. I'll be back to help as soon as I can. In any event, Shelly will be in at eleven."

"Anyone left to check out today?"

"No. Checkouts are gone. See you later," he said as he headed for the door.

I went into the laundry room and started a couple of loads. I carried the hotel phone with me as I checked the pool area. No one was there, but there were some wet towels and some empty pop cans on the ground. I gave the area a quick clean and went back inside. The early afternoon was a good time to get little jobs done before people started checking in.

I was surprised when Pastor Martin and Bill Kent walked into the lobby. "Well, hi guys. What brings you to our happy establishment?"

"We called your place, and Sue told us you were here. I hope you don't mind us coming by," said Bill.

"Not at all. The boss is gone so, I've got all the time in the world. What can I do for you?"

"The Pastor here reminded me you had a fundraiser for the church last year out at your place."

"I did. Was glad to help. So, what's up?"

"It's my brother." Bill started to say more, but his voice trailed off.

"His brother's farm has been flooded out. The family's in a difficult financial spot. They've lost everything."

"There's been so much flooding this year. We've been lucky, just one small part of a field underwater," I said.

"Bill came to me for advice, and I thought of the fundraiser we had at your farm last year. I was surprised how much we raised for the church annex building fund. Anyway, I was wondering if you would consider offering your farm as a location for a get-together. I thought some of the ladies from church could have a bake sale, and we could set up games for the children. You could do as little or as much as you want. Anything would help," finished the Pastor.

"I'd be proud to help. What's your brother's name, Bill?"

"Vic."

"Vic Kent. I don't think I know him. Where's he live?" I asked.

"Over by Spencer," Bill answered.

"Oh, no," I said. "Near the dam. No wonder." The ice jams on the rivers were bad enough, but when the Spencer dam failed, entire towns were washed away. "Is everyone in Vic's family OK?"

"Yeah, no one hurt."

"I guess that's the thing to focus on. Sit down, and I'll be right back." They went into the area just off the lobby where we served breakfast. I walked to the front desk and pulled a few blank sheets of paper from the printer. I came back over and sat down at the table. "First, we need a date. When do you want to do this?"

"As soon as we can, I guess," said Bill.

I laid the hotel phone on the table, then took my phone out of my pocket and called Sue. She looked at our calendar and told me that the Williams family would be here through the weekend, leaving early next week, and the Stevens family was due tomorrow. Those were the only bookings we had until the following weekend. "How about Thursday night? That'll give us two days to put things together, but still avoid the weekend when people have things going on."

"That's pretty quick," said Pastor Martin.

"That brings focus and urgency," I said. "How about we start at eleven a.m. and go late. People with kids can drop in at any point in the day. We can sell them food, pony rides, hayrack rides, and whatever else we can think of, with all the proceeds going to Vic and his family."

Over the next 40 minutes or so, we came up with more ideas. The Pastor said he'd spread the word through church email and, for those without internet connections, the good old phone tree. When I suggested he call around to the other churches in the area, he was quiet for a moment. He didn't object, but I could tell he was uncomfortable with the idea. Most of the congregations in the area got along fine, but there were a few of the smaller churches that were really out there: the snake handlers come to mind. I laughed and told him to consider my place as Switzerland; everyone could come without it feeling like it was someone else's home turf.

A family walked into the lobby, and I excused myself to take care of them. After I got them checked in, another man walked into the lobby. He didn't have a reservation. I told him we were full for the night and asked which direction he was going. He told me he was headed toward Denver, so I made a couple of calls to interstate motels to our west. I found him a room about 25 miles away at the next exit. He thanked me and left. When I walked back over to the table, Bill and Pastor Martin were standing.

"You're starting to get busy. We'd better let you get back to work. I just want to thank you so much," said Bill.

"You're more than welcome," I said. It made me feel good to help the guy out. The look on his face now compared to when he had come in was as different as night and day. It wasn't all that important how much money we raised. What was important was that Bill now felt like he was doing something to help his brother. Also, I knew it'd be an uphill battle. Bill had only lived in the area for 25 years; that's a newcomer by local standards. I'm keenly aware of this as I've only been here for 30. The locals still call my farm the Westerville place. My last name is Comstock.

"One last thing," said the Pastor. "How are we going to keep people around for more than an hour or so? The longer we hold them there, the more money we can get by selling things."

"We just need a main attraction for the evening so people will stick around," I said.

"What would that be?"

"I think I know where I can get a band on short notice."

AUGUST 1970

"I can't believe she would say that to me!" Sarah told Abe. "We're trying to help this poor boy, and they don't want him in church. What's wrong with people?"

"It's not everyone, Sarah."

"No, I know it. Monica is the only one who has said anything. At least, she's the only one who's said anything to my face. But you know there's more that think that way."

"You and I both know who's behind it: George Newport."

"You'd think controlling all the money in the county would be enough for him, but no. He's got to say who can and who can't go to the Methodist Church. I'm calling Reverend Jones."

"Don't do that." Abe had never seen his wife this mad. He knew he had to stop her—or at least slow her down—before she did or said something others could use against her later. He also knew that the Reverend Jones hadn't even been here two years yet. A thing like this would split the church at best, and destroy it at worst, right along with the young minister. "I'll go into town and talk to him tomorrow."

"Who, Reverend Jones or George Newport?" asked Sarah.

"Reverend Jones is who I meant. But come to think of it, I might just call Jeff."

"What good would the sheriff do? Besides, he's Catholic."

"He told me once that his job was all about handling disputes and dealing with stupid people. I think we may be dealing with both here."

"He's just a little boy who's lost his parents." Her voice trailed off, and her anger slowly turned to sorrow for Marcus. She began to cry.

Abe wrapped her up in his arms, "Let me fix this," he said.

June 2019

I didn't get home until almost midnight. I'd stayed for a few minutes talking to Shelly about the fundraiser. She said it sounded fun and she'd stop by with her boy before work on Thursday.

As I drove in past the barn, I thought I saw something moving out in the field. The car headlights only hit it for a split second as I turned. I parked the car and went to have a look. As I walked behind the barn, I saw Mr. Williams standing there, looking up at the sky. "You okay?"

"Oh, hi. I'm just soaking it in." He held his arms up.

It was a clear, cloudless night. "Mr. Williams, I want to thank you," I said as I looked at the night sky.

"For what?"

"For reminding me that I have a million-dollar view."

"That you do."

"Why don't you have your telescope out?"

"I did earlier. I put it away after the kids went to bed. Your kids enjoyed seeing the craters on the moon."

"I'm sure of it. Thanks for that."

"You know, I enjoy being a university professor, and my wife loves telling people her husband is a professor, but my favorite students are young children. They stand in awe of the cosmos. Most people, as they get older, just take it for granted, or stop looking up altogether."

"Or live in a city where the light pollution is so bad, they can no longer see the stars?"

"I couldn't have said it better myself."

"You know, professor, the night after tomorrow we're going to have a crowd of people out here. I was thinking I'd really look like a big shot if I could tell everyone that I had a university professor lined up to give a kid-friendly lecture about the stars."

I went on to tell him what I was planning, and he actually seemed excited about his part in it. I went on to say that his lodging rate covered all the food and activities, such as they were. I just wanted to make sure he didn't feel like we were shaking him down to donate to strangers, although I figured he'd probably contribute a few bucks anyway. He just seemed like that kind of guy.

"Oh, by the way, my girls love the country night light. I think they enjoyed catching the fireflies as much as looking at them in the jar in our cabin with the lights out."

"Good. That's what I'd hoped. If you remember, you might want to let the bugs go in the morning. They don't last long in the jar. If your Alisha is anything like my Katie, she might get upset by dead lightning bugs."

"You're even concerned with the well-being of fireflies. You're my kind of guy, Bob."

AUGUST 1970

"Are you sure that this is about the boy?" asked the sheriff.

"What do you mean? What else could it be about?" said Abe.

"Don't you think George Newport might just harbor some ill will towards you?"

"You mean because I dated his wife back in high school?"

"In part."

"I can't believe you'd listen to idle gossip."

"I didn't say I believed it, but you know that Newport has heard the tongues wagging, too. He's got to hate everything about the situation."

"There's no situation, Jeff. I dated Miss Hagar back in high school. She was interested in me because I was supposed to be a big deal football player. I was interested in her because she was pretty."

"And her father was the local banker," added the sheriff.

"Come on. You know better than that. Social status has never made any difference to me. Whether a person has money or not doesn't matter either. In fact, if her father had just stayed out of it, we wouldn't have dated for very long. We had nothing in common. Miss Hagar was always way too interested in her clothes and hair to suit me. But then, her father didn't approve of his little girl dating the son of a poor dirt farmer. I didn't care much for that, so I kept on seeing her. Then, when he forbid his daughter from dating me, she had a very natural teenage reaction. We snuck around together for more than a year after that. I'm sure we wouldn't have if he hadn't stuck his nose in."

"I'm glad to see that it doesn't bother you anymore." Jeff grinned at him.

Abe laughed in spite of himself. "I still get mad when I think about old man Hagar. It doesn't mean anything."

"And you still call his daughter Miss Hagar."

"That's to remind me. The help always called her that, and that's what I was: the help."

"I always thought you were more to her than that."

"We stayed friendly, but that's all there was to it."

"That's not what the rumor mill says."

"Dammit, Jeff, I don't care what the rumor mill says. She married George Newport, the rising star at her father's bank, and had his son. That's the end of it."

"I always heard Newport was her father's choice, not hers. And there is some real interesting debate about who the father is."

"There's nothing to that," Abe said as he looked away.

They stood in silence for a moment. Jeff thought it best to return to the original topic.

"Well, now, you'd better keep in mind that most of the members of your church owe money to Newport's bank," Jeff reminded Abe. "At least some will follow his lead if he doesn't want a Black kid in his church."

"I know it."

"Anyone with a business or a house in this corner of the county probably has a loan at his bank," said the sheriff.

"I know. I'm still paying the loan my dad took out to set up our dairy operation. Anyway, what do I do? Sarah's pretty upset about it all."

"She's really taken to Marcus, hasn't she?"

"Yes."

"Why do I get the feeling that you haven't?"

"Oh, he's a good enough kid, but we've got our own coming."

"Meant to ask, how big a surprise was it?"

"Well, I mean, we gave up trying almost ten years ago. I just figured it wasn't meant to be. I'll be forty-seven years old when the baby is born, and Sarah just turned forty-five."

"I guess that'll make you a geezer parent." Jeff put his hand on Abe's shoulder. "Now, my advice, don't do what you think will be easier or balance things out a little better than worse. Just do what you know is right. You don't need anyone to tell you what that is because, I suspect, you already know."

JUNE 2019

"Slobber." I looked around. Usually, our dog was the first one to greet visitors. The car had pulled up to the house, but there was no sign of him. I figured he was off playing with the kids somewhere.

"Mrs. Stevens?" I asked.

"Call me Jackie, please." She turned back to the car, opened the back door, and got her little girl out of the car seat.

"Have a good weekend, Mommy," the little girl said as she ran toward the swing set.

"I guess her plans don't include you," I joked.

"I guess not," she laughed.

"What made you come to visit us?"

"My brother's recommendation. Do you remember him? He and his family stayed with you last summer. Bob Mason?"

"How could I forget someone with a great name like Bob?

"I take it your name is Bob, too."

"It is indeed. Welcome." As I said this Sue walked out onto the front porch with Mary and Isabella, her two KP helpers of the day. Both girls were ten years old but couldn't be more different from one another. Mary enjoyed being around people, was mischievous, and was quite the chatterbox. Isabella preferred to be by herself. I pointed at the two of them, then pointed at my eyes, and then pointed at the little girl trying to get on the swing.

"On it, Bob," Mary said happily as she rushed toward the swings.

Isabella's shoulders slumped as she followed.

"They'll make sure she's safe," I said.

"Bob told me that your kids are terrific."

"Most of the time. This is my wife, Sue." I said as I stretched out my arm toward her. "Sue, this is Jackie Stevens. Her brother, Bob Mason, and his family stayed with us last year."

"Good morning," said Sue. She seemed especially talkative today.

"I'll show you to your cabin whenever you're ready."

"Oh, there's no hurry. I'm sure Abbie will want to run around for a while after our car trip," she looked over at her daughter being bracketed in the swing by Mary on one side and Isabella on the other.

"Do you want to go really high?" asked Mary.

"I think she's fine as she is, Mary," I said, shooting her a look.

"Whenever we go any distance in the car for some reason, Abbie thinks it's the weekend," said Mrs. Stevens.

"I won't tell her it's Wednesday if you don't," I said.

"My brother said his kids just had the best time last year. They talked about the pony rides and fishing in the pond, but they just kept coming back to how much they loved picking their own corn right out of the garden for dinner."

"We plant two rows of corn as early as we can and then keep planting two more rows each week for about a month or so, so we'll have a fresh supply all season. I doubt even very wealthy folks have experienced the pleasure of picking their own ear of corn off the stalk, shucking it as they walk toward the house, and then plopping it into an already boiling pot of water. When you sit down to eat, it's as fresh as it can possibly be. That said, I'm afraid it's a little early in the season yet."

"And here you went and got my hopes up," she laughed. She had a nice laugh.

"Sorry about that, but maybe we can make it up to you with some warm cookies."

"Hey, Abbie," she called to her daughter. "Do you want a warm cookie?"

Abbie hopped off the swing and came running with all the athletic grace a four-year-old can manage. Mary and Isabella fell in behind.

SEPTEMBER 1970

T he sheriff had been right. Abe and Sarah did what they thought was right, not what would have been easy. As it turned out, all they did was what they'd been doing. They kept going to church with Marcus every Sunday. Several people grumbled about it, and two families left the church and began attending the Methodist Church in Lowe. As for George Newport, he made a big show of pulling his financial support from the church. When asked, he told people he and Mrs. Hagar-Newport were attending church elsewhere with their son, George Jr. He never did say what church or where it was. He was certain he was the most important man in this part of the county, and not being able to get the congregation to do what he wanted made him angry.

George Newport had heard the gossip for years. It ate away at him. How could these stupid bumpkins think for one minute that his son wasn't his? It made for a good story, that's why. Abe had dated his wife briefly back in high school. So what? That was more than two decades ago. Abe and Sarah were happily married; he knew that. There was certainly no problem with his own marriage. But the gossip wouldn't die. Each time he walked into the store or café and the conversation stopped, he knew they were slandering his family. He hated Abe for this, even though he knew that Abe had nothing to do with it.

That was why he tried to get the congregation to keep that Black kid out. It seemed like a slam dunk. Such a simple thing: point these local idiots in the direction of their own bigotry and nurture their hate. But, apart from a few, there was no hate in them. George Newport didn't care about the kid, but it had seemed a good way to get at Abe. What he couldn't believe was that the church didn't beg him to come back. As he pointed out to the young minister, he provided almost 10% of the church's income. All the Reverend Jones would say was, "All are welcome to attend church." The young pup should have been intimidated and afraid for the future of his church. But the minister and most of the congregation would actually have let him leave. He couldn't believe they didn't ask him, no, beg him to come back. But they didn't. Eventually, the Newports returned to Crossroads Methodist Church. Everyone pretended that nothing had happened, but George Newport felt as though he had lost a lot of his influence. No matter how long it took, he knew he'd have things the way he wanted them. He would get back at Abe and Marcus, as well. After all, the kid had made him look bad.

Abe would have just as soon stayed home, but church was important to Sarah. She said it was good for Marcus, though Abe could see every little unkindness directed at the boy. He could tell that the boy knew something was wrong, but couldn't figure out what he'd done. Abe tried to reassure Marcus but wasn't very good at it. After all, he didn't understand why people would act this way toward a kid, so how could he explain it to a little boy?

Back at home, Abe asked Sarah, "Why would the Cummons family get up and move two pews farther away from us?" After her initial battle with Monica, Sarah had begun to take the actions of others in stride. Now it seemed to be Abe's turn to take offense on Marcus's behalf.

"I hope you noticed that the Johnsons and Morrows moved closer to us."

"What gets into people? These are good folks. Why do they act like this?"

Sarah started to say something, then closed her mouth. She thought for another moment and finally said, "It's easy to see the flaws in others, but much more difficult to see them in yourself. No one thinks of themselves as prejudiced."

Abe didn't realize Sarah was talking about him as much as some of the people in church. It would take Abe decades to understand that prejudice can be much more insidious in its subtle forms, often residing in otherwise decent people.

Things seemed to find a level. People didn't change so much as they adapted. Life went on as new and juicier scandals came along.

June 2019

A t breakfast on Thursday morning, I addressed the troops.

"I have no idea how many people will show up today, but we'll start setting up like we would for a big birthday party, a wedding, a fishing tournament, and Halloween all rolled into one. We're trying to raise some money to help a farm family that's been flooded out. But the important thing for us to remember is that we want everyone to have a good time. Oh, and don't be shy about letting people know we can host a party for their anniversary, graduation, or whatever. If they want to know more about what that might cost, tell them I'd be more than happy to talk with them about it." I looked at Mr. Williams, "Do you think I'm being too mercenary about this?"

"I don't think so. You're offering the use of your place to raise money for someone you've never met. If you get some benefit from this at a later date, I don't see the harm," answered Mr. Williams.

"What can I do to help?" asked Jackie Stevens brightly.

"Now, I've already roped Mr. Williams into giving a star lecture. I want to be clear; you are all guests here. You don't have to pay for anything; it's all included in your rental. That said, Sasha, I wonder if you'd be willing to lead a pony if we get busy enough to have all four going at the same time. That is if it's alright with your parents," I added quickly.

Before her parents could say anything, Sasha said, "Sure!" And then in a quieter voice, "If Charlie will show me how."

"Sure, I will," said Charlie, his face going red.

Mr. Williams and I exchanged a look, and Mrs. Williams looked as though her daughter's last statement had disquieted her, but she said nothing.

"Can I help with the ponies, too?" asked Leah.

"You may be a little young, Leah," I began, and then saw the dejection on her face. "But you could help me feed and water them later if you want to." That seemed to perk her up.

I heard Slobber barking and got to the front door before Bill Kent had a chance to knock. "Good morning, Bill. Who's in the car?"

"Karen. You remember my wife?"

I was off the porch and headed for the car, "Slobber. Slobber, don't eat that woman." I reached down and scratched behind his ears. "Karen, how are you? I haven't seen you in forever."

She got out and said, "Hi, Bob. I wasn't too sure about your dog, so I decided to risk Bill. I figured if he didn't get bit, then I'd probably be safe."

"Good thinking," I said.

"Thanks again for doing this," Bill said as he walked over to us.

"No trouble at all," I said. "Come on into the house. We were just talking about our plans for today." We walked into the kitchen, and I introduced everyone around the table. "How about a cup of coffee?"

"No thanks. Look, I'm real sorry for interrupting your breakfast. I just wanted to get here early to help you set up."

"I'm glad you did. We have lots to do before people start showing up. Sure you won't have some coffee while I finish mine?" They both declined, and I slugged mine down. "Charlie, Jake, join us outside when you finish your breakfast. Katie, Isabella, Mary, you three help Sue clean up."

We were only a few steps into the barnyard when Charlie and Jake came flying out of the house after us. "What do you want us to do, Bob?" asked Charlie.

"You boys bring two sawhorses from the barn, will you?" They were off at a run. I turned to Bill, "I wish I had half their energy."

"I know what you mean," he said.

"Karen, in that little building, we have all sorts of toys and games. Somewhere in there we've got a box with those old-time milk bottles and some wooden rings. Would you see if you can find that?"

"Sure thing, Bob."

"Bill, I've got some scrap lumber in this building over here. I think I've got a big piece of plywood we can put on top of the sawhorses." We found a thin sheet of plywood, but it seemed flimsy to me, so I dug around and pulled out some boards. "I think we'll put these on top of the sawhorses, then put the plywood on that."

"Sounds good."

The boys brought the sawhorses out of the barn. "Where do you want them?"

"Let's set them up here," I said. Bill and I put the boards and plywood on top just as Karen walked over with a dusty old box.

"I think this is it," she said.

The Williams and Stevens families came walking over. "How can we help?"

I was about to tell them again that they were guests and weren't expected to help, but I knew I was fighting a losing battle. "Girls, in that playhouse, we have paper and crayons. Could you make some signs that say free will donations?"

"I'll make sure they spell it correctly," said Mrs. Williams.

I was about to tell her that it might be more effective if the signs, drawn in crayon, were misspelled, but I thought better of it. She seemed happy to spend time with her girls. Off they went to the playhouse, Leah holding her mother's right hand and Alisha holding her left.

"Abbie, could you tell Karen and your mom how the ring toss game should be set up?"

"Yes." She dug through the box and pulled out a bottle. "Put this one in the middle, Mommy." She pulled out another bottle and handed it to Karen. "Put this one over there," she said, pointing. "No, it gots to be closer!"

"Charlie and I will go check on the ponies," said Sasha.

"And your father, Jake, and I will go too," I said. Sasha rolled her eyes, and Charlie blushed again. Mr. Williams smiled and said nothing as he briefly put his hand on my shoulder. We all walked to the barn.

When we got inside, Charlie began telling Sasha about saddling and leading a pony. Mr. Williams seemed most interested in observing, so I asked Jake, "Do you know what happened to those white, five-gallon buckets we used to have? I was thinking that instead of handling the money for rides, games, and food, we'd just put a bucket by each, and people could drop whatever money they wanted into it."

We looked around, but only found three of the old buckets. Jake pointed to my old barn boots: rubber boots that came up almost to my knees. "We could use them, you know, like the firefighters do."

"That's a good idea, Jake."

"Those are too muddy," said Katie. Apparently, she and Mary had been released from KP.

"Yeah, ah, muddy," I said. Turning back to Jake, "Let's use them, but first hose them off, will you? Buckets, too."

"That's not mud. That's pony poop," said Mary.

"Come along with me, please, girls. Is Isabella still helping Sue?"

"No. We finished," said Mary.

"Where does that girl get off to? Katie, can you go find her?" As we walked out of the barn, a car pulled into the driveway. "I wonder who this is?"

A woman got out and looked around the barnyard. When she saw me, I said, "Good morning. It's Mary Anderson, isn't it?"

"Well, you sure have a good memory. I think we met at the Bass wedding, didn't we?'

"Yeah, I think you're right. Oh, Mary, meet Mary," I turned to my foster daughter.

"I know Mrs. Anderson. Sue takes us to her store all the time."

"How are you, Mary?"

"I'm fine."

"You're just like all the other men in this part of the county, Bob, making their poor wives do all the grocery shopping. If you'd stop in to buy some eggs occasionally, I'd know you as well as I know Mary," Mrs. Anderson joked.

"Guilty as charged," I said, "But, in my defense, we have chickens."

Bill and Karen came over. Karen hugged Mary Anderson. "Thanks for coming, Mary."

"Oh, of course. Sorry, I can't stay. Pastor Martin said we were having a bake sale, so I came to drop off some pies." She opened the back door of her car. "Bob, where can I put these?"

"Mary, would you run up to the playhouse? I think we have a couple card tables behind the door. Bring those down and set them up by the house, will you?"

The girl was off like a shot. Bill said, "I'd better help her carry those," and he followed her.

"Let me help you with those pies, Mary," said Karen. Mary reached into the back seat and handed a pie to Karen, and then turned and handed one to me before pulling the last one out. We carried them to the porch as Mary and Bill approached the house, Bill carrying the card tables and Mary carrying some paper.

"I got the signs," Mary, the girl, said.

Bill put the legs down and stood the card tables up. "This a good spot?"

"That's perfect." We put the pies down on one of the tables.

Sue came out of the house, "Hi, Mary."

"Good morning, Sue. I'm sorry I can't stay, but I've got to go open the store. I'm already late."

"Good thing you don't have to worry about the manager yelling at you," joked Karen.

"That may be the only good thing about owning your own business," she laughed. She said her goodbyes, walked to her car, and waved out the window as she drove away.

Katie walked out onto the porch and announced, "I found Isabella. She's hiding in her room and said she's not coming out."

"I'll go," said Sue as she turned and disappeared into the house.

"What's next?" asked Bill.

"Let's move the cars into the field east of the driveway. If we park them next to each other, as people pull in the driveway, they'll see where to park. Hopefully, we won't need to have anyone standing out there parking cars all day."

"Mary, would you ask Mr. Williams, no wait, ask Mrs. Williams to follow us with her car?"

"But she's playing Candy Land with Leah and Alisha."

I smiled. "I'm a Chutes and Ladders man myself. Still, we wouldn't want to interrupt. Go ask Mrs. Stevens if she could move her car." Mary ran across the barnyard to where Mrs. Stevens was setting up milk bottles to Abbie's precise specifications. Mrs. Stevens waved and started over. It looked as though Mary was now Abbie's ring-toss game worker.

I got in my car. Our other vehicles were all in the tractor shed, which served as our garage. Bill hopped into his car, and Jackie Stevens climbed into hers. We drove back through the barnyard, across the driveway, and into the field. We parked next to each other, forming a little row. As we got out of our cars, I said, "Well, now, that was a perfectly executed parade." I walked into the barn. "Mr. Williams, we're parking cars in the east field."

"I guess I can spare a minute to do that." He pointed to Charlie and Sasha. I understood that I was now on guard duty.

"Just pull up next to the others, like you were parking in a lot at a big store."

Jake came into the barn. "I've got the boots and buckets washed off."

"Take them up to the house. Ask Sue for a rag and make sure the insides of the buckets are dry; that's where the money will go. Oh, and Mary has some signs to tape onto them."

Another car came down the driveway and pulled in front of the house. A woman got out, put a cake and a plate of cookies on the card table, got back into her car, and drove away.

"Who was that?" asked Mrs. Stevens.

"I'm really not sure," I answered.

"My brother was right about this place. It must be wonderful to live in a community where everyone helps each other like this."

Another car came down the driveway. "Oh, no," I said to Karen, who had walked over to us. "Is that...?"

"Yes. It's Mrs. Higgs. No wonder the last car just dropped and ran."

"Who's Mrs. Higgs?" asked Jackie Stevens.

"She's a person of strong opinions," said Karen.

"And lots of them," I added. "Mrs. Higgs thinks that charity, mercy, and forgiveness are divine qualities, so she doesn't practice them herself." I thought she would drive up to the house if she were dropping something off for the bake sale, or park by the cars we had lined up in the field, but she just seemed to sense where I was and drove right up to the barn.

"Now then, Bob, I told Pastor Martin that I would oversee the bake sale; I know you mean well, but your organizational skills do leave something to be desired. As I told the Pastor, when you held the fundraiser for the church last year, and you know how much we appreciated it..."

I knew exactly how much she appreciated it.

"... it was all just a huge, disorganized mess. We could have raised so much more money if you'd just taken a little more time and thought things through," Mrs. Higgs began as she got out of her car.

"I'm going to check on Abbie," Jackie Stevens said as she turned and fled. I would have introduced her if I thought I could have gotten the introduction in.

"I can tell just by looking that, like always, you're not ready for an eleven o'clock opening. It's a good thing I'm here to bring some order. Why don't you have those children help? I know they're from broken homes, and we shouldn't expect too much of them, but really, you could be teaching them personal responsibility and community involvement." She was building up steam.

I have never hit a woman in my life, but at that moment, all I wanted to do was drop Mrs. Higgs where she stood. Karen stepped close to Mrs. Higgs and said, "I'm so grateful you're here, Alice. Could you help me organize the bake sale table? I'm afraid I have things all over the place." Then she spun Mrs. Higgs around and pulled her toward the house, and most importantly, away from me.

In my life I've had many people help me in many ways, but no one had ever jumped on a grenade for me before. I didn't know Karen all that well, but from this moment on, I would always count her as a friend.

I figured it was time to get the porta-potties ready. I didn't like this job much, but knew that today's job would be much easier to deal with than tomorrow's cleanup. Besides, this job would be much more pleasant than my last conversation. I walked over to the west side of the barnyard, and Bill caught up with me. As he fell into step beside me, he said, "I was waiting for Mrs. Higgs to leave you alone before I came over. Sorry."

"If the roles had been reversed, I'd have done the same. Grab that tarp, would you?" My four porta-potties were covered with a heavy tarp. I undid the straps that held the tarp in place, and we pulled it off the plastic outhouses. Then we rolled it up and carried it over to the work shed.

"That's heavier than I would have thought," said Bill.

"Yeah, but the hard part will be covering them up tomorrow. I'll clean them out first, of course, and then I'll need to get step ladders out and have the boys help me get that old tarp up and over those things. That's heavy work." I got a couple rags out of the shed and wiped cobwebs out of the johns. I shouted for Jake to bring two rolls of toilet paper and some sanitizer from the house.

"Why do you cover them at all? The weather would have to be terrible to hurt those plastic things. And you could use the cable ties to hold them in place during high winds."

"You are correct, sir," I said. "But I once had a guest who told me they were unsightly. So, now, I cover them up. Well, except for days when we'll be using them, of course."

Jake came running up with two rolls of toilet paper and a gallon jug of hand sanitizer. "Sue said that this is all the sanitizer we have left."

I swirled the liquid around in the bottom of the jug. "This will have to do for now. Put the TP into those two johns," I pointed to the first and third ones.

"This one already has a roll in it," said Jake.

"They all do. I want to make sure they all have two rolls in them. The dispenser rod can hold three rolls, but that's probably too much for just today." I poured what was left in the gallon jug into the empty dispenser on the wall of the porta-potty. "I'm going to have to get more of this. It probably won't last the day."

"I'll run into town and get some more," said Bill.

I turned to tell him that there was no hurry, but he was already well on his way. A moment later, I saw why he'd left: Mrs. Higgs was upon us.

"The children say that you had them make the donation signs. Well, they simply won't do. And taped haphazardly to buckets and boots? This just looks ridiculous. If you would put forth a little effort..."

I looked around, hoping that Karen would once again come to my rescue, but she was nowhere to be seen. Not that I blamed her. She'd just spent the last several minutes with Mrs. Higgs. Karen had more than earned a break.

"Just like my sister and her husband over in Brighton. They just won't listen to me. The trouble that family has, if it's not one thing, it's another. He drinks, you see. I tried to warn my sister all those years ago, but would she listen to me? No, she would not. And now, look what's happened: their son is in trouble with the bottle. He was arrested and spent the night in jail for DUI and public intoxication. My sister wanted to bail him out, but her husband wouldn't hear of it. He said that the only way for the boy to learn was to pay by spending the night in the lockup. That boy learned, all right, learned from his father, I tell you. That man has been a terrible influence on that boy ever since he was born. It's only surprising it took this long for him to get into trouble with the law."

"Has the boy been in trouble before?" I asked.

"Nothing like this, I'm here to tell you. But I've said for years that it is only a matter of time. The apple doesn't fall far from the tree, you know. My poor sister, I just don't know what she's going to do with those two."

"It's difficult raising children," I managed to say.

"Oh, I've never had that difficulty; my children never got into trouble. Certainly not like that. My Glenn and I raised them in the faith and gave them good role models. Yes, that's probably the most important thing a parent can do. You and your wife should consider that. I know your wife was raised Methodist, not Lutheran; still that's no excuse. My children are off living their lives in different parts of the country and are very successful. Although they don't seem to get back to visit, not even during the holidays. I try to tell them that family gatherings are important, but they say the travel is hard during holiday time, especially with small children. Now, though, their children are older, you'd think they could make more of an effort to get back and visit me, especially now that Glenn is gone. Yes, I think that's the last time they were all here was for their father's funeral."

"We have wanted to visit our son, Carlos, in San Diego..." I was cut off.

"Oh, I don't mind it for myself, but I'm sure I could set an example for the grandchildren. I send them cards for their birthdays, and I get no response. I'd like to know that they got my well-wishes, at least. I just don't know how to correct this behavior. My children were brought up to acknowledge gifts, but they don't seem to think that is important in their own children. Perhaps, if

I moved closer, I could help out a little. Just being there might be enough to remind my children of the importance of good manners and letting others know that you appreciate their efforts on your behalf."

"But we'd all be so sad if you moved away," I said, not trying to hide my sarcasm. Mrs. Higgs didn't notice.

"Oh, I'm not sad for myself, mind you. My grandchildren, now that's another matter. Sometimes I think I owe it to them to move closer and help raise them. My children are so busy, you know, with important careers."

My ten-year-old, Mary, came running up to me. "Bob, come quick. We need you in the barn!"

I started running for the barn, or what I call running these days. I heard Mrs. Higgs shouting something, but couldn't tell what, and furthermore, didn't care. My mind was running through all the horrible possibilities that could happen to children in a barn. Nothing is quite as ugly as an agricultural accident. I burst into the barn and shouted, "What's happened?"

Mr. Williams, Charlie, and Sasha turned and looked at me.

"Is someone hurt?" I asked.

"We're all fine," said Mr. Williams.

"Well then, what…" I started to say.

Mary came walking up behind me. "Sue told me to save you from Mrs. Higgs," she said matter-of-factly. Then she went skipping off towards the house.

"What's going on?" asked Mr. Williams.

"I never seem to know," I answered him, and then said to Charlie, "Saddle one of the big and one of the small ponies."

"Already done," said Charlie.

"Charlie is really good with horses," said Sasha.

"He is indeed," agreed Mr. Williams.

"I'm going to go check on, uh, something, now, I guess." I was still a little confused, but at least my heart wasn't racing anymore. I walked out of the barn and toward the house. We have quite a large barnyard, so I was calm by the time I walked into our small living room. Sue was sitting on the sofa with Isabella. Karen was sitting in a chair, and Mary was standing in front of them. Sue was laughing. Karen was hysterical.

"Did you instruct this child to lie?" I asked Sue.

"No," she said, still giggling.

"Sue saw you with Mrs. Higgs and said someone needed to save you," explained Mary.

"Better than the seventh cavalry," Karen managed to say between laughs, tears rolling down her face.

"Where is Mrs. Higgs now?" I asked.

I turned to the sound of Mrs. Stevens' voice. "She's currently arguing with Abbie about the proper setup for the ring toss game. While I don't know Mrs. Higgs well, I'd still say she has just met her match for stubbornness."

SEPTEMBER 1975

Marcus and Sue walked to the school bus. He held Sue's hand as she skipped along by his side. This brought unwanted attention and taunts from some of the other boys, but nothing too bad. In fact, having Sue with him had kept him out of fights so far this school year. Not that he worried much about fights. He'd been in way more than his share ever since he started school here six years ago. The boys in his class had learned that he was not someone to be taken lightly. Marcus had taught them this lesson on many occasions. He didn't pick on kids but he had quickly learned that backing down was seen as weakness.

The first day Marcus came home with torn clothes and other signs of a fight, Abe told him that he and Sarah would talk to the principal and teacher, but he would have to take care of himself. Sarah had hugged and kissed Marcus when he got home after his first fight. Marcus had squirmed away from the mothering, feeling uncomfortable, and sought out Abe and Jeff. Abe wasn't all that helpful because he was a big man. His schoolboy fights involved taking a lot of punishment just to get in one good punch, which always ended the fight. Jeff, on the other hand, was a smaller man who had seen combat in World War II. As the sheriff, he was occasionally challenged by some young tough guy. No matter how big or strong, the young tough guy always got a ride in handcuffs in the back seat of the sheriff's car. Out here, with backup a long way off, a sheriff could never, ever lose a fight. Jeff told Marcus to avoid punching someone in the head unless he learned about boxing because a skull is very hard and can break the small bones in your hand if you hit it the wrong way. Punch the soft places instead: the stomach, sides, and lower back just under the rib cage. Use your fists, elbows, and knees. If someone gets you down on your back and gets on top of you, jab them in the throat with your thumb, and gouge at their eyes.

Abe thought this was dirty fighting, but knew that Jeff was pragmatic. In the schoolyard, as in life, you either won the fight or you lost it; either way, you still got hurt. Jeff was patient and kind, but he had no tolerance for bullies. He told Marcus that, when attacked, you make the attacker understand that he'd just made a big mistake. Abe's advice, when facing more than one bully at a time, had been to go after the biggest, mouthiest kid. Marcus took some beatings, but soon enough gave better than he got. The fights became fewer and farther between. Now that he walked his sister to the bus after school, there had been no fights this year. Until today.

In the town of Crossroads, the entire school district comprised three buildings: the grade school, the junior high, and the high school, all side by side. The school bus pick-up and drop-off area was in the parking lot beside the high school. George Newport Jr. and two of his friends were headed to George's car. They saw Marcus and Sue together and couldn't resist taunting them. They fell in on both sides of the much smaller children and began pushing Marcus. For his part, Marcus was uncertain what to do. Normally, he would tear into the biggest one, but with Sue by his side, he didn't feel he could start anything. One of the boys shoved Marcus from behind, pushing him to the ground. Another boy stood over Marcus and said, "What's the matter, Sambo, can't you walk?" Marcus decided this boy would be his target.

Marcus charged up from the ground and tackled him. The boy was several years older—and bigger and stronger—than Marcus, but he had been taken by surprise. Marcus took him to the ground, but George Jr. and the other boy pulled Marcus off and began beating him. As they knocked Marcus to the ground, they kicked him and then got down on their knees and continued to punch him.

Sue shouted, "Get off my brother." She tried to jump on George Jr.'s back, but he shoved her. He pushed her down much harder than he had intended to. Sue hit the ground hard, and it knocked the wind out of her. She lay there for a moment, caught her breath, and then screamed.

A bus driver shouted, "Hey, what's going on there?"

The three boys took off at a run for George Jr's car. Marcus was in pain, but managed to roll over and say to Sue, "Are you all right?"

Sue didn't answer for a while. She cried for a couple minutes and then sniffed. Finally, she said, "I'm OK. I'm not hurt."

Marcus struggled to his feet. He helped Sue up and brushed off her clothes. Marcus held his side as they walked to the bus. He didn't know what he would tell Abe.

When the school bus dropped them off at the end of the driveway, they started the long walk up to the house. Marcus thought it would be best not to mention the fight at all. That was usually what he did and only talked about it if Sarah or Abe noticed that he was hurt, or his clothes were torn or had blood on them.

"I'm going to see daddy," Sue said as she proceeded to the dairy barn.

"He's going to be busy milking right now. You shouldn't bother him."

"He likes to see me. He wants to know about my day at school." Sue walked to the barn with Marcus following behind her. He hoped she wouldn't mention the fight. She told her father the moment she walked into the barn.

"Three boys were mean to me and Marcus today."

"Are you alright, honey?" Abe asked Sue.

"I'm OK. I'm not hurt," she answered the way her mother had instructed her to when she fell, but wasn't in pain or cut or injured in some way. "I was very brave. I only cried a little."

Now Abe stopped what he was doing and turned to face the children. "What happened?"

Marcus told him about the fight and how Sue was pushed down. "Who was it?"

"George Jr. and a couple of his friends." Marcus held his side. He couldn't quite stand up straight without feeling a sharp pain.

"Who were the friends?"

"I don't know them."

"You're sure you're not hurt?" Abe asked Sue.

"I'm OK, Daddy."

"Marcus, take Sue into the house," Abe said as he turned back to his milking duties. Marcus couldn't see Abe's face, but the ears under his feed cap were turning a bright red. When Abe finished the milking, he walked slowly to his truck and drove into Crossroads.

There weren't a lot of after-school hangouts for kids. Abe found the boys at the café. When he walked in, Norma said, "Hi, Abe. What brings you into town this time of day?"

Abe didn't answer or acknowledge her; he moved to the table where the boys sat. "I hear that you three high school men pushed my five-year-old daughter down." The café went silent. Abe was a powerfully built man, but was known to be friendly and calm. As Abe glowered at the boys, everyone in the café knew something bad was about to happen. When a large man who is slow to anger stands and balls up his fists, you know you are about to see something serious.

"So, what if we did?" smirked George Jr. "What are you going to do, call the sheriff?"

"You don't get it, do you, kid?" said Norma, who had moved to Abe's side. "I don't think he's going to bother the sheriff."

"So, what are you going to do?" taunted George Jr.

With a quick swipe, Abe toppled the heavy wooden table onto the boy sitting to his left. The boy on his right tried to push his chair back to get away, but tumbled over backwards. Abe locked eyes with George Jr., who was just starting to stand. In the split second it took George Jr.'s eyes to go from malicious glee to fear, Abe wrapped his huge farm boy right hand around George Jr.'s neck, slamming him against the wall. Abe began to squeeze. George Jr.'s face went through all the shades of red, each in turn, and then began turning purple.

"Stop it, Abe! Let him go!" shouted Norma. She grabbed Abe's left arm and pulled. Norma was by no means a small or weak woman, but she didn't move Abe at all. She slapped him over and over. Abe turned to look at her with the expression of a man waking up from a trance. She stopped hitting him when she saw him return to his senses. "If you're going to kill him, take him outside. I don't feel like cleaning up any corpses today."

Abe lowered his hand from the boy's throat. Norma said to the three boys, "Get out and go home. You've caused enough trouble today." The two boys ran for the door while George Jr. coughed and tried to get his breath.

Abe bent over the boy and whispered, "If you ever lay hands on my daughter again, I'll kill you. Do you understand me, boy?" George Jr. understood. He stumbled toward the door.

Abe picked up the chairs and set the table back in place. He bent over and picked up the cups of soda that had spilled onto the floor. "I'm sorry, Norma. I shouldn't have done this, here."

"You shouldn't have done it at all."

"I'll pay for any damage."

"What damage? You already straightened up. I just need to get the mop for the spilled pop." She stepped into the back and returned with a mop bucket. As she cleaned up the spilled liquid Abe put his hands into his pockets and hung his head.

"I'm sorry," he said again.

"Are you alright?"

Abe nodded.

"You had better get on home, now."

As Abe walked out, an old man in a back booth said to Norma, "It's a good thing you did what you did when you did it. Abe might have killed that boy."

"You may be right," said Norma. But she hadn't done it for those boys. She didn't like the two followers very much and she actively disliked George Jr. She had done it to protect her cousin, Abe.

"What do you think our local banker is going to do?" asked the old man.

"When he finds out about this, he'll do something, that's for sure," she answered. George Newport couldn't let anything go. He would respond to the smallest slight, real or imagined. There was no way he would let this pass, Norma knew.

Later that evening, the sheriff paid a visit to the farm. Abe was waiting on the porch. As Jeff walked up, Abe stood up, turned around, and put his hands behind his back. Jeff laughed. "That won't be necessary."

"I thought George Sr. would insist," said Abe.

"Oh, he wanted you arrested, all right."

"Well, don't you get in trouble covering for me."

"I don't think I've got to worry about that. I talked to Norma and some of the other folks who were in the café. They said you'd heard that George Jr. had laid hands on Sue. Is she OK?"

"She seems to be."

"That's good. George Jr. tells an interesting story about the after-school fracas. He says that Marcus attacked him for no good reason, and his friends joined in to protect him from that crazy kid. The girl must have just been in the way and got knocked over by accident. How old is Marcus now?"

"Just turned twelve in June."

"That's what I thought. Anyway, I told George Newport that no one would believe his son's story because there were several witnesses to the whole thing."

"How many?"

"I don't know if there were any. I didn't go looking for them, but George Sr. didn't know that. I talked to him for a while and let him threaten to call the State Patrol if I didn't do my duty. After he carried on that way for a few minutes, and it seemed like he'd made all his threats, I reminded him of a couple of things.

"What?"

"That if he pressed charges against you, you'd get your day in court. And, most likely, it would come out that you'd punished

George Jr. because he and two other boys had attacked a much younger boy and an even younger and smaller girl. I went on to tell him that if there were any parents on the jury, they would acquit you. Shoot, they'd probably deliver your acquittal with balloons and a cold beer. Further, George Jr. would then have a county-wide reputation for beating up little kids. That would reflect badly on his boy, on him, and on his bank. That seemed to make him stop and think."

"Thanks, Jeff. You're a good friend."

"Don't thank me yet. I have a feeling George Sr. will think of some way to get back at you."

"I'm sure of it," said Abe, frowning.

June 2019

That afternoon at the fundraiser, we had dozens of kids, but few adults. Charlie and Jake led ponies with their riders around the grounds, while Sasha followed Charlie. I grilled hot dogs and hamburgers and sold them to raise donations. Sue, Karen, Jackie Stevens, and Peg Williams watched the kids play in and around the swing set, in the bounce house, in the playhouse, and everywhere else they went. When it looked like everyone who wanted to had eaten, I hitched the wagon to the tractor and asked if anyone wanted to go on a hayrack ride. That met with many little hands in the air. After I made a loop around the pond and back, it was time for the smaller children to go home for their afternoon naps. I waved goodbye as about a dozen kids were loaded into vehicles, crying and screaming that they didn't want to go. Mrs. Stevens carried Abbie to their cabin for a nap while Mrs. Williams did the same with her youngest, Alisha. Sue had already taken Katie for a nap about an hour before. Now, Katie was back outside looking for someone to play with. Finding most of the remaining kids were older she went to swing by herself, although Slobber kept her company.

It seemed like a mid-afternoon lull in our all-day party, so I got a couple envelopes and walked over to Charlie. "How are ride sales going?"

"I haven't really paid any attention. Some of the moms drop money in the bucket and some don't." We had used the buckets regardless of Mrs. Higgs' thoughts on the matter. She was mad about it and, of course, voiced her disapproval. Fortunately for me, after a few hours with little to do she ran out of things to comment on, got bored, and left. I took the money from the bucket and put it into an envelope.

"When you think all the pony riders are off doing something else, unsaddle Trinket and Colt and make sure they get some water. Later on, we'll saddle Speck and Randolph."

"Remember, you said I could help you feed and water the ponies," said Leah.

"Good heavens, gal, you snuck right up on me. Where'd you come from?"

"I was playing Candy Land with Mommy and Alisha, and then I had two pony rides, and then I jumped in the air house, and then I played with Slobber, and then I ate lunch in your house, and then I went on the hayrack ride, and then I had two more pony rides, and then I helped Daddy with the ring toss, and then I told Mommy I didn't want a nap because I'm bigger than Alisha and I don't need one, and now I'm ready to help with the ponies," she said all in one breath.

"Did you happen to have a cola with your lunch?"

"I had two. I was thirsty."

"I don't doubt it," I said. "Well, boys, looks like you've got plenty of help with Leah and Sasha here." I walked over to the ring toss table. Bill and Mr. Williams were talking as a girl tried to throw a wooden ring over a bottle.

"Oh, almost," Mr. Williams said. "Here, try again." Turning to me, "Step right up, sir. Three shots for a quarter. Win a free pony ride or a jump in the bounce house."

"You know if being a university professor doesn't work out, you'd make a first-rate carney."

He laughed in that friendly, easy way of his and said, "I think you've just insulted carneys everywhere."

I handed Bill the envelope of cash. "Don't worry, I know it's not much, but most people won't be here until tonight."

"This is...." his voice trailed off, then he simply said, "Thanks, Bob."

"Glad to do it. This is good for me too, you know. I want as many people as possible to know about my place. I'm hoping I'll get some bookings from today."

"I hope you do, too," said Bill.

"Have you thought about what you'll say tonight, professor?" I asked Mr. Williams to change the subject.

"I thought I'd wait and see who wanted to listen to me. If it's mostly children, I have a standard introduction to the night sky. For older teens and adults, I can offer something a bit more advanced." Bill and I exchanged a look. "Don't worry. I'm not as boring as you think," he said with a laugh.

"I'm sure of that. It's just that folks around here might not sit still for a lecture," I replied quickly.

"I'm happy to share what I know with anyone who might be interested."

A car came down the driveway, turned into the field, and parked by the other cars. I recognized Shelly from work as she got out of her car. I excused myself from Bill and Mr. Williams and walked toward her. As I got closer, I saw that her son had gotten out of the passenger side and run around to his mom. They started walking towards the barnyard. Shelly saw me and waved. I waved back, and we met by the barn.

"I thought you only came out at night," I said.

"I thought the same of you until the other day," she answered back. Most of the time the eleven-to-seven overnight shifts went to one of us, usually to Shelly five nights a week and to me twice.

"You must be Todd. Your mother brags about you all the time."

"Do you have ponies?"

"I sure do. Would you like to see them?"

"Yes," Todd said with a big smile.

"Then let's go into the barn. It's the ponies' nap time, but we'll see if they're still awake." As we walked into the barn, I asked Shelly, "How long can you stay?"

"I figured an hour or so, then I've got to take this one into town to get some new pants, then back to Mom's."

"It's nice of your mom to watch your boy while you work."

"I don't know what I'd do without her help. Five nights a week, Todd sleeps in the same bedroom I grew up in."

I thought about how hard it must be for a single parent, and then I thought about Sue. I barely saw my wife today. She had been watching the kids, cooking breakfast and lunch for the Williamses and Stevenses and had even found time to laugh at me. She is amazing.

"Hey, Charlie, saddle a pony for cowboy Todd here, will you?" I said to the tallest of the four kids standing by the stalls. It looked like Charlie and Jake had gotten the saddles off Trinket and Colt. Leah was as good as her word and was watering the ponies while Sasha stared moonily at Charlie.

"OK, cowboy Todd, do you want to ride a big horse or a little one?" asked Charlie.

"A big one," said Todd.

"Randolph it is," said Charlie as he put a blanket across the pony's back.

"So how has your mom been?" I asked Shelly.

"She's been doing pretty good. I think having Todd eat supper with her five nights a week is nice for her. She don't get so lonely now, you know, since Dad died."

"I'm sure she enjoys the time with her grandson."

Charlie had Randolph saddled and led him outside. We had a two-step ladder for the kids to stand on to reach the stirrup. I usually just lifted the kids up, but Todd climbed the ladder and then pulled himself onto the pony.

"It looks like you've done this before," I said as Charlie led the little horse and rider away.

A few hours later, things began to pick up. Several dozen cars were parked in the field. More than thirty children were running and playing. Everywhere I looked—at the swings, bounce house, ponies, and games—people were talking, laughing, and generally having a good time. A couple of the old timers were playing horseshoes. I asked them about the rules because I could never remember the scoring system. They explained the number of points for a ringer, or if the horseshoe was leaning against the post, touching the post, or close to the post. I thought I might get roped into a game, but was saved when a couple of their grandkids came over and wanted to play. The T'N'T cowboy band set up, played a couple of songs, and then decided they needed to get something to eat. I tossed some hamburgers on the grill, and they promised to play some more later (the band, not the hamburgers). Sue's brother Marcus dropped by, still wearing his uniform, but then, I couldn't remember the last time I'd seen him wearing anything else. Pastor Martin and my boss Gene showed up. Best of all, Big Mike and his wife, Lottie, honored us with their presence.

I have long thought, but have no way of knowing, that Mike and Lottie are the richest people in the county. I have also thought, and know for sure, that they are among the nicest. They own the sale barn. If you want to buy or sell livestock, that's where you go. When I first moved here, they went out of their way to make me feel welcome. Big Mike is the smartest businessman I know. Lottie is a great accountant, but she says she's just a bookkeeper. She may not be a CPA, but her knowledge of business, taxes, and especially agricultural accounting is impressive.

Big Mike's name is not ironic. He is 70 years old and must weigh in at over 300 pounds. I worry about his health, but he tells me that he's always been this size and not to bother him about it. So, I don't. Instead, I talk with him about ways to grow my business. I've lost track of how many suggestions he's made that have made or saved me money. Often they are small ideas, but sometimes the smallest ideas make the biggest impact. I once told him I was thinking of borrowing money to build a new reception hall. He told me I was nuts to borrow money for something that wouldn't generate enough cash to pay the monthly loan payment. Instead, he told me to remodel the old dairy barn. I thought he was nuts, but it turns out he was right. Over time, I knocked out a wall, put down new flooring, and did a lot of painting. It didn't happen right away, but it did happen. We paid for it out of cash flow, and it has made money for us ever since.

"When are you going to put on that guitar and play for us?" Big Mike asked Billy Joe.

"We already played, and you missed it."

"Tom told me they'll play some more, later," I explained unnecessarily. Big Mike didn't really care. He and Billy Joe just enjoyed arguing with and insulting one another.

"Are you going to keep me waiting 'til I'm old and grey?" asked Big Mike.

"Too late," said Billy Joe.

"I'm not old. I'm just now hitting my prime," said Mike.

"Big Mike is so old he doesn't buy green bananas anymore," Tom offered.

"Be careful, Tom. That could be considered elder abuse, and the sheriff is standing right over there," said Billy Joe.

"I'll bet he's off duty. I'm probably safe," said Tom.

"Don't be too sure. The law never sleeps," said Pastor Martin, joining the fray.

"You'd better listen to the pastor."

"I don't have to. Big Mike and I are Methodists," said Tom.

"Well, nobody's perfect," said the pastor.

"Yeah, I think the sheriff is here to make sure you wild Lutherans don't get out of control," added Big Mike.

"I'll try to behave myself," said Pastor Martin.

"I'm sure glad to hear that," I said.

The T'N'T cowboy band played a couple more songs and then took another break. Billy Joe said that they didn't want to peak too early. Big Mike let him have it for that, and the good-natured ribbing continued as before. Much as I enjoy listening to insults —when they're directed at others—I thought I'd better walk the grounds to see if anyone needed anything. I made a big, slow circuit of the barn yard, talking with everyone I met. We talked about whatever they felt like talking about. I was their host after all, so if they wanted to know why the band wasn't playing, we'd talk about that. If they wanted to know if it was true that I had a university professor set to lecture about the stars, we'd talk about that. If they wanted to know about Bill's brother, we'd talk about that. But as is usually the case here in farm country, we mostly just talked about the weather.

I stopped to talk to Jackie Stevens. Abbie was playing on the swings with some other little ones.

Billy Joe's wife, Jenny, saw me. "Have you seen my husband?"

"Yeah, Jenny. He's somewhere over by the ring toss game. At least, he was a few minutes ago. Oh, say hi to Mrs. Stevens, here."

"Please, call me Jackie. The name Mrs. Stevens just reminds me that there was once a Mr. Stevens." I made a mental note to call her Jackie from now on.

"What did yours' do?" asked Jenny.

"Ran off with a coworker."

"Hey, I think I see Billy Joe," I said.

"Well, that's OK. I didn't really want to talk to him anyway."

"What's he done?" Jackie Stevens asked.

"Well, he hasn't run off with a coworker, because that would be me, but I think he'd run off with his music if he could." She frowned. Turning to me, she said, "All you men marry up. You know that, right?"

"I'd argue that if I could," I said. I could tell she wanted to be mad, but I saw the beginnings of a smile as she and Jackie walked off into the crowd. Now we had Jenny and Jackie—J'N'J to compete with the T'N'T cowboy band—I thought.

John Stapleton asked if it was safe to let his little girl play on the swings while that "big ole dog" was there. I assured him that Slobber might lick a kid to death, but otherwise, he was terrific with kids and was as safe as he could be.

I made it back to the ring toss table just as Big Mike was trying his hand. His last toss settled perfectly over a milk bottle, and Big Mike let out a whoop.

"And the gentleman wins a free pony ride," said Professor Williams.

"Grandpa, you're too big. You'll kill that pony," said Big Mike's granddaughter, genuinely alarmed.

Big Mike swept the little girl up in his arms and gave her a big hug. "Well, maybe you'd better go in my place. What do you think?"

The girl seemed to agree and went skipping off toward the ponies.

"That was mighty nice of you to give up your pony ride like that," said Billy Joe.

"Don't you have some music to play?"

"Oh, yeah, we're gonna play all night."

"You can't play all night unless you actually start playing at some point."

"You'd complain if they hung you with a new rope."

"And another thing: why did you change the name of your band from Triple T to T'N'T?"

"I thought you knew. Back when the high school principal, Ted, played with us, we had Tom, Tim, and Ted: Triple T. Then Ted up and had a heart attack and died on us. My boy, Roy, was learning to play fiddle, so I roped him into playing with us. We only had the two Ts, Tom and Tim, so we became the T'N'T cowboy band."

"I think back when Ted was playing with you, the band name should have been 'Triple T and One Odd Ball.'"

"Hey, that's kind of catchy. Wish we'd've thought of that back then."

"I just saw Jenny a minute ago," I said to Billy Joe. "What did you do?"

Billy Joe looked at the ground. "I've done something terrible."

"What?"

Billy Joe looked me right in the eye. "With God as my witness, I don't know."

"I hate it when that happens," said Big Mike.

"I've been working on the stage in the old dairy barn. Do you want to see it?" I asked Billy Joe. I felt bad for bringing up any unresolved unpleasantness and thought the stage would be a welcome change of topic.

"Sure. I didn't know you'd finished it."

"I didn't say it was done. I'm not entirely sure it ever will be."

"Let's have a look," said Big Mike.

We walked between the playhouse and the pony barn. John Stapleton caught up with us and said, "You were right about the dog being safe for kids. But you didn't tell me that he might take the leg off an adult."

"What happened?" I asked.

"I left my little girl with the other kids on the swings and went to talk with some friends. When I came back there to fetch her, that dog of yours didn't want to give her up."

"Slobber get a little protective, did he?" Billy Joe laughed.

"I came walking up towards the kids on the swings, and that dog locked his eyes on me, raised his hackles, and started the most frightening growl I've ever heard. I mean way down deep in this throat. I just backed away slowly, and that seemed to satisfy him."

"Well, John, you are a pretty desperate-looking character," said Big Mike, helpfully.

"I'm sorry, John. Slobber hasn't met you before, and he doesn't let anyone he doesn't know get near his charges. I'd forgotten how serious he can get in a situation like that."

"Oh, that's all right. I'll stay twenty or thirty yards away and shout to my daughter that it's time to eat. That'll bring her running when she gets hungry and save me from being dinner for your dog."

"If that doesn't work, just track me down and I'll run interference for you while you collect your little one."

"No hurry. We'll be here a while. I'll let her swing, for now." With that, John peeled off from my two companions and me and walked back towards the fun and games. We continued past the pony barn toward the old dairy barn so I could show off my new stage.

I was going to ask Billy Joe's opinion about the stage when he was out earlier in the week, but I forgot all about it when the Williams family began to enjoy the campfire cookout and music. As we got up to the old dairy barn, I opened the door and turned on the light. Mr. Claws hissed, jumped out, then darted past us and disappeared around the building.

"Holy crap," said Big Mike. "I thought that thing would give me a heart attack."

"Sorry about that," I said.

Ignoring the cat, Billy Joe said, "You've really done a lot of work in here. This place looks great."

"This was Big Mike's idea, you know," I told Billy Joe.

"I just suggested you use this old building for your receptions. You haven't had cows on the place since Abe died, so why not remodel this old barn? It's plenty big enough inside here. You could put up tables and host a big sit-down reception, or clear out the tables and have a huge dance floor. I thought the band would just be tucked into a corner, though. Don't know why I didn't think of using the platform for a stage."

"So, we'll be up on the concrete platform?" asked Billy Joe.

"If you want to be. Take a look and see what you think."

Billy Joe went up the ramp on the left side of the stage and looked down at us. "You obviously didn't just pour this big, huge slab of concrete. Why was it here?"

"Back when Abe milked, he would open up the doors on each side of the barn, and the cows would walk in and up the ramp. Abe stood on the floor and hooked the milking machine up to the cow's udders. He said it was easier than bending over all the time or using a stool. When each cow was done, he would unhook the milker, and the cow would just walk out the other door."

"How did he get the cows to do that?"

"You're just a special kind of stupid. I thought you was a farmer?" said Big Mike.

"I am, just crops, not cows," answered Billy Joe.

"Somehow, the cows just knew to do it," I said.

"Cows are smart animals. They know they need to be milked twice a day, where to go to get milked, and what times to do it. Once you get them into a feeding routine, you don't need to herd them much. Just wait, they'll be along," explained Big Mike.

"I guess you learn a thing or two running the sale barn," I said.

"Ah, even a blind hog finds a truffle every now and then," said Billy Joe.

"I need to find something to hit you with," Big Mike said, while looking around.

"You two are in rare form tonight," I said. "How do you like the light bar?"

Billie Joe looked up and noticed the long row of colored lights I'd suspended from the ceiling with chains. I walked over to one side of the stage, opened a box, and flipped a couple switches. The lights came on, then just the blue ones, then different combinations.

"That's pretty neat. Where'd you get these?"

"At Big Mike's auction." He had an auction every month at the sale barn and sold all kinds of stuff.

"I should've guessed. Unless cows like the spotlight," was all Billy Joe had to say.

We walked back down toward the barnyard, and I excused myself from Billy Joe and Big Mike. I thought I should check in with the pony wranglers. They didn't need my help with anything. I noticed that a couple of dozen more cars were parked in the field. As I looked around, I saw that things were picking up again. I started for the grill when I noticed Bertha, the Catholic church secretary, was now running the ring toss game.

"Win big bucks, Sister," Bertha said in her brassy voice to a nun who was looking around.

"Bertha," I said. "How are you?"

"Just great. This is quite a shindig you've got going on here."

"Yeah, it seems to be going well. How'd you get roped into running the ring toss?"

"I met the professor. We got to talking, and he wanted to check with you about something. I told him to go find you and I'd hold down the fort. I don't teach at a fancy university, but I think I can manage the ring toss game. Oh, there he is. Over by the sheriff."

"Thanks, Bertha," I chuckled and walked over to where Mr. Williams and Marcus were standing.

"There are about 11,000 people in the county. At over 2500 square miles, that works out to be a little over four people per square mile," I heard Marcus say as I walked up.

"Filling Mr. Williams in on the scope of your job?" I asked Marcus.

"That's a lot of ground to cover," said Mr. Williams.

"Bertha says you were looking for me."

"Yes. What time did you want me to give my lecture?"

"I don't really have a time in mind. I think what we'll do is feed people, then gather them in the reception hall for an old-fashioned barn dance. The first time the band takes a break after dark, I'll announce that astronomy class is in session. Is that OK?"

"Sure. I can play it by ear."

"Alright. Excuse me, gentlemen, I've got to fire up the grill again and burn some hot dogs and hamburgers."

I tossed some hamburger patties and hot dogs on the grill. It was supper time for most folks, so I figured the smell of cooking meat would soon attract a crowd. Pastor Martin came over with Bill and Karen.

"It looks like quite a good turnout," said the Pastor.

"Yes," I said, "I'm pleased. I saw Father Paul earlier. The Methodists are here, but I haven't seen the Presbyterians yet."

"Ah, they're just a bunch of sore heads," joked Bill.

I was stunned. Bill wasn't the kind of guy who tried to joke around. Not that he was especially funny in the best of circumstances, but lately he'd been downright glum. I think the pastor noticed, too, and I know that Karen did because she beamed a big smile.

"You know, I have to take that back. I saw Melissa Grafton out here with her boys this afternoon. She's a Presbyterian, isn't she?"

"Oh, yeah," I said, "She was here with her boys earlier today. Her older son had a birthday party here just a couple days ago. I guess they didn't get their fill of pony riding and had to come back."

"Can we get two hot dogs and three hamburgers, please? Oh, and two of those burgers with cheese," said a man who walked up with his family.

I didn't recognize him. I gave a quick glance at my three companions, but if they knew who this guy or his family were, they weren't telling.

"Coming right up," I said. "I'm Bob, and this is my place." I had hoped he would take the hint and introduce himself, but he didn't.

"What's the damage?"

"It's a free will donation. We're raising money to help with flood expenses for Vic Kent. This here is Vic's brother, Bill." They shook hands, but the man still didn't introduce himself. "Just drop whatever you think it's worth into that bucket over by the table and grab yourself one of those little bags of chips, and an apple. Condiments are on the table, and bottled water is in the cooler. Help yourself. Here you go," I said as I put the dogs and burgers on paper plates and handed them over.

As the mystery family headed off to the table, I asked my trio, "Do you know who that was?" All three just shook their heads *no* in response.

"Maybe you should charge a set price for the food," said Pastor Martin.

"You might be right about that, but usually when people know it's for a good cause, they'll be generous. At least, more times than not, it works out that way," I said, hoping I was right.

I started doing a pretty good business and the three moved out of the way. Slowly, they moved into the crowd and when I looked back, they were out of sight. As I looked around, I saw Sue bring another variety box of chips out to the table. Mary was close behind with a bowl full of apples, and Isabella brought up the rear with another ketchup bottle. The boys had saddled another pony, and now Sasha was leading Trinket around the grounds with a very happy-looking little girl on his back. Charlie was leading Randolph, and Jake had Speck. I really hadn't counted on it getting this busy. Lots of kids were waiting in line for a ride. I really should saddle Colt and join the wranglers, but I had a grill full of meat and lots of hungry people waiting. From somewhere behind me, I caught little bits of the conversation Marcus was having with Mr. Williams.

"...about 12% in poverty."

"You sure know the county numbers," said Mr. Williams. "So, how many of us are there?"

"Blacks and Asians together make up about one-quarter of one percent of the county population as of the last census. Hispanics are about five percent. All the rest are white."

"Over 94%?"

"Yes."

"I have no right to ask you a personal question, but I don't understand why you choose to live here."

"Well, Henry, I guess the simple answer is, this is home. I've been around the world in the Navy. As a young man, I thought I might never come back except to visit. But..."

"Hey, sheriff. Come flip some burgers, will you?" I shouted over my shoulder.

"Do you really expect the high sheriff of the county to take on the menial tasks of a common innkeeper?"

"As a taxpayer, I'd like to see some return on the princely salary you're paid."

"I better empty the money out of those boots so I can put them on. It's getting pretty deep over here. Besides, it looks to me that you're getting everyone else to do all your work for you."

"It's called leadership, Marcus," I said.

"Then I'm going to have to warn those kids not to step in the leadership."

I laughed. "OK, that was a good line. Now come flip some burgers, will you? I've got to saddle another pony."

"Marcus is still wearing his uniform, Bob. I'll cook for a while," said Sue.

"I can help, Sue. I was just giving Bob a hard time," said Marcus.

"No, now, you'll get grease all over your uniform."

While the brother and sister argued, I took a fast walk to the barn. I saddled Colt, one of the larger ponies, and led him outside. The children were excited to see another pony join the circuit. I tossed the next kid in line onto Colt's back and fell in behind Jake and Speck. We made a slow trip around the barnyard, and as soon as we made it back to the starting point, I replaced one rider with another and began the orbit once again. In about 20 minutes, the line began to dwindle.

"Jake, why don't you unsaddle Speck, get him some water, and take a break. Get something to eat."

"Mary brought us sandwiches already."

"When did you eat?" I asked.

"Charlie and I ate while leading the ponies."

I was so proud of these kids I could about bust. They had worked pretty much non-stop since breakfast without complaint. Jake led Speck into the barn as Sasha brought Trinket around.

"Do you want a break, Sasha?"

"No. This is fun."

We loaded two more kids onto our mounts and started around again. I caught up with Charlie when a boy was having trouble getting onto Randolph. The little fellow finally got his foot into the stirrup, and with a little help from Charlie, climbed happily aboard.

"Why don't we have this be Randolph's last trip. Then you can put him up for the night and take a break."

As I led the pony around the barnyard, I began to tell everyone within earshot that we were going to put the ponies away soon, so if they wanted a ride, they needed to line up now. In less than two minutes, we had an additional twelve children in line. I figured I'd be doing this for a while, but Charlie came out of the barn a few minutes later and offered to take over for me. I asked him if he was sure. After all, he'd been doing this most of the day.

"Yeah," he said. "Besides, I'd feel bad leaving Sasha here after I asked her to help."

So, I left Colt in Charlie's capable hands and headed into the tractor barn, our garage, and picked up our two-gallon gas can. I walked out to where the cars were parked and unscrewed the gas cap on the sheriff's cruiser. As I emptied the contents of the gas can into Marcus' car, I heard a child's voice behind me.

"What you doing?" asked Alisha.

I turned and saw she was with her father. "I just want to make sure that the sheriff doesn't run out of gas. What are you doing out here? All the fun stuff is over there."

Mr. Williams said, "Alisha left her stuffed animal in the car."

"Well now, we wouldn't want him to miss all this fun, would we?"

"Marcus strikes me as a numbers and statistics guy. He wouldn't by any chance keep a close eye on the gas mileage of the sheriff department vehicles, would he?" The professor asked, while smiling.

I knew I'd been busted. "Yeah, inconsistencies in the numbers make him crazy."

"Doesn't it get expensive adding gas all the time?"

"Not really. Next week or the week after, whenever I get the chance, I'll bring an empty can and a rubber hose..."

"I don't want to know," Mr. Williams cut in.

I headed over to the old dairy barn. Billie Joe and the T'N'T cowboy band had set up, and I was surprised to see amplifiers on the stage with them.

"I thought you guys were strictly acoustic."

"If you'd ever come see us play anywhere but your place, you'd know we use amps."

"When you're right, you're right," I admitted.

As they did a sound check, I wheeled out the old carnival wagon popcorn machine. It is just what it sounds like: an old wagon, about the size of a large desk, with a big popcorn popper on it. I plugged it in and went looking in the storage cupboard for some paper bags or cones to put the popcorn in.

"Where'd you get that?" asked Billy Joe, his voice booming over the mic and echoing around the old barn. He turned a dial and then spoke into the microphone again, "No, wait. Don't tell me. That's another one of Big Mike's auction deals."

I gave him a thumbs-up in response and carried some paper bags back over to the cart. I pulled out some cubes of—well I'm not sure what they are—from a drawer on the side of the cart. I unwrapped one and dropped it into the popper. When it melted, I poured in a cup of popcorn. In a minute, the popping began, and a wonderful smell started to fill the big room. I dumped the first load of popcorn into the warmer and started another batch as people began wandering into the building. I filled several bags with warm popcorn and set them out so people could help themselves.

The band played half a song and then made some adjustments to their sound levels. I opened the big barn doors, hoping the sound would reach those in the barnyard. I didn't need to worry. As I looked out, people were streaming toward the old barn. Billy Joe counted off, and the band launched into a series of western classics.

Sue walked up to me and said, "We're out of buns."

"Hamburger or hot dog?"

"Both. So, I used bread."

"Is Marcus cooking?"

"No. After we ran out of buns, I just finished what was already on the grill and served it on bread. Then I shut it down."

"Had most folks eaten?"

"It looked like it."

"So, what's it look like?" Sue knew what I meant by this.

"Over $400, our cost, in food, bottled water, and paper products."

"Ouch."

"Maybe, we need to consider recouping the cost of what we provide."

We do about four fundraisers a year. I always like to say that 100% of the money raised goes to what we're raising money for, but I could certainly see Sue's point. "Yeah, maybe." Then I asked, "How much did we bring in?"

"From the ponies, games, and food, a little over $900. I don't know about the bake sale."

"So, we could have given Bill $400 and just sat around and enjoyed a day off."

"We helped him get another $500 for his brother. That's something, isn't it?"

"Yeah." If I were any more charitable, I might bankrupt us. "Still, we gave almost half of the total. I thought people would be more generous."

"Bob, it's June in farm country. All the money is invested in crops that aren't ready, yet."

"I suppose you're right."

I walked up to the stage and thanked everyone for coming out, thanked the band, and mentioned the reason we were all there. I reminded folks about the astronomy lecture. Then I got out of the way and let Billy Joe and the boys get on with it.

I walked back over to Sue, put out my hand, and asked her to dance. Sue doesn't say much and doesn't like attention, but she loves to dance. We rarely get out, so this was the first dancing we'd done in a while. I have two left feet to begin with, but Sue is pretty good. She had taught every kid we had ever fostered to dance.

"I had better make some more popcorn," I said.

"You had better dance with me one more time. The popcorn can wait."

After one more dance, I saw Mary in the crowd and knew I'd better find something for her to do before she thought of something herself. I asked her to dance with Sue. She happily obliged as I went off to make more popcorn. The sheriff and professor were standing by the popcorn wagon, talking away.

"How many Blazing Saddles jokes do you get every day?" asked Mr. Williams.

"Not many anymore, but for about ten years after I became sheriff, I got a couple a day," replied Marcus.

I started some more popcorn going and surveyed the scene. It looked like people were having a good time. I spotted Charlie leading Sasha onto the dance floor. Then I realized he was teaching her to two-step. That's pretty brave, especially considering several of the kids from his school were watching. The boys were pointing and poking at each other and just generally being knuckleheads, but then, they are teenagers; it's their job.

"Do they give you much trouble?" Mr. Williams asked Marcus. I seemed to drop in and out of their conversation. I wasn't trying to eavesdrop, but as I turned my head, I picked up sounds from all over the large room.

"Come election time, it mostly seems to balance out. I think there are as many people who vote for me because I'm Black, in some kind of weird reverse racism, trying to convince themselves that they aren't racist, as there are people who will never vote for me, just because I'm Black."

"Sounds complicated."

"Not really. Just nuanced. I'm certain most people vote for me for the right reason: because I do the job to the best of my ability."

The popcorn started to pop, and I lost the conversation. A few people stopped, got popcorn, and said they had a good time. I gave them all my sales pitch, although I tried to hide the fact that it was indeed a sales pitch. Yes, we host weddings, anniversaries, birthday parties, and all sorts of get-togethers out here. That sort of approach.

Big Mike came over and said, "I've had a good time, but Lottie says we have to get our grandbaby back to her folks."

"Thanks so much for coming out. What's going on in the next few days?"

"Livestock sale tomorrow. Then our monthly auction on Saturday. I've got some stuff you might like."

"Oh, you know I'll be there. I can't resist."

"See you then. Goodnight."

"Goodnight. Drive safe."

It was coming up on nine o'clock. Usually we'd just be getting started, but it was a weeknight, even if there was no school tomorrow. Billy Joe must have been thinking much the same thing. From the stage, he said, "If you want to dance, you'd better lace up your dancing shoes and get out on the floor because we're going to play a couple more until it gets good and dark. Then the professor will take the show outside and tell us about the stars. I can't wait." He waved at Mr. Williams. The professor waved back. It wasn't until that moment that I realized just how good Billy Joe was at this kind of thing. He'd just gotten the whole crowd to look back at the professor; now they all knew who was giving the lecture and they knew that Billy Joe thought it would be so good that he'd stop playing so he could hear it.

As the band launched into a reel, I unplugged the popcorn maker. As I looked up at the stage, Billy Joe was puffed up with pride. The reel is all about the fiddle player and his boy, Roy, nailed it. I could see Jenny standing with Jackie Stevens. Jenny, smiling, pointed out her son, the fiddle player, to Jackie. Maybe Billy Joe had just gotten out of the doghouse, thanks to his son.

The band played "Cotton-Eyed Joe" and "Good-Hearted Woman." The crowd called for them to play one more, which they happily did, finishing with "Happy Trails."

"I guess you're on, professor," I said to Mr. Williams. "Where do you want people?"

"I thought the north side of your pony barn, where we were the other night. The barn shields a lot of the light from your barnyard."

"I'm going to see if anyone has car trouble or needs help," said Marcus. "See you a little later."

As people began leaving the barn, some headed for their cars. I waved and thanked them for coming out. Others followed the professor as he walked around the corner of our old converted dairy barn and headed into the field just north of the pony barn. One man told Mr. Williams that giving all that money to NASA was a big waste. I didn't hear everything Mr. Williams said in response, but I was surprised and impressed with what little I did hear.

"Many people share your view, but I would ask you to consider what our nation gets in return for the funding. NASA is hiring smart people to invent things to solve problems. Right now, they're working on ways of deflecting meteors to prevent the extinction of all life on Earth. That alone is worth the budget, to me. Since the 1960s, there have been over 2000 spin-offs, either directly or indirectly, from NASA inventions: smartphone cameras, GPS, the computer mouse, wireless headphones, CT scans, and LEDs. Improvements in everything from baby formula to artificial limbs to water purification systems to the memory foam in your mattress. Laser eye surgery is possible because of NASA inventions. I could go on, but if you still think the half a penny of your tax dollar that goes to fund NASA is a waste, we'll have to agree to disagree."

Mr. Williams didn't belittle or insult the man. He didn't try to impress him with his massive intellect. What he did do was acknowledge the man's opinion and then present his own opinion in a thoughtful and intelligent way. Our nation could sure use less arguments and a whole lot more of this kind of discussion, I thought.

The lighting bugs were out and putting on their own show. The last glow of the sun on the horizon was gone now, and I marveled at how the place could look beautiful even in the dark. Mr. Williams turned from his debate to address the crowd.

"Good evening. My name is Henry Williams, and I teach astronomy at the University of Nebraska. Can everyone hear me?" People nodded yes, and he continued, "First, I'd like to thank Bob for giving me the opportunity to do what I love: talk about the cosmos."

"Thank you for doing it," I said loudly. Looking around, I was surprised by the number of younger children who were here with their parents. I thought we'd probably have an older crowd, but as it turned out, the kids outnumbered the adults by nearly three to one. The professor noticed the demographics, too.

"Who can tell me what the closest star is to Earth? I'll give you a hint, we could see it all day until just a few minutes ago."

"The sun?" ventured a girl at the front of the group.

"The sun isn't a star," another child interjected.

"Actually, it is." Mr. Williams turned to the girl, "You're quite right." Turning back to the child who had rejected the answer, he said," I know it seems funny that the sun is a star because we are used to seeing stars at night. When I was your age, I didn't know it, either. But in my junior high science class, we got to watch a recording of a show called Cosmos. It had been on TV back in the 70's and was hosted by a man named Carl Sagan. It changed my life. Maybe some of you saw the remake of the show a couple of years ago with Neil deGrasse Tyson."

A couple of the kids said, "I did."

"Good. Anyway, the sun is 93 million miles from Earth." He looked down at a little boy. "That's a long way, Jack." The boy giggled. "But light is so fast that it gets here in about eight and a half minutes. Do you think you could run 93 million miles in under nine minutes?"

"Some days it sure seems like he can," said the boy's mother. The crowd laughed. This was going better than I had expected.

"Now look up at the stars. What you see isn't the actual star, but the light from the star. The light rays from those stars have been traveling toward us for years. What's really weird: Some of those stars aren't there anymore. What we are seeing are the light rays that left the star many, many, many years ago and are just now getting to us. Some of those stars collapsed years ago and then exploded"—Mr. Williams brought his hands together and then threw them apart—"throwing star guts everywhere."

This brought a delighted "Eew" from the kids.

"The star guts swirl around and form gas clouds which contain all the elements needed to form galaxies." He looked at the smallest girl in the audience. "So, when you feel little and think everything around you is so big, just remember that the atoms in your body are made up of carbon and oxygen and other elements from those old explosions. You are"—he looked up at the group—"we are all made of star stuff."

I felt a tug on my shirt. I turned around to see Jake; he had a concerned look on his face. "Marcus wants to see you," he said.

We were at the back of the group, so I don't think anyone noticed when we turned away. I followed Jake back to the barnyard, where Marcus was talking to a group of boys.

"He called her a name," Charlie was saying in response to a question from Marcus.

"What did he call her?" Marcus asked.

Charlie wiped tears from his eyes and then looked Marcus directly in the face. "You know what he called her."

I could see the muscles in Marcus's jaw working. Then he said simply, "Yeah, I guess I do." Marcus turned and looked at the three boys standing together at the side of our group with a look that would melt iron. Then he turned to me. "I found these three beating on Charlie."

"You all right?" I asked Charlie. He nodded but said nothing.

"Apparently, these three heroes made some remarks about Sasha. Charlie stepped between her and them." Marcus turned and looked at the three boys with disgust. "And then, even though each one of them is older, bigger, and stronger than Charlie, it took all three of them to fight him. Sasha ran and got me."

"Where is Sasha now? Is she all right?" I asked.

"She was pretty scared, so I told her to go find her parents or go back to the cabin. I stayed here to talk with the boys and find out what happened." He turned to the three boys. "Are your parents here?"

"No. I drove us out," said the oldest boy.

"Driver's license," Marcus held out his hand. The boy handed it over. Marcus took out a small notebook and copied down the information. He turned to the other boys and asked, "You two have ID?" They each shook their heads. "What are your names and date of birth?" They told him. He asked for their parents' contact information, and they reluctantly provided that as well.

Marcus turned to the oldest boy and handed his license back to him. "Take these two home and then drive yourself straight home. I'll be in touch with your parents."

"Yes, sheriff." They walked, heads down, toward the parking area.

"Let's get you cleaned up," I said to Charlie. As we started for the house, I saw Jake stop Marcus.

"I saw those boys hitting Charlie, but I didn't help him. I wanted to, but I was too scared," Jake said, and then he began to cry.

I started to turn back to him, but Marcus wrapped him up in a big hug and said, "That's my job, not yours. You didn't do anything wrong, and this isn't your fault."

I kept on walking to the house with Charlie. We walked into the kitchen, and I dug out the first aid kit. He had a split lip and a bloody nose, but with three bigger kids pounding on him, it could certainly have been worse. I cleaned him up as best I could and asked, "How do you feel?"

"I'm OK, I guess."

"I'm proud of you, you know."

"What for? I just got beat up."

"I don't think even Marcus would do very well against three guys who were all bigger and stronger than him."

"If three guys want to fight Marcus, they'd better bring more guys."

Marcus and Jake entered the kitchen. Jake sat beside Charlie and asked, "Are you all right?"

"Yeah."

"I'm sorry I didn't help."

"Not much you could have done."

"I should have done something."

"Then your face would look like mine."

"At least we would match," said Jake.

Charlie laughed and then said, "Seriously, it's OK."

"I want to tell you two something I've learned about bullies and being bullied," said Marcus. "Bullies make you feel bad about yourself. They make you feel weak. They make you feel like you should have done something more. What you have to remember is that what they do has nothing to do with you. Bullies can only feel good about themselves when they're putting someone else down. There is something in them that makes them miserable, and they spend their lives trying to make everyone else feel just as miserable. It's almost enough to make you feel sorry for them. Almost. Most of the bullies you'll meet in your lives won't threaten you physically. They will be coworkers or insecure bosses who can't climb the ladder without stepping on you or can't feel like they're in charge unless they're holding you down. The internet age was made for these jerks. You can say terrible, untrue things about others without revealing your own identity."

Professor Williams entered the kitchen, but before he could say anything, Charlie asked, "How is Sasha?"

"She is fine. She's in the cabin with her mother and sisters. How are you?"

"I'm OK."

"I feel like I need to say something to you." Mr. Williams paused for a long moment, looking straight at Charlie, and then said, "I wasn't sure I liked my daughter being around you. It made me nervous in a way you can't understand unless you're the father of a daughter. Sasha told me what happened with those boys. When you stepped between her and them to protect the girl you were with, well, that's what a man does. I didn't expect that of you. I was wrong about you. I'm sorry. I'm grateful to you. Thank you." He turned to me and said, "You've got a good one there, Bob."

"I know," I said.

SEPTEMBER 1975

Sarah had taken Marcus to see the doctor. Abe finished the afternoon milking while Sue played.

"How was school today?" Abe asked her.

"It was fun. We got to finger paint."

Sue was in the afternoon kindergarten. Marcus took the school bus in the morning. Sarah drove Sue to school and then picked up Marcus early from school to drive to the county seat. Sue understood that she would ride the school bus home by herself, like a big girl. The trip was uneventful.

"Sounds messy," said Abe.

"Billy got the paint all over his shirt, but nobody else did. We washed our hands, and Miss James said we were good painters."

"What else did she say?"

"She said we tromped upstairs like elephants."

"When did you do that?"

"After recess."

Abe had finished milking and was putting away his equipment. "Sounds like you enjoy school."

"Uh-huh."

"Are you making friends?"

"I like Sally. She's my best friend. But I already knew her before school."

As Abe finished his chores, the ones he could do while keeping one eye on Sue, he said, "Are you getting hungry?"

"Not now."

"Well, how about a snack?"

"OK."

They walked toward the house. "I'm not sure when your mom and Marcus will be home. If they're late, we might have to figure out supper for ourselves."

"I can make supper for you, Daddy."

"I didn't know you could cook."

"Yes. I help Mom all the time."

"What would you like to do until Mom and Marcus get home?"

"I know what we can do. Let's be pretty-pretty princesses."

"That sounds like something you should play with your mom."

"No, Daddy, you."

A few moments later, Abe was sitting on his daughter's bedroom floor. Sue had dug into her play clothes and put together an outfit that only a little girl would recognize as a princess costume. "Now you need to be a pretty-pretty princess." Sue looked around and quickly realized that none of her clothes would come anywhere close to fitting her father. She got out her art supplies and pulled out a large piece of construction paper. After she rolled it into a cone, she taped a scarf to the top. Although she taped the cone along the seam, the paper was too heavy and kept popping open and reverting to a flat piece of paper. Abe rolled it back up and held it in place with his thumb on the inside of the cone and his fingers on the outside. Then he took off his feed cap with his other hand and put it on the floor. He held the damsel-in-distress hat on top of his head. That still left him one hand free to drink his imaginary tea Sue had poured for him. He thought about all the things he had tried to be in his life and all the things he had been mistaken for. This was a first. For this one shining moment, he was a pretty-pretty princess.

"How about we have a glass of milk and a cookie right now," Abe suggested.

"I can pour my own milk."

"Can you, now?"

"Uh huh."

They walked into the kitchen, and Abe got out the milk, glasses, and cookies. He was wearing his feed cap. Sue was still in her princess clothes. A moment later, Abe wiped up the milk Sue spilled on the table while trying to pour her own glass. He turned on the radio and listened to the evening farm report. After the news, the station switched over to music.

"Show me how to dance again, Daddy."

The big man got up from the table and lifted his daughter up so they could dance cheek to cheek.

"No, Daddy, like the big girls."

Abe lowered his daughter down until her feet were on top of his feet. Her little right hand was in his enormous left. She hugged his leg with her left arm, while he held her in place with his right hand on her shoulder. Abe did a slow box step as he counted, "one together, two together..."

Sarah and Marcus came in through the front door and into the kitchen. Marcus sat down gingerly while Sarah hovered over him.

"Look, Marcus, I'm dancing."

Marcus just smiled and nodded.

"I can see that, honey," said her mother. "I'll need your help in a minute when I start supper. Abe, I need to talk to you." Sarah cocked her head toward the living room and Abe gently lifted his dance partner off his feet and onto her own.

In the living room, Sarah told Abe about the visit to the doctor. "They X-rayed him. Two cracked ribs. The doctor said Marcus must have been in a lot of pain."

"The fight was three days ago. He never said a word to me," said Abe.

"Or to me either. They wrapped his ribs but said there isn't much they can do about cracked ribs. He needs to keep as still as he can, but it's going to hurt for a while."

"I broke a rib playing football. It hurts to bend over, pick stuff up, laugh, even breathe. I can't believe he wouldn't tell us he was hurting."

"It's lucky, I guess, that I saw him struggling with his book bag," said Sarah.

"I didn't notice at all." Abe looked down at the floor and put his hands into his pockets.

June 2019

The next morning, there was trash everywhere. Paper plates, napkins, plastic water bottles, and all manner of miscellaneous garbage spread across the barnyard. I picked up some of it before breakfast, dreading what I would find in the old dairy barn dance hall. I saw Jackie Stevens and Abbie come out of their cabin and head for the house and breakfast. I stopped the cleanup and walked into the house with them.

In the kitchen, Sue had pancakes on the griddle. The smells of sausage and pancakes made my mouth water. The boys weren't up yet, but all the girls were at the table. Mary and Isabella were waiting for pancakes, while Katie had her usual bowl of cereal. I walked over to Sue, put my hands on her shoulders, and kissed the top of her head. In her ear I whispered, "The place is a wreck."

"I know. I saw out the window." To Mrs. Stevens and Abbie, she said, "We have pancakes or pigs in a blanket."

"What are the pigs?" asked Abbie.

"That's a pancake with a sausage rolled up in it," said her mother.

"I want that."

"How many?" I asked as I pulled the links out of the warming compartment on the stove.

"Why don't we start with one, just to make sure she likes it?"

"I want many pigs," said Abbie.

"Well, here's the first one," I said as I slid a plate in front of her. "Would you like a glass of milk to go with that?" She nodded her head, yes, but didn't take her eyes off the pig in a blanket. She examined it closely. "Coffee, Mrs. Stevens?" I asked. Then corrected myself, "Sorry, I mean, would you care for coffee, Jackie?" She flashed that wonderful smile of hers, and I couldn't help but think that her ex was an idiot.

"Yes, please. Last night was great fun. It was like a county fair and barn dance rolled into one."

"That pretty much describes it," I said, placing a cup of coffee in front of her. "Help yourself to sugar or cream."

"I was happy to meet Jenny last night. She watched over me at the dance. I almost asked a handsome young man to dance, but Jenny warned me off. She said he was, now let me see if I can remember her exact words. 'He's all hat and no cowboy.'" Jackie laughed at the thought of it.

"Probably Pete," said Sue.

"I think that is the name Jenny told me," said Jackie.

"I believe the saying is 'all hat and no cattle,'" I said.

"Jenny probably wasn't talking about his ranching abilities," said Sue.

I turned to look at Sue as she looked away and busied herself setting a short stack of pancakes in front of both Mary and Isabella. "Eat up, girls, we've got a lot to do today," I said.

"Oh," came a groan from Isabella.

"What do we get to do today?" from Mary.

"After chores and clean up, I thought we'd go fishing," I said.

"I like fishing," said Katie.

"I like fishing, too," said Abbie.

"I didn't know you had been fishing before," Jackie said to her daughter.

"Yes. You need a hook and a string," Abbie informed her mother.

"Is that right? Well, can you help me learn to fish?" Jackie asked Abbie.

"Sure, Mommy, it's easy."

Jake and Charlie came into the kitchen. Charlie had a small, swollen lump under his left eye and a fat lip, but he looked better than I thought he would.

"What happened to you?" Jackie Stevens asked when she saw Charlie.

"Oh, I hit a bully in the fist with my face," Charlie answered.

"Looks like you hit him more than once."

"He'll probably have to put some ice on his knuckles today," Charlie replied. He seemed to be in pretty good spirits. Much better than I would be in his place.

I wondered when the Williams family would come to breakfast. As I usually do, I began to worry that they might be packing up and checking out a few days early. I wouldn't blame them if they were hopping mad about last night. I was most worried about Mrs. Williams. What would she have to say about all this? I know this wasn't her idea of a great vacation to begin with, so I figured she was working on her husband right at this very moment. "You've had your nights in the country looking up at the sky; now it's time to go home." Or "I will not stay another night in a place where my children aren't safe." How could he argue with that? I guess I'll just apologize and hope for the best.

"I'm done," said Katie, rousing me from my thoughts.

"Very good," I said. I asked Sue, "Who's on KP?"

"Jake and Isabella, this morning."

"All right. Charlie and Mary, when you finish breakfast, grab a couple trash bags and join me outside. Let's go, Katie."

Katie and I walked outside and began picking up trash. I held the bag open and Katie put a bottle in, and then attempted a cartwheel. She went over a little crooked and fell onto the grass, but recovered nicely with a somersault. Apparently, Slobber is attracted to children playing because he came running up to greet us. Katie began playing with the dog, and I knew I'd lost my helper for now. With a youngster like Katie, I only try to keep her on task for a few minutes at a time. As the kids get older, I require a little more work and attention to detail, each according to age. After a few minutes of picking up trash by myself, Charlie and Mary came out, trash bags in hand. Before I could say anything to them, I saw the Williams family emerge from their cabin. I figured I'd better face this head-on, so I started walking toward them. We met about halfway between their cabin and the house.

"Look, I just want to apologize for what happened last night. I'm so sorry..."

"And just what do you have to apologize for?" Mrs. Williams said, cutting me off.

"You are my guests, and your comfort is important. But more than that, I want you to enjoy every minute of your time here."

"So, are you responsible for those loutish boys?"

"Well, no."

"Do you think we had to drive all the way out here to Boondocks, Nebraska, to find out there are cruel, vulgar, coarse, callous people in the world?"

"Well, I, uh..."

"I suppose you think racism started last night. Lord, white people." She glanced at Charlie, and the hint of a smile played across her lips. "Good morning, Charlie," she said in a tone that was decidedly less sharp than what she had used with me. In fact, her voice almost sounded musical.

"Good morning, ma'am," said Charlie.

As Sasha walked by, she didn't say anything, but she gave Charlie a small wave, which he returned in kind.

I sometimes think I understand people, or know how to read them, but every now and then I get a lesson about how much I have yet to learn. This morning had been another such lesson.

"I know what happened last night," Mary said to Charlie. "You loooooove her," she teased while stretching the word love out for several seconds. "You want to marrrrrry her."

"Shut up, Mary," said Charlie.

Mary wasn't quite done and began making kissing sounds. Charlie threw an empty plastic water bottle at her. I sent them to separate parts of the yard.

About an hour later, the grounds looked pretty good, and the dairy barn dance hall was back in shape. I went into the kitchen and found Sue making a grocery list.

"I've got to stock up on supplies. We went through a lot of our surplus last night. I've also got to return a library book that's delinquent," said Sue.

"Is it a young adult book?" I asked.

"No, this isn't one of the kids' books, it's mine. Why do you ask?"

"Because if a YA book was overdue, that would make it a juvenile delinquent," I said.

"You're not all that funny, you know," Sue said, although the corners of her mouth turned up.

"Then why are you smiling?" I asked as I moved in and kissed her. I had intended to give her a quick kiss and then head out, but it turned into a long, slow, soft kiss. When I opened my eyes, I saw Jake's back. Apparently, he had walked in, seen us kissing, and turned to retreat.

From the next room, I heard him tell someone, "Don't go in there. They're kissing again."

"Oh, great," said Mary. "Now we'll never get to go fishing."

I reluctantly left Sue to her shopping list. I went outside, hitched the wagon up to the tractor, and gathered up our fishing gear and tossed it on board. The kids were excited about having an afternoon off from the usual summer duties. Jackie and Abbie climbed aboard with my kids and the Williams family, and away we went, chugging along at speeds approaching four miles an hour. Slobber trotted happily alongside.

When I asked Mr. Williams if he and his family wanted to go fishing with us, he told me he hadn't been fishing since his dad took him fishing as a boy, and he'd never taken his girls. I told him it was way past time for him to wet a line. He smiled and somehow talked his wife into going along.

When we got back to the pond, Mr. Williams got his family set up with our well-used fishing poles. I helped Jackie and Abbie while my kids, veterans of many fishing trips, fended for themselves. Charlie helped Katie put a worm on the hook. Only Isabella rejected fishing and went for a walk around the pond by herself.

Jake found a turtle and showed it to the other children. Abbie and Katie touched its shell; Alisha wanted to have a good look at the turtle, but wasn't interested in touching it. Not to be outdone, Mary caught a frog to show the little girls. None of them wanted to touch it. "Don't worry. He won't give you warts," Mary said.

"They don't have to touch the frog if they don't want to, Mary," I said. "How about we start fishing?"

Mr. Williams sat on the dock with his feet in the water. His daughters Leah and Alisha joined him and sat on each side of him.

"Your grandpa Williams taught me that the best way to catch fish was to put your bare feet in the water." His girls took off their shoes and socks and followed suit.

Slobber walked up, lay down on the dock, and put his big head on Alisha's lap. "Slobber," she laughed, "get off. You're too heavy." She giggled while pushing Slobber's head with her little arms. I thought Alisha had a year, maybe less, of that great laugh, and then it would turn into a more grown-up sound. But, for now, she still had that little kid laugh, the sound of pure joy.

"Is there a trick to getting him off Alisha's lap?" Mr. Williams asked.

"I don't know if I can. He looks pretty comfortable," I said. Then I patted my leg, "Come here, Slobber."

He was up and over to me in an instant. I rewarded him by scratching behind his ears. "I've got to go take care of some stuff," I told Mr. Williams. "If you need anything, use one of the kids as a runner, and send me a message. I'll be in the barnyard."

"I thought you'd done all the cleanup."

"Almost. The kids worked so hard yesterday, I figured they should have a break. My next couple hours will involve a garden hose, a wet/dry vac, and four plastic porta- potties."

"Oh. Right. I forgot about that."

"I'll see you later," I said, and began walking back toward my task. Isabella fell in beside me. "Would you like to go back to the house and read for a while?" I asked.

"Yes."

We walked back to the house. I figured she should get the quiet time she wanted, just as the other kids got the noisy fishing party they wanted. Besides, I'd be right outside if she needed anything.

After the better part of an hour, I completed my disagreeable task. I went into the house, and took a quick shower, changed my clothes, and brought a cup of coffee into my office. From one disagreeable task to another, I thought, as I looked through the bills. It had been a slow month; only a few cabin rentals and a few parties. We receive money every month for fostering the children, but Sue and I decided years ago that whatever money was left over after feeding and clothing the kids would go into a savings account for each child. Our first foster child, Carlos, joined the Navy after he graduated from high school years ago. When we presented him with his savings account as a graduation present, he was overwhelmed. It was only a little over a thousand dollars, but it meant the world to him. He is married now with kids of his own, but to this day he tries to get us to visit him and his family in San Diego. He has made it back here a couple of times in as many decades, but we never have managed to visit him in his home.

I flipped over another bill. I couldn't see how we'd be able to put much, or any, money into the kids' accounts this month. The Fourth of July was two weeks away, but we had no bookings for it. We don't shoot fireworks because it scares the animals. Sometimes the hens don't lay for several days afterwards. In these parts, the Fourth is all about fireworks. I would hasten to add that we take the kids to see the big public display at the county seat in Lowe.

My mind was wandering a bit. I've got some work with George Grant next week. George is a licensed plumber and contractor. When he has a big job, he throws some work my way. I'm handy and have my own tools. George is a great plumber, but not quite as talented as a carpenter. So, we are a good match.

The phone rang. Mrs. Avery wanted to book a birthday party for her daughter. She had never booked with us before, so I explained the cost would vary depending on the number of kids and whether we fed them. She said she'd get back to me when she had a better idea of the size of the party. I thanked her, hung up, and penciled her in for the date in July she'd requested.

No sooner than I'd flipped the calendar page back to June, the phone rang again. Mrs. Rogers, who had also never booked a party with us, booked a party. I was thinking about what a coincidence this was when the phone rang yet again. Another booking, only this time they wanted to reserve the dairy barn dance hall for a sit-down dinner and asked if it would be OK if they brought their own food and entertainment. I told them that would be fine, but to let me know how many people so I could set up tables and chairs for them. I blocked out the evening of the 28th for the barn.

The phone rang again as Jake came into the office. An anniversary party. I made the note on my calendar. "What is it, Jake?"

"I think everyone is ready to come back from the pond, now."

"Have Charlie drive the tractor and wagon back."

"Charlie?"

"Yeah, he knows how. I can't leave right now; I'm on the roll of my life."

Jake took off as the phone rang again.

After two hours, I'd booked over twenty parties, and the calls kept coming. Charlie had successfully piloted the tractor and wagon back with my kids and guests. As I took yet another call, I looked out the window and saw Sue drive up.

Sue walked into the office. I couldn't wait to tell her the good news. I got out of my chair as she crossed the room, threw her arms around me, buried her head in my chest, and burst into tears. I was too startled to even ask what had happened. I held her for a few minutes, and she began to get control of herself.

Mary looked into the office. "What's wrong?"

"Nothing," I said. "There're supplies from town in the car. Get the other kids to help you bring it in and put it away. You know where it all goes. Go on now."

Mary left just as Sue said, "I've ruined everything."

"I don't believe that for a minute. Tell me what happened."

"I lost my temper."

"You?"

"Yes, I did."

"What happened?

"I was shopping at Anderson's grocery. I was checking out when Mrs. Higgs came into the store. I don't remember exactly what she said, but it was a left-handed compliment followed by criticism and insults. You know, the usual. But then she said something about you being lazy and the kids being no good. I just lost it. Oh, Bob, it was bad. The store was full of women, and I was shouting. People will think I've gone crazy."

"Were Mrs. Avery and Mrs. Rogers there?"

"They were behind me in the checkout line. We had just been talking before..."

I went to the desk and started reading names off calendar squares, asking if each had been there.

"Yes, I think so. How did you know?"

The phone rang. "Excuse me," I said and answered the phone. It was George Grant. "Hello, George. Do you still need me for that job next week?"

"Yes, but that's not why I'm calling. My wife just got off the phone with her sister, and she was at the store a while ago. I guess everyone is talking about how your wife blasted old lady Higgs. I couldn't believe it. I don't claim to know your missus well, but I've never known her to string more than two sentences together. Oh, you should've heard it. It was a thing of beauty. Like a momma bear defending her cubs."

"You sound like you were there."

"Oh, no, I wasn't there. My wife's sister was there afterward, when everyone was talking about it. Then she called my wife to tell her about it. Then my wife told me."

"Well, you shouldn't believe everything you hear third or fourth hand."

"Oh, I didn't hear about it third hand. Well, OK, I did, but, I mean, I saw it."

"What? How?" I asked, truly baffled.

"You know Norman Lewis' little girl, Alice?"

"No, but I know Norman."

"Well, anyway, she got one of those fancy phones, you know, not like mine that just makes phone calls, but one that you can not only take pictures with, you can make movies. Records pictures and sound. Just real clear, too. It's amazing what they come up with. What was I saying, oh yes, anyway, Alice was filming inside the grocery store when Mrs. Higgs walked in."

"So, Norman's girl showed you a video from her phone?"

"Oh, no. I seen it on the Facebook."

"What?"

"Yeah, my wife showed me. You know, I don't have much to do with that kind of thing, but Martha is a wiz at it."

I turned to Sue, "Apparently, you're an internet sensation, honey." Her hand went to her mouth as she gasped.

"Martha says over 200 people have seen it. I guess there's a way of knowing that. I don't really understand it myself, but it's not just on the Facebook, it's on other things, too."

"There are all sorts of social media accounts you can post on, all right," I said. "Thanks for letting me know, George."

"See you next week," he said and hung up.

I felt lighter than air. As our phone rang, I threw back my head and laughed.

"It's not funny."

"Maybe not, but it is probably the best thing that has ever happened to us." Instead of answering the phone, I turned on the computer. Our internet connection is spotty out here, but I was determined to see this video.

"You're not watching that," she said, still upset.

127

"I guess you're right. I need to answer the phone, and then I'll probably have to clean some fish."

SEPTEMBER 1975

George Newport asked the state patrol to investigate the incident at the diner. They talked to the sheriff first. Jeff called as soon as they left his office to warn Abe they were on the way. When they got to the farm, Abe offered them coffee. The two officers declined, but Abe sat down at the table and drank a cup. The two officers stood in the kitchen and questioned him for a while, then, after a few minutes, they sat down, and each had a cup.

Maybe it was the fact that several witnesses saw the three boys beat Marcus. Perhaps it was the fact that the officers couldn't find anyone other than George Jr. who would say they saw Abe lay hands on the boy. Or, it could have been the medical records of Marcus' injuries. At any rate, the officers finished their coffee and left.

The mid-seventies were like that. The whole country was tired of upheaval. A couple of small-town fights didn't seem like much.

The state patrol only investigated it because a banker claimed that the county sheriff wasn't doing his job. The patrol officers came to the same conclusion as the sheriff. They stopped by his office on the way out of town and told him so.

George Newport began working on other plans.

June 2019

"Looks like you had a good day fishing. Quite an impressive catch," I said. Charlie and Jake had already cleaned all the fish by the time I got outside. I'd spent quite a bit of time on the phone, then explained to Sue what had happened, or what I figured had happened to cause the avalanche of bookings. Sue was mortified, of course. For my part, I couldn't wait to see the exchange with Mrs. Higgs, but I'd have to wait until Sue wouldn't catch me watching it. So, I left her to answer the phone while I checked on our guests.

"Yeah, the kids had a great time. It really took me back to when I went fishing with my dad. Your kids really know how to fish; you must take them a lot," said Mr. Williams.

"As often as I can, but not often enough. I keep pretty busy."

"The sheriff told me you have several side jobs. What all do you do?"

"I don't do all that much, really," I said. "I work a couple overnights a week at a motel down on I-80. I pick up some odd jobs here and there. I'm a decent carpenter, so the contractors in the area call me if they need something built to a specific size, or they need extra help on a job site."

"And you run this place, take care of your guests, host fundraisers, and foster five kids. When do you sleep?"

I laughed. "I could use a publicist. Interested?"

"I'm serious. What you and your wife do with these kids is nothing short of amazing."

"That's mostly Sue. Over the years, the kids just respond to her. I think it's because she is one of the few adults in their lives who listens more than she talks."

"How many children have you fostered over the years?"

"Dozens. Most of them have been for just a couple of weeks. All five, now, are long-term, but we've had kids for only two days, all the way up to 18 years when they age out."

"What got you started?"

"It was Sue's idea. We didn't have kids of our own, and she felt we could make a difference."

"You obviously have. Your kids are terrific."

"That's more the kids than us. Sadly, we've had some failures and heartbreaks. I haven't always handled things as well as I might."

"How so?"

"Are you sure you want to hear this?"

"I'm curious about everything. That's probably why I study the universe. But I don't want to pry. If this is too personal, just say so."

Every time I talked with the professor, I liked him a little more. I hit the high points of fostering children: the difference between licensed and approved homes, dealing with the foster care agency, caseworkers, counselors, family members, attorneys, healthcare providers, and the ever-changing rules. We had as many as nine kids at one time. A few years ago, the rules changed, and now you can only have six children at a time and only four under the age of twelve. I told him how awful it is to split up large sibling groups, when legally we could only take a couple of the kids, and then the other siblings went to another home or homes often a hundred miles away. I told him about the long-term successes, like Carlos, but I didn't say much about my failures. We've had kids who were so violent that we couldn't keep the other kids safe from them. They were moved out. We've had kids who came to us abused mentally and physically, and who needed almost daily medical attention. It's more than a 30-minute drive to the doctor. It's over an hour, one way, to see a mental health professional. The logistics didn't work, so they were moved closer to the help they needed. The problem wasn't the long drive. The problem was either Sue or me driving and then sitting around waiting, then driving back, while the one who wasn't driving couldn't take another job or go anywhere because there were other kids to watch.

I told Mr. Williams about how our current crop of kids came to be with us. Charlie and Jake have three parents between them.

They share a mother, and each has their own father. You would think that out of three parents, they would have one responsible adult to take care of them. You would be wrong. Charlie's father is White, while Jake's is Black, and neither father can be found. Their mother, who is White, gets out of rehab long enough to get into trouble, gets locked up, and then gets sent back to rehab. The cycle repeats as the boys are brought into family court to be put through a kind of emotional hell every year or so.

Mary's parents were taken in a car wreck. I'm not sure if it is a good thing that she was only two years old at the time. Her aunt was supposed to take care of her. Her aunt would rather drink. I know that's judgmental. Addiction is a disease, but I see the effects on the children. I find it difficult not to blame adults when they don't do right by the children who need them.

Isabella's mother died from cancer. Her father can't seem to make it through the day without drugs or alcohol or both. I'd like to throw all the drugs and booze in the world into the Grand Canyon and cover it over.

Then there is Katie. Her father murdered her mother. I'm not sure she understands, but I know that one day a kind of horrible realization will dawn on her. I hope she will be strong enough to withstand it.

I didn't tell Mr. Williams about my biggest failure. A boy named Allan. I've failed other foster children in the past, but usually it was because they were with us for such a short time. I need time to build rapport with people. Sometimes I can build a relationship in a few months, but usually it takes me years. The children who come to us have had at least one terrible thing happen to them. Usually, more. A lot more. And many of them have gotten into trouble at school or in town while they lived with us. Allan is the only one who has gone to prison.

Allan was 17 when he cracked a man's skull with a piece of pipe and stole his car. He was tried as an adult and sentenced to 20 years in prison. I can only imagine what would have happened if the man had died. Marcus was shaken to his core. He had spent more time with Allan than I did. He stopped by several times a week to check on his progress in school, help with homework, take him fishing, or just talk. He was a true mentor in every sense of the word. Whenever Allan got into trouble, Marcus was there to set him straight. Whenever Allan was down, Marcus was there to encourage him. When Allan assaulted a man and stole his car, Marcus arrested him.

Allan was Black. That seemed to justify all the old ways of thinking and undo all the work Marcus had done for decades to get the people of the county to look beyond race when judging others. Marcus would make the long drive once a week to visit Allan in prison. When he was stabbed to death in a prison riot, Marcus withdrew into himself for almost a year.

I didn't tell Mr. Williams any of this. I did tell him that some kids come to us who are too broken to help. At least, I don't know how. There is a wonderful feeling when a parent wins their battle with their personal demons and reunites with their kids, but then there is a flip side. I told him that the worst thing is often when the court turns the child back over to the parent. This sounds like the best thing. It's supposed to be. But all too often, the parent isn't up to the task. The damage done to the child in cases like this is horrifying.

Mr. Williams looked at me in stunned silence. I hadn't told him the worst of it, and yet the milder tales of the trauma inflicted on the children were too much for him. "I'm sorry," I said. "I shouldn't have told you any of that."

"I asked for it," he managed to say.

"I'm working at the motel tonight. I'd probably better get a few hours' sleep. Do you need anything before I turn in?"

Mr. Williams shook his head but said nothing.

MARCH 1980

M arcus was helping Abe with the milking. They had just finished and were starting to clean up when Marcus asked, "Why do you think my parents left the interstate and came north 30 miles?"

"What left field did that come from?" asked Abe.

"We were going to see the mountains. We would have driven I-80 across Nebraska to Colorado. Why did we leave the interstate and come 30 miles north? If we were stopping for something to eat, there are plenty of restaurants at every exit. Same thing for hotels. So, what were we doing up here?"

"Well, I don't know."

"I want to know."

"Tell you what, how about I call Jeff and see what he knows?"

They walked to the house, and Abe dialed the phone. "Hey, is Jeff there? Tell him it's Abe." He stood quietly for a few moments and then said, "Hi, sheriff. How you doing?" He laughed at the answer and then said, "Marcus had some questions about—" he turned and looked at Marcus, "—the day his folks passed." After a minute, he continued, "I think it might be better in person. Could you stop by in the next couple of days, whenever you have time?" He paused. "I'm sure tonight would be great. How about supper? Sarah is making fried chicken." Another pause, and he said, "Well, she'll be disappointed, but, I wouldn't want her mad at me. Around eight will be fine." Abe looked at Marcus again. "Thanks, Jeff. See you then. Bye."

Marcus went to the fridge and got out the milk. He poured a glass and sat at the table. Abe sat down but said nothing. He hoped the boy would say what was on his mind. Sue walked in with Sarah.

"Help me with supper, Sue," said Sarah.

"How was school today, sweetheart?" asked Abe.

"It was OK, I guess."

"Well, that's not a ringing endorsement."

Marcus got up and left the room. Sue said, "Maria can't go to the dance with Marcus."

"What dance?" asked Abe.

"Why?" asked Sarah.

"I don't know. I heard some of the high school girls talking about it after school."

"I think I left my billfold in the dairy barn. Sue, would you see if you can find it for me?"

"Sure, Daddy," she said and ran out the door.

"So, what is it you want to tell me in private?" asked Sarah.

"My clever ploy didn't fool you, huh?"

"It never does. Just remember that. Now, what is it?"

Abe told Sarah about Marcus's questions and Jeff's visit that evening. "I guess getting turned down for a school dance stirred up a lot of stuff."

"It's tough enough at that age, but it sounds to me like he asked the girl, she said 'yes' and then her father told her no. At least, she couldn't go to the dance with Marcus."

"Probably so," agreed Abe.

"I've got an idea, Abe. What if we went to the mountains this summer?"

"I can't get away for that long. Who would take care of the livestock?"

"How many times have you helped the neighbors? We could drive out in a day. Spend a few days in the mountains and come back. We wouldn't even be gone a week."

"I don't know," said Abe, unconvinced.

"It'll be good for all of us to get away for a while. And Marcus will finally get to see the mountains his parents were taking him to see," said Sarah.

At supper that evening, instead of the usual easy communication, they all made halting attempts at conversation.

"Abe and I were thinking that maybe this summer we'd all drive out to the mountains."

"What would you two think about that?" asked Abe.

"Cool," said Sue.

"I don't care if I ever see the mountains," Marcus stated flatly.

Jeff stopped by a few minutes after eight o'clock. After they exchanged greetings, Marcus asked if he could talk to the sheriff alone. Abe offered the den and closed the door behind them. About twenty minutes later, they emerged from the den, and Marcus stuck out his hand. The sheriff shook it.

"Thanks for taking the time, sir," said Marcus.

"Anytime, Marcus. Whatever I can do. You know that, right?"

"Yes, sir. Thank you. Goodnight." Marcus went up the stairs to his bedroom.

"I guess I'd better run along."

"What's your hurry, Jeff?" asked Sarah.

"I'm afraid I've got a very early morning facing me."

"I'll walk you out," said Abe.

The two men walked outside and over to the sheriff's car. Abe didn't ask. He just waited. The sheriff looked at Abe for a minute and finally said, "I'd say that's the loneliest boy in the world."

June 2019

It was quiet at the motel for a Friday night. Interstate highway motels are typically full of travelers who check in late and check out early to get back on the road. I was the only employee on duty and had a list of tasks to get done by morning. I'd gotten to work just before eleven o'clock and started on the list. But, in the wee hours of Saturday morning, I took a break to surf the world wide web to find one particular video.

The picture went from one item on a shelf at Anderson grocery to another, and in and out of focus with sound from all sides. You couldn't tell what Norman's girl, Alice, was trying to record. She must have been standing in the perfect spot to capture the front door and checkout stand, though. I watched as Mrs. Higgs entered the store and saw Sue paying the cashier. As Mrs. Higgs strode over to Sue, the camera zoomed in on the two of them. I couldn't hear what Mrs. Higgs said at first, but after a few seconds the background noise all but stopped.

"...only $40 from the bake sale. Not that I'm surprised. The whole affair was a disorganized mess from start to finish. If your husband had just put a little thought, effort, and planning into it, we could have raised so much more for Bill's brother, oh, what's his name?"

"Vic," said Sue, her face flushed.

"Well, I suppose, even with more planning, not very many people would have come out to your place, what with those children of drug addicts you have out there. Young hoodlums, all of them, I wouldn't be surprised. We've seen the effect on this community from those children of yours in the past. Prison is none too good for them. And you and your husband keep bringing in more. I don't know how you can do it in good conscience. If the two of you would simply think about what you could do for the community instead of what you are doing to the community."

I have known my wife since we were kids in college. She has always been quiet. She actively avoids the spotlight, and I've never seen her speak in front of a group of people. In conversation, she tends to listen much more than talk. But, at this point in the video, she roared. "You bloated old busy body! How dare you criticize my family! You do no good for anyone, ever, but you find fault with us? Those kids worked all day yesterday to help raise money for someone they don't even know. As for Bob, he works three jobs to keep our heads above water! And when I told him that we'd cleaned out our food supply to sell for donations he insisted that all of it, every penny, go towards helping Vic's family. We kept none of it! He is the most generous, the most kind man I've ever...." Her voice began to falter, but then she gathered herself and blasted out, "Don't you ever say another word about Bob or those children again! Not another word to me, and I'd better not hear about you talking them down to anyone else! Do you hear me!?!" With that, Sue pushed past Mrs. Higgs, grabbed her groceries, and left the store.

"Well, I never," sputtered Mrs. Higgs.

"And it sounds like you better not ever again," said Mrs. Avery. Behind her, Mrs. Rogers tried to stifle a laugh. Mrs. Higgs stood there for a moment, started to say something, then turned and left the store. The aftermath could only be described as a celebration.

I closed the computer and went back to work. The video answered the few remaining questions I had. I'd guessed why we got all those bookings from the folks in and around Crossroads after Sue told me what happened, and I'd gotten the phone call from George. Mrs. Higgs doesn't just criticize us; she freely distributes her opinions and advice to everyone. The only surprise is that she was told off by the quietest, sweetest woman in the county. I suspected that at that moment, Sue could have run for any public office and been elected by a landslide.

I smiled to myself as I started to pull together the motel breakfast. It was supposed to be ready for our guests by six a.m., which is about the time Gene gets in, but I like to have it ready sooner. We usually have early birds who like to get up and get on the road. I want to make sure that they can grab a quick bite and a cup of coffee before they begin their journey.

When my boss walked in, the first thing he said was, "Saw your wife on the internet."

"You know, that's not something a man usually wants to hear, Gene," I said, but couldn't wipe the dopey smile off my face. He laughed, and I changed the subject by bringing him up to date on work stuff. We made it to breakfast and the first few checkouts when the morning desk clerk and two maids showed up.

"Looks like you're good to go," Gene said.

"OK. See you later." I walked out of the motel lobby, got into my car, and drove home. I felt gratitude. My wife was loved and even protected by her community of friends and neighbors. Perhaps I'd be accepted too, someday.

April 1980

M arcus could have given up and shut down. What he did was focus on what he knew he could control. He became an exceptional student, getting A's in almost every class. He excelled in math and science, but struggled with writing. Words didn't come easily to him, though with the effort he put forth, he was in the top five percent of his class. He had participated in every sport the school offered his freshman year. Marcus was tough and strong, but small-town politics largely dictate who coaches can start and who sits on the bench. He realized this when he overheard his track coach, who was also the football coach, say to a group of men, "Yeah, you're right. The one slow Black kid in America, and he plays for me." Marcus finished the track season and didn't go out for a single sport in his sophomore year. His teammates made half-hearted attempts to get him back into sports, but they knew why he turned his back on it, and they didn't blame him.

The kids in school saw the attitudes of their parents and all the adults around them. Just a few years before, these kids were guided by those opinions, but now they saw the ugliness behind them. Still, they didn't know what to do about it. Marcus didn't have close friends, but most of his classmates liked him. He didn't ask another girl out on a date or to a dance. Marcus couldn't see the point. He understood he was different. He was an orphan, and he was Black. People might pay lip service to equality, but he knew that they were either naive or fools. When they said, "It doesn't make any difference," he would correct them by saying, "It shouldn't make any difference, but it does." He didn't think about changing the little part of the world in which he found himself. He had only a burning desire to get out. He pursued anything that would bring him closer to his goal or give him more or better options. As hard as he worked at school, he worked even harder on the farm. Abe commented more than once that he had to work at a slow run just to keep up with the boy.

When Big Mike bought the sale barn in 1980, he was struggling to make a go of it. Abe and Marcus would come and help as much as they could. Marcus knew that there was plenty of work on the farm to keep them occupied. He asked Abe why they were driving out several times a week to help. After all, they weren't being paid. Abe told him that he would rather drive a dozen miles to buy and sell livestock, farm machinery, and other household odds and ends than drive over 50 miles to do the same thing. "A man should do all he can to keep his community strong." After six months, Big Mike finally started to see a positive cash flow.

At fifteen, Marcus could drive on his own to and from school (although he still rode the bus with Sue most days) and to any after-school or summer job. Big Mike hired Marcus as part-time help. Marcus outworked every other employee at the sale barn. Big Mike put out the word: the kid was a worker.

At the barber shop or at Norma's Cafe, Big Mike would say, "In the time it takes two guys to talk about how to unload a truck, Marcus can have the thing unloaded and put away." Despite the overt racism from some of the old guard, people revered hard work. Marcus earned respect.

JUNE 2019

O
n the way home from work, I wondered if I could get Sue to look at the last couple of minutes of the grocery store video. I thought it would make her feel better if she saw how other people responded to what she had said. I had tried to explain to her that all those bookings came from her telling off Mrs. Higgs. While I was sure she understood that what she had said had benefited us, I also knew she was embarrassed about raising her voice publicly. Perhaps I could get her to look at the video someday, but I realized it wouldn't be any time soon.

I got home somewhere between 7:30 and 8:00 a.m. Breakfast was well underway. Sue was working away in the kitchen, serving the kids and the Williams family. The wonderful smell of Sue's breakfast hash filled the kitchen. Cubed sweet potatoes, onion, and sweet maple sausage fried in a skillet and topped with a fried egg is one of my favorite things. Less than a minute after I walked into the kitchen, I was joined by Jackie Stevens and Abbie. "How was everyone's evening?"

"I spent it stargazing," said Mr. Williams.

"What a big surprise," said Sasha. Teenagers are far and away the world's largest producers of sarcasm.

"Sasha," Mrs. Williams offered as a one-word rebuke.

"It's OK, Peg. The girl is just teasing," said Mr. Williams. Sasha smiled at her father and studiously avoided her mother's gaze. I think he was trying to avoid tension by quickly adding, "So, what's the plan for today?"

"Well, now," I said, "There are just no end of things to do. We can work on the treehouse." The boys eyes lit up. "We can make homemade ice cream." My eyes probably lit up at the thought of it. "But what I'd really like to see are Alisha and Abbie on ponies."

"OK," said Abbie simply.

Alisha looked just a little bit alarmed. I looked at her and said softly, "You don't have to ride a pony if you don't want to, but if you did want to, I'll bet your parents would walk right beside you." Alisha turned quickly and looked inquiringly at her mother. Mrs. Williams looked back and nodded her head at her youngest daughter. Alisha offered a big smile.

"I'm ready now," said Abbie.

"We just this minute got here for breakfast," said Jackie. "Eat some breakfast, and we'll ride a little bit later."

"But I'm not hungry."

"You need energy to ride a pony," said her mother. "Eat a little bit and, I promise you'll get to ride after breakfast." Jackie looked over at me, and I mouthed the word 'Sorry.' She smiled, and I knew she wasn't mad.

Mrs. Williams took a bite of the hash. She closed her eyes as she savored it. Then she said to Sue, "My momma used to..." She stopped herself and began again. "My mother made something very similar to this when I was young. What do you put in it?"

"Just regular sweet potatoes and onions, but the sausage is a local product. It has a sweet maple flavor that I haven't found anywhere else. Oh, also rosemary and thyme that we grow ourselves. Fry up an egg over easy and put it on top, and that's it."

"May I see your recipe card when you have a moment?"

"If I can find the card. I mostly go by memory."

Mrs. Williams looked thoughtful, as though she was considering something. Then she said, "I haven't tasted this for thirty years."

An hour later, Trinket and Speck were saddled, with Alisha on one and Abbie on the other. I must admit that the point of this is a photo opportunity. Parents love to get a picture of their child on a pony. We took a few pictures with Jackie standing next to Abbie on Speck. Then we took the picture that I'd been planning for a couple of days. Alisha was on Trinket. Sasha was holding the lead with her parents standing on each side of the pony. I told Leah to get into the shot, and I took several pictures of the whole Williams family on and around the pony.

This would be a great reminder. What I tried to do with all my guests was to take a picture of the family enjoying themselves and then send it to them about ten months later. My hope, of course, was to encourage them to come back to stay with us. But if not, they would be reminded of a pleasant time the family had together, and maybe they'd tell others about what we had to offer in the way of family fun. When you offer a family-friendly vacation experience in the middle of nowhere, you must use every marketing trick that you can think of.

I had several activities planned for today. I hoped they would be fun for parents and children alike. All my plans included being outside. As I looked to the west, I could see a storm headed our way. The property line is only a hundred yards west of my house, and beyond that is a corn field. You can see a very long way out here on the prairie, and I could see a dark blue wall of clouds coming toward us. "Sue, could you get one or two of the kids to help you put together some sandwich stuff and maybe grab the ingredients for homemade ice cream and take it all to the fridge in the dairy barn?"

"Yes. I see it coming, too."

"Thanks," I said to Sue. I turned back to the group and said, "You have all worked so hard, I think it's only right and proper that we have a special movie day." Our guests looked at one another, but my kids seemed to be very happy with the idea. "Boys, put the ponies back in the barn."

"Mary and Isabella, please come with me," said Sue.

"Katie, can you show Alisha and Abbie where we watch movies?" I was more than pleased when Katie took their hands and the three of them started skipping toward the dairy barn dance hall movie studio. Sasha and Leah fell in behind the little girls out of curiosity. I pointed to the west and told the adults, "In about twenty minutes, we're going to get very wet if we're still outside."

"Yeah, looks like it will be a pretty big storm," Mr. Williams said to me. We could see the clouds boiling up over the corn, filling the horizon. "Do you see that, Peg? This is why I wanted to come out here. The views are extraordinary day and night." For the next few minutes, we watched the storm roll toward us. Sue and the girls came out of the house. They each had an armful of food, along with disposable plates, utensils, and cups.

"What can I help carry?" I asked.

"Get the cooler I left on the kitchen table. It has everything else in it."

I went to the kitchen and retrieved the cooler. It was very heavy. I wondered if Sue had left anything in the kitchen. As I lugged it out of the house, I saw the Williamses, Jackie, Sue, and the girls were almost at the dairy barn. The wind picked up, and I felt the temperature drop. The weather can be dramatic out here. Slow as I was moving with my burden, I tried to pick up the pace. I walked across the barnyard, past the pony barn, and got to the dairy barn just as the first few raindrops started to fall. They were very cold as they hit my skin and wet down my shirt. As I stepped inside, I could hear the rain on the roof. It began to intensify as I carried the cooler into a side room where we kept a small refrigerator. Sue was already putting things away. "I'm glad that you packed enough food for a week, but I don't think we'll be holed up here that long," I joked.

"The cooler is full of ice. You did want to make homemade ice cream, right?"

"Oh," I said. I went to the closet and pulled out the old projector. It was on a small cart, and I rolled it into the big room. I went back to the closet for the movies and picked up a box full of old reels. "I'm working with George next week. What would you think if I asked him what it would take to turn this room into a kitchen and add two restrooms just off the main room?"

"I'd say you must have come into quite a bit of money," answered Sue.

"Well, it doesn't hurt to ask." Before she could comment, I scurried into the big room. I should have waited to hear what she had to say, but the box was heavy. That and she would probably try to talk some sense into me. I couldn't help myself. I wanted to keep improving the place. I wanted it to be as wonderful in fact as it already was in my head.

I set the projector up and turned it on. The light hit the wall. Usually, I'd show movies outside at night, but with the storm moving in, I figured it would get dark enough to show movies inside today. "Bear with me, folks," I said. "It may take me a couple minutes to find the best spot and get everything in focus. I have shown movies in here before, but this time of year, what I really like to do is show them outside. I find a good spot and project onto the side of the barn. The kids sit on blankets, and we have movies under the stars. I guess we'll just have to rough it inside here with tables and chairs."

"Movies under the stars sound nice," said Mr. Williams.

It was dark enough inside that I asked Charlie to turn on the lights while I got set up. I got the film threaded into the projector and said, "OK, turn off the lights." The wall showed a countdown of "three, two, one" and then the famous Looney Tunes logo and theme music burst into the room. Bugs Bunny's face appeared on the wall.

"Who is that?" asked Abbie.

I looked at Jackie in mock horror. "And here all this time I thought you were a good parent. Don't you believe in a classical education for your child?" Fortunately, she laughed.

"Just watch," she said to Abbie. "He is a very funny rabbit."

I fiddled with the focus and sound during the cartoon. By the time it was over, I thought I'd about gotten it right. As I rewound the film, the rain really started to pound on the old barn. I put on the first reel of a Laurel and Hardy two-reeler. Our heroes were having a terrible time getting a piano up a very long and very steep hillside of stairs. The first reel finished, and I rewound it before starting the next reel.

"Where did you get these old cartoons and movies?" Jackie asked.

"At the sale barn," I said. "Did you get a chance to meet Big Mike the other night? It's his place, and he has an auction once a month with all kinds of things people want to sell. I got this projector and all these cartoons and movies, but I don't know who gave them to Big Mike to sell." We watched a couple more short features, and then it dawned on me that I had a popcorn machine sitting idle against the wall. "Who wants to spoil their lunch with some popcorn?"

"Bob," Sue warned.

"I'm not hungry, but I'm thirsty," said Leah.

"Mary, would you show Leah where the fridge is?" I asked. "Hey, does anyone else want something to drink?" A few others said that they did, so I enlisted the aid of a couple more kids to distribute the bottled water. I plugged in the popcorn popper and dropped in one of those mysterious orange squares and waited for it to get hot and melt.

Mrs. Williams came over and asked, "So, what is the plan for the rest of the day?"

"Well, the rain kind of changed things. To tell the truth, I'm making it up as I go along." A thought occurred to me. It was the kind of thing that I shouldn't have even considered. If I'd thought about it for a few seconds, I'd have never mentioned it, but, sadly, I so often don't allow myself the time needed for intelligent thought before speaking. "We can watch your kids. They seem to be having a good time. We'll watch some cartoons, eat some lunch, and later, I thought we'd make homemade ice cream. You and your husband could go back to your cabin and, uh, take a nap." How is it I manage to stumble into these situations? I know it's hard for a young couple with children to get any adult time alone. I meant well. I really did. Mrs. Williams fixed me with a look. She was going to kill me; I was sure of it. I hadn't just stepped over the line; I'd gone two states past it. I blushed; I could feel the heat in my cheeks, and knew my face must be bright red.

Without looking away from me, she called for her husband, "Henry." Then she turned to him. "I'd like to see you back in the cabin."

"Are you kidding? It's pouring out there. We'll get soaked."

"Do you remember Jessup?"

"Vermont?" He paused for a moment, and then an enormous smile erupted across his face. Whatever their secret code was, they both knew very well what they were talking about. "Kids, your mom and I are going back to the cabin. Behave yourselves. We'll be back after a while." They walked out into the downpour.

I turned to Sue and put my arms around her. "One of these days, you and I are going to take a whole day for ourselves. Just the two of us." I kissed her as the popcorn started to explode in the popper.

APRIL 1980

A be had finished the milking and his other morning chores. Just like clockwork, the postman arrived and put the mail in the mailbox. He was always there about this same time every day. Abe took the long walk down the driveway to retrieve the mail. As he walked back up toward the house, he looked through the sale ads, letters, and bills. He noticed a letter from the bank. He wondered what this could be about. Abe walked into the kitchen and opened the letter with a butter knife. He read the letter but didn't think he understood it. After he read it a second time, he picked up the phone and called the bank.

"Crossroads Bank, this is Gladys speaking."

"Hi, Gladys, this is Abe. How are you today?" Abe was happy to get Gladys because she had been at the bank for nearly 35 years. She had started as a teller right out of high school when old Mr. Hagar still ran the bank. Over the years, she'd done every job at the bank, and everyone in town knew that she really ran the place.

"I'm just fine, Abe. How are you doing?" Gladys was more than happy to have a reason to speak to Abe. He had been the big high school football hero when she was a freshman. Gladys had never married, and while she would never admit it even to herself, she still had a crush on Abe.

"Oh, I'm OK."

"And how is Sarah?"

"She's fine. The reason I called, uh, well, I got a letter that I don't really understand."

"Oh. What is it?" Gladys asked. Abe read the letter to her. Gladys was confused for a moment and then said, "This must be some kind of mistake, Abe. You and Sarah have never missed a loan payment. In fact, your line of credit goes back to when your dad owned the farm. It sounds a little like one of our form letters, but it isn't one of those. Give me a few minutes to check on this. I'll call you back."

Abe thanked her and hung up. He poured himself a cup of coffee and looked at the other pieces of mail while he waited. About 15 minutes later, the phone rang. Abe picked it up and said, "Hello."

"Abe, it's Gladys."

"Thanks for getting back to me."

"I don't know what to say."

Abe stiffened in his chair. Gladys was as friendly a person as he had ever met, and she liked talking. If she was at a loss for words, the news couldn't be good. "Just tell me what's going on."

"Most of the bank's loans have a clause, a balloon payment, that allows the bank to call the loan at any time after a set number of years. Usually, we just refinance at a higher rate if interest rates have risen or simply continue as before if rates have remained flat. You haven't done anything wrong. There is no reason for this, but Mr. Newport has called the loan."

"What does that mean?"

"It means that you owe the balance of your loan, in full, well, now."

"Let me talk to Mr. Newport." Abe put an unpleasant emphasis on the *mister*.

"Right after I talked to him, he left. He said he wouldn't be back today, but for you to make an appointment if you wanted to talk to him. Abe, I just don't know what to say. I've seen him make some decisions that seemed wrong, or that hurt people, but I've never seen him make one that was so clearly a disservice to the bank itself."

"This has been a long time coming, Gladys. George Newport and I have been at odds for a lot of years. He has finally figured out a way to get at me and wants to face me on his home field." Abe thought for a moment. "I guess I'd better make an appointment. Think he'll be available about 10:30 tomorrow?"

"I'll put you down in his appointment book. I'm sure sorry about all this, Abe."

"Nothing for you to be sorry about, Gladys. Thanks for your help." With that, Abe hung up and began thinking about what he'd say to George Newport.

The next day, Abe was in the bank about ten minutes early for his meeting. He spoke briefly with Gladys and then sat down in the waiting area. Gladys had buzzed Mr. Newport's office phone and told him Abe was waiting. George Newport told Gladys that he'd tell her when he was ready to see him. Eleven o'clock came and went. Gladys couldn't keep her mind on her work. She kept apologizing to Abe and offering to get him coffee.

Abe stayed calm. He sat in his chair reading a two-year-old fishing magazine. He knew Newport wanted the meeting on his home turf. Abe also figured that Newport would make him wait.

George Newport was nervous. He had come in early — which he never did — to set his trap, but wasn't sure if he could pull it off. Before anyone else arrived at the bank that morning, he had adjusted two cameras, so his entire office was on the security monitor. Everything visual would be recorded, but with no sound. He could say anything he wanted to provoke Abe, and when the big man reacted, it would be captured on film. It wouldn't matter if Abe was the best friend of the sheriff; the video evidence would be enough for the state patrol, if it came to that. George Newport was only concerned that Abe would overreact. He wanted a dramatic video so that Abe could be charged with a crime, but Abe was a very big man. An overreaction by Abe could mean severe pain for him. The best-case scenario would be Abe tipping over his desk or throwing and breaking things. At a quarter after eleven, he buzzed Gladys' phone to tell her to send Abe in.

George Newport made an elaborate show for the camera, standing and gesturing for Abe to take a seat. Both men sat down, Abe in a chair that was a bit too small for him, and George behind a huge black desk. Newport started with a small needle, "So you wanted to see me. What can I do for you?"

"For starters, you could get some new magazines for your lobby."

"I'm quite sure you didn't come here to discuss my magazines."

"No. I came to ask why you want to end a profitable relationship."

"You give yourself too much credit. The bank doesn't make much money on you."

"So, rather than make money, you want to do what?"

George Newport couldn't wait any longer. "I want to take your farm."

"This isn't business, is it? This is personal." Abe knew very well that this whole thing was personal, but he kept calm. "Besides, if you're going to go around saying things like this, you need to grow one of those long black mustaches that you can twiddle between your fingers."

"Of course, it's personal. You tried to kill my son!" Newport spat out the words.

"Speaking of, how is George Jr? Does he still need help to beat up children?"

"He's in college and doing better than your boy ever will. One day, he'll take over this bank, but he won't have to deal with you. You'll be gone. You'll be the man who lost his family's farm." He smiled malevolently. He hadn't gotten the reaction he had planned for. In fact, Abe had been pushing his buttons. But he knew he could still salvage the situation. He could give Abe something to think about. "Unless...." He let the word hang in the air.

"OK, Newport, I'll play. Unless what?"

"I've never liked that boy of yours. Send him away."

"And just like that, all of my problems with the bank will go away."

"It will be better for you, and it will certainly be better for the community."

Abe had a dozen thoughts flash through his head. He thought of how Marcus was earning respect in the community and was more valuable than anyone in the Newport family. He thought about how spreading the word of this outrage should cripple the bank. He thought about how much he would like to pick up that big, ugly desk in front of him and beat George Newport with it. And finally, though he would never say it to anyone, he thought of sending Marcus away. This was the thought that shook him. "I guess we're done here." Abe stood.

"Not quite. Your loan is due. By law, I'm required to give you 30 days, but I'm a generous man. I'll give you until the end of next month. Get the total from Gladys on your way out." George Newport's face was a mask of hate. He had accomplished almost nothing of what he had planned, but he had released some of his venom.

"I can't believe it took you five years to come up with this," Abe said over his shoulder as he walked out of the office.

"I've been thinking about this for much longer than five years," said George Newport to the walls of his now-empty office.

After getting the information he needed from Gladys, Abe decided to treat himself to lunch at the café. The cost of a burger, fries, and a cup of coffee wouldn't make much difference at this point. The payoff amount on the loan was almost $38,000. It might as well be a million. He had less than a thousand dollars in his savings account. What would he tell Sarah?

Abe waved and said hello to all the familiar folks in the café as he walked in and sat at the counter. Norma smiled and said a quick hi, but she didn't have time to talk. It was almost noon, and the café was filling up. One of her waitresses had called in sick, while another had run away with her boyfriend, becoming the new hot topic of conversation in this small town.

Abe sat and sipped his coffee as he waited for his food. He tried to think about his situation, but the lively atmosphere kept distracting him. At two big tables, the coffee loafers were holding forth. These were the old, retired guys from around the area who met every day to talk and trade insults. Most of them ate breakfast at home and then went to the café. They drank coffee all morning, right up until the lunch rush, when they would order lunch or Norma would diplomatically tell them she needed the tables for her lunch crowd. They enjoyed giving Norma a hard time, but they didn't mean any harm.

"Norma, I need a menu," one of the old guys shouted across the room. He could see how busy she was.

"What do you want with a menu?" asked another coffee loafer as he got up to go home for lunch. "You're only going to order the same thing you do every day."

"I'm trying to broaden my horizons."

"Broaden your waistline, more like."

"You're dumber than a bag full of hammers, do you know that?"

"Well, you're dumber than a second coat of paint."

"Oh, yeah, well, you're dumber than a box of rocks."

"And you're dumber than a sack of barber hair."

"I think we can agree that you're all dumb," said Norma, bringing menus. "Now who's staying and who's going?"

"I gotta head home, Norma. My wife is probably wondering what happened to me."

"We all been wondering that," said one of the old guys.

Yet another of the coffee loafers got up and said, "What do I owe you?"

"Just drop fifty cents in the jar by the cash register, would you, Clint?" Norma said.

Another coffee loafer joined the fray, "Fifty cents for a cup of coffee? I'd expect that kind of price out of a place that had crystal chandeliers."

One of the guys sitting a few stools down from Abe shouted, "Knowing you guys, that's fifty cents for a coffee and a dozen refills. Now, will you leave Norma alone so she can get the food served? My boy and I are hungry."

"Be right there, Jim," said Norma.

A man sitting at the counter turned to Jim and said, "I see you've got a helper with you today. How old is he now?"

"He's four," said Jim. "My wife's sick, so I brought him to the shop with me. Tell Bert, here, what we've been doing today."

The little boy went from sitting on the stool to kneeling on it. "I hand my Daddy tools," he said proudly.

"And I'll bet you do a fine job of it, too," said Bert. "I wonder if your wife has what one of Norma's gals has. She's sick, too."

"Could be. There's probably something going around."

"Hey, I heard a good one the other day. An Iowan is flying to London. Halfway over the Atlantic, one of the engines flames out. The captain comes on the intercom and says, 'Ladies and gentlemen, we have lost an engine, but I want to assure you that the three remaining engines are more than enough to get us safely to London. However, it will take us an additional two hours.' A little while later, a second engine burns out. The captain comes back on and says, 'Ladies and gentlemen, as you have no doubt noticed, we have lost a second engine, but there is no need to fear, our remaining two engines are enough to get us safely to our destination. Unfortunately, it will now take us an additional four hours.' Well, wouldn't you know, just a few minutes after that, another engine burns out. The captain comes on the PA and says, 'Ladies and gentlemen, we have just lost our third engine. While the situation is dire, I want to assure you that the remaining engine has enough power to get us to London, but it will take us an additional six hours.' Of course, the fourth engine flames out. The Iowan stands up and shouts, 'Doggonit, now we'll be up here all night!'"

Norma slid a plate with a burger and fries in front of Bert. Turning to Jim, she said, "Yours will be right out." She raced back to clean off one of the tables just as the cook rang the bell in the kitchen. She left the heavy plastic tub with dirty dishes on the table and retrieved the food from the kitchen. As she set it down in front of Jim and his boy, Bert took the top bun off his hamburger to add ketchup and mustard from the containers on the counter.

"Man, that's a tiny burger," Bert joked.

Jim lifted the top from his hamburger and joined in the fun, "Where's the burger?"

Taking his father seriously, the little boy said, "It's under the pickle, Daddy." The little voice carried all over the café. The coffee loafers howled with laughter. Abe snorted in spite of himself. Norma put down the pitcher of iced tea she had just picked up and walked into the kitchen.

Still laughing, Bert said to Jim, "I think we may have hurt her feelings."

"Yep. We probably went too far," said Jim. The boy didn't understand what was happening, so he just ate his food.

Abe got up and walked over to the table that Norma hadn't had time to bus. He began to fill the tub with dirty dishes and utensils. One of the old guys said, "You're the biggest busboy I've ever seen." The others at the table had another laugh.

"You haven't got your food yet," Abe said as he nodded toward four more guys coming in for lunch. "Help me clean off these tables. You guys get that one over there, and I'll wipe this one down." The old guys got up and did as they were told. When they finished, they sat back down at their table, and Abe carried the overflowing tub of dirty dishes to the washroom beside the kitchen. Norma was wiping off a plate. "You all right?" he asked her.

"Most days, I can take all the jokes. But some days...." She didn't say any more. Abe knew what she meant. He sat the tub down and put a big hand on her shoulder. Without saying another word, he walked back to his stool at the counter, sat down, and took another sip of coffee.

When Abe first came in, he had thought about telling everyone in the café about the bank calling in his loan. He knew if he had, he wouldn't have to tell another soul, because the news would be all over this corner of the county by sundown. The old guys made jokes about women gossiping, but no group of women anywhere could hold a candle to them. Now he was glad he hadn't said anything. He didn't like public speaking to begin with, and airing his problems in public just wasn't his style. It was probably a good thing he spent most of his time working alone. He liked to talk to people every so often, and even enjoyed it sometimes. But if he had to do it every day, he'd probably go crazy. He knew what to do. He would go home and talk with Sarah, and the two of them would figure it out.

Abe drove home, did some of his chores, and started the afternoon milking as Marcus and Sue got home on the school bus. The kids came out to the dairy barn and began helping Abe without being asked or told to. While he was proud of the kids and liked having them around, he felt that he needed time to think. "Why don't you two go get your homework started. I can finish up here." Marcus and Sue looked at one another. This was unusual. Abe always had work for them to do around the farm. To be sent away to do homework within a few minutes of getting off the bus was out of the ordinary, to say the least. They did as they were told.

After supper was made, eaten, and cleaned up, Abe sat in the kitchen with Sarah. He told her about his meeting with George Newport. He told her most of his thoughts, but not all of them. He asked her what she thought they should or could do. She was at as much of a loss as Abe. They talked about ways of raising $38,000. All the options seemed to be anywhere from bad to extremely bad.

Marcus heard it all.

Marcus wasn't in the habit of eavesdropping, but he was almost in the kitchen when he heard his name in the conversation. He stopped just outside the kitchen doorway, heard the story, and the pain and even fear in the voices. Marcus was a quiet and watchful boy. He had done everything in his power to help on the farm; he worked part-time jobs to the best of his ability, excelled in school, and honored his foster parents. Now, they were in trouble, and he just knew it was all his fault.

Marcus needed a plan. He was good at setting goals and then planning to attain them. His goals were easy: to protect his foster parents and find where he belonged in the world. Nothing to it, right? He needed time to figure things out, and the only way to gain more time was some sort of delaying tactic. He would have to see George Newport and come up with an offer that appealed to the banker, enough for him to offer Abe more time. He could meet with the school guidance counselor — which he dreaded more than meeting with George Newport — and ask about early graduation options, colleges, trade school, and maybe the military. If these ideas didn't pan out, what would he do? Run away? No, that seemed like something a little kid would do. Find a long-lost relative? The sheriff had made a thorough search when he was orphaned. No grandparents, no aunts or uncles, no distant relatives. Well, the lack of distant relatives was a lie. He had pressed the sheriff quite hard a few years ago, and he'd admitted there were cousins. Marcus insisted on calling them, and Jeff had allowed Marcus to make the expensive long-distance calls from his office. He had been hopeful that they would want him — that they would welcome him to their home. What he heard was what the sheriff had learned years before: his call was met with suspicion. Perhaps they thought this was a scam, or a shakedown for money. But, whatever the reason, they denied knowing him and having any responsibility for him. This came at a time when Marcus was shown every day that he didn't belong. He was looking to belong somewhere. His foster mother, Sarah, was so kind and loving. His little sister, Sue, was usually fun, sometimes a pest, but loved him and looked up to him. His foster father, Abe, never showed him affection but would offer compliments on good work. Perhaps that's what prompted Marcus's great work ethic.

The next day, Marcus made an appointment with the school guidance counselor and assistant principal, Mr. Clarke. Mr. Clarke was extremely happy to have any student show an interest in their own future or ask for his help and advice. Marcus asked about an apprenticeship in carpentry. He liked woodworking and had taken a shop class at school, but was disappointed that all he got out of it was a birdhouse. He spent time in Abe's father's old shop. Abe was a decent carpenter, but he always said that his father was the best carpenter he had ever seen. Marcus could tell by the intricate carving on the furniture in the house and all the outbuildings that Abe's father must have been great at it. He couldn't figure out the house, though. The rooms were all different sizes, and the house just didn't look like anyone had put a lot of planning into the outcome. Abe had explained that his father built onto the old house when he had materials and time. Sometimes years would go by before another wall was knocked out and a room added. While the inside of the house looked good, the outside looked as if several building blocks had been pushed together. It seemed to Marcus to be a kind of Frankenstein's monster house. It made some sense, though. Each outbuilding was built with a particular purpose in mind. The house, on the other hand, just kept growing.

Mr. Clarke woke Marcus from his reverie and suggested that he consider college. Marcus wasn't done with the apprenticeship idea. "Is there some place I could go to learn the craft that would teach me and provide room and board in exchange for my labor?"

"I'm not aware of any place like that outside of a Dickens novel. A trade school would teach you the basics, but going to work for a master carpenter would probably be best. Still, you could get a job in a cabinet-making shop, or something like that, but you would likely be stuck making cabinet doors all day, every day."

"So, I'd still need a place of my own to live while I studied or worked?"

"Yes, most likely."

"What about the military?"

"I don't think the military would be a good fit if you want to become a carpenter." Mr. Clarke thought for a moment. "I get the feeling what you do isn't as important to you as getting away from here. Am I right?"

Marcus met his gaze and answered directly, "I want to graduate as soon as possible and move away from here. I need ideas on how to house, clothe, and feed myself with the least amount of money possible."

"I think college is your best bet. Your grades are very good. You could be accepted by many schools, and then choose the one that offers you the best deal. You probably won't get a free ride, but don't lose sight of the long term just because it'll cost you a few dollars up front. I'm sure Abe and Sarah would be happy to help you get started."

"No, they have money troubles of their own," Marcus said before he caught himself. He hadn't wanted to say anything about the family and the problem with the bank.

Mr. Clarke thought he knew what was going on, but he only knew part of the story. "I have a friend who is a Navy recruiter. It used to surprise me how many of our Nebraska boys went into the Navy; more than the Army and Air Force combined. I guess the thinking is that the Navy will be as far away as they can get. Anyway, I'll set up an appointment so you two can talk. Think about what you want and need now, but think about your future, too. I'll let you know when he can meet with you."

Marcus thanked him and went back to class. After school, he met Sue and told her that she would have to ride the bus home by herself. Then he walked to the bank. He asked Gladys if he could speak to Mr. Newport. Gladys looked surprised and then somewhat alarmed. "Oh, Marcus, I don't think that's such a good idea. Does Abe know you're here?"

"No, ma'am, he doesn't."

George Newport walked out of his office and stopped in his tracks when he saw Marcus. He only paused for a few seconds, but it seemed a very long time to each of the three forming an uncomfortable triangle in the bank lobby. Finally, Newport asked bluntly, "What do you want?"

"I'd like to speak with you privately, if I may, sir."

George Newport thought about saying that he was far too busy to be bothered. He considered telling Marcus to make an appointment with Gladys for another day. He thought about many things, but his curiosity got the best of him. "Come into my office."

Marcus turned to follow and bumped into a table, toppling it and spilling loan applications, new account ads, and various circulars about money markets and certificates of deposit onto the floor. Clumsy idiot, Newport thought, but said, "Just leave it." Then he nodded to Gladys. The unspoken message was for her to clean it up. He needn't have bothered, as Gladys was used to cleaning up all kinds of messes around the bank.

Newport sat down behind the barricade of his desk. He didn't ask Marcus to sit down, so Marcus stood. After appraising him for a few more seconds, he said, "I didn't think Abe was the kind of man who would hide behind a boy, but I guess that's just what he's doing, isn't it?"

"No, sir. He doesn't know I'm here."

"So, why are you here?"

"To tell you about my future plans."

"Why would I care about that?"

"I know you want me gone. My plan is to graduate early and join the military. I won't be out of here as quickly as either one of us wants, but I'll be gone sooner rather than later. All you have to do is leave my foster parents out of it."

Newport was about to laugh in his face and throw the kid out. Then he had a thought. He could use this. Yes, this might work out better for him. "You're smart; I'll give you that. You knew exactly what I needed and offered me just enough. So, if I don't call Abe's loan, you'll leave town as soon as you possibly can?"

"Yes, sir."

He picked up the phone from his desk. "Gladys, call Abe and tell him I was a little hasty. We'll go back to the original terms of the loan." He put down the phone and looked at Marcus. "So, we have a deal?"

"Yes, sir. Thank you, sir."

After Marcus left his office, George Newport began putting some details into his plan. Yes, this would be better. He wasn't the bad guy at all. He didn't have to call the loan and try to take the farm; that would make him the bad guy to everyone who banked with him. Abe was right about that much: it would be bad for business. But, interestingly enough, the boy was desperate to get out. Hadn't he just said he won't be out of here as quickly as either one of us wants? So, the story to be told is that Abe and Sarah want the boy gone. They are pressuring him to graduate early, and they are forcing him to join the military. No one would believe that Sarah would do that. Some, however, would believe that Abe might. That was all Newport would need — just enough people to think the worst of Abe.

Now, how best to spread this story? The old guys at the café could spread the word very quickly. Except Newport couldn't think of how to approach them, let alone strike up a conversation with them. He disliked them all, and he was sure the feeling was mutual. Also, he didn't want to tell the story himself. At least, not more than once. This needed to get into the general conversation around town in the most natural way possible. So, who would be the conduit for his slander against Abe? He was painfully aware that Abe was a generally well-liked man in this part of the county. It had to be someone who enjoyed talking about others and didn't care if they were hurt by idle gossip, or who was too stupid to realize the harm of telling tales out of school.

George Newport had another light bulb moment. Mrs. Burton, the biggest gossip in church, would be perfect. She always approached him after church. The woman seemed to have a pathological need to tell all about the horrible things others said and did. Not only was she brimming with rumors about who was seen drunk, or what couple was fighting and would probably divorce, but she especially loved scandal. What was more scandalous than a couple arguing about a child's welfare? Sarah, a good-hearted woman, was fighting her brute of a husband. He thought about including more details and then decided to leave it to the expert, Mrs. Burton. She would embellish the story perfectly. It could very well grow much more damning if he didn't try to direct it. This Sunday, he would plant the seed. Mrs. Burton would tell him of the latest goings-on about town and try to pry what information she could from him about who was struggling financially. This would work.

JUNE 2019

We had a wonderful time in the dairy barn dance hall movie studio. We took a break from films to eat lunch, and then Leah thought we should put on a talent show. I suppose what she really wanted was to get up on the old concrete milking platform that was now a stage. I told her to go on up. While she was looking around, I opened the light box and turned on my new stage lights.

"Sasha, come sing with me," Leah shouted from the stage, ready to perform, just not by herself.

Sasha shot a quick look over at Charlie and then said to her sister, "I don't know what to sing."

"You're a good singer. I know you want to sing. You sing all the time at home. Sing whatever you want, I'll help," came the response from the stage.

I leaned over Sasha's shoulder and said so only she could hear, "It's just your sisters and a few friends here. If you want to sing from the stage, go ahead, but you don't have to if you don't want to." Sasha thought about it for a minute and then walked up to the stage. She and her sister sang a song that I thought I'd heard on the radio, but I wasn't sure. After a second, I understood it was a love song. Charlie was very attentive.

"Your turn, Charlie," said Sasha.

"I don't have any talent," he replied.

"Oh, sure you do, come on," she urged. Charlie just shook his head, but instead of looking down, he kept his eyes on her. Sasha turned and looked at me, "What about you, Bob? What's your talent?"

"He can make a rotten, rainy day into a fun day," said Jake, smiling at me.

"Why, thank you, Jake," I said.

"He's quite right, you know," said Jackie.

"Actually, I have one great talent which I will share with all of you if Abbie, Katie, and Alisha will help me." Abbie and Katie were ready for anything, but Alisha seemed less than certain, probably because she was sitting by herself while her sisters were on stage and her parents were in their cabin. "I make great homemade ice cream. Let's get started." I led the girls into the side room where Sue, who had been doing all the work all afternoon, had finished putting away the lunch leftovers and already had the ice cream maker out and the ingredients in the canister. I lifted the canister into the big bucket and attached the motor to the top. Then I pulled the cooler with all the ice over by the bucket and told the girls to start putting ice around the canister. They each picked up a few cubes at a time and dropped them into the bucket. Even Alisha joined in. Within about a minute their hands were cold, so I took a metal scoop and quickly filled the bucket and then I turned on the motor. As the canister turned, I explained that we had to melt the ice to get the canister cold enough to make ice cream. I told them each to get a handful of rock salt from the bag that Sue brought over. They each took a turn dropping the rock salt on top of the ice. "Good. Well done. Now, we just have to let the machine work and add more ice if it gets below this level," I said as I pointed at a spot on the inside of the bucket.

It didn't take long for the ice to melt a little, and the girls added more, a cube at a time. That was alright, of course, because the goal was not efficiency; the goal was keeping the littlest kids occupied.

When Sasha stood in the doorway next to Mrs. Stevens, Alisha turned to her sister and asked, "Where are Mommy and Daddy?"

"In the cabin."

"They've been gone a long time. What are they doing?" Alisha asked her sister.

"Whatever it is, it must be worth skipping lunch for," Jackie said as she looked over at Sue and me and smiled a playful smile.

As it turned out, Mr. and Mrs. Williams got back to the dairy barn dance hall movie studio ice cream parlor just as the ice cream finished. We dished it into plastic cups and issued a plastic spoon to everyone, and I sat back to soak in the praise. As everyone remarked how good the ice cream was, I was quick to respond that they should thank Abbie, Katie, and Alisha for doing such a good job adding ice and rock salt.

It was about nap time for the little ones, but it was still raining outside. We got out some big towels and wrapped up the three little girls. Abbie snuggled into her mother's lap, Katie into Sue's lap, and Alisha into Mrs. Williams' lap. I turned off the lights and started another film, but with the sound turned way down low. As I walked by Mrs. Williams, she asked," So, what do you have planned for tonight?"

I rubbed my chin. "Well, what do you think about going to an auction?"

April 1980

Sunday, after church, Mrs. Burton approached George Newport just as he knew she would. He was only surprised it took her so long; he had to drink two cups of coffee in the church basement before she got to him. His wife was off talking to a friend. Abe and Sarah had left with the kids after the service. This was his chance. "Mrs. Burton, what's going on in our fair city today?"

"Well, I hate to say it, but Mr. Wallace stayed too long drinking at Norma's café last night. That's why he isn't in church today. He needs to realize that he is no longer a young man. That much drinking is going to catch up with him. He doesn't just restrict his drinking to Saturday night, either. He's missing more than church. I hear that his work is suffering."

"Has he been in trouble at work before?" Newport asked.

"Not like Otto Brady. I guess Otto got into it with the foreman at the locker plant and almost got fired. I heard that they almost came to blows. Isn't that terrible? I think what's really bothering

Otto is his children. His son is having trouble in school, and his daughter, well, I'm sure you've heard about his daughter. I can tell by your face that you haven't. Now, I'm telling you this is in the strictest confidence. Brenda was doing so well after high school. She got that job as a waitress at Norma's and then what do you know — she ran off with the Maxwell boy."

"It is difficult raising children. Sometimes it's hard to know what to do. Recently..."

"Oh, I haven't told you the whole story. They say that if those two end up getting married, it'll be a shotgun wedding, if you know what I mean. I hope for their sakes they elope and leave the area. Otherwise, everyone will do the math about how many months between the wedding day and the birth of their first child. And I don't think the math will work out, if you know what I mean."

George Newport looked just beyond Mrs. Burton. Two teenage boys were making fun of her behind her back. One boy said to the other, "One too many ducks on the pond, if you know what I mean." They dissolved into laughter as they walked off toward the snack table. Mrs. Burton was completely involved with her stories and didn't notice the boys.

"Mrs. Stapleton has already volunteered to direct the Christmas pageant again this year. She works so hard on it. She sewed all the costumes herself last year. It must have taken all her free time for months, the poor dear. Just between you and me, though, I thought the angel and the shepherd costumes looked the same. I was so embarrassed for her."

Newport wasn't sure how to introduce his topic. Every time he saw an opening, it slammed shut an instant later with another stream of consciousness pouring out of this vapid woman. "It is sad when it happens so close to home."

"Oh, there seems to be no end to the sorrows here in Crossroads. Mrs. Hershey's husband, John, has been stepping out on her, if you know what I mean. They say he has been keeping time with that little blonde bookkeeper at the Ford dealer in Lowe. As her friend, I feel I should tell her. She is such a sweet, unsuspecting person. I can't seem to bring myself to do it, though. Still, I feel so bad for her. Such a sad thing when families break up."

"I heard a sad story myself this week about..."

"They say Mr. Sutherland may have to go back into the hospital. Lung cancer, you know. He should have seen it coming, all those years of smoking. His wife begged him to stop, but he just couldn't. It is just the most awful thing when a person harms themselves. I suppose he couldn't help himself. We all know several people who should stop unhealthy activities but just can't. Maybe there isn't that much difference between smoking too much and drinking too much. Some people just can't help themselves."

"I wonder if I might ask for your advice." Finally, he found his way in.

"If I can help you in any way, I'm always most glad. I've been blessed with a good head on my shoulders. People are always asking for my advice and I'm only too glad to give it, if I feel I can be of any help at all."

"Thank you, Mrs. Burton, but I hesitate to ask."

"Oh, but you must. I mean, I'm only here to help. Aren't we all put here to help one another?"

"Since you put it that way, I suppose it would help to unburden myself."

"Yes, that's always the best thing, Mr. Newport. Now, what is it? Trouble at home?"

"Not me!" His voice rose a little bit, but he quickly caught himself. He just had to set the hook. He just had to remember what it was he was trying to do. Back under control, he said, "You see, that's the difficult thing: this is about another family. A family here in church. I want to help, but I don't know the full story."

"Tell me what you know," Mrs. Burton ordered, and amazingly, she allowed him to proceed without interruption.

"This week I got an unexpected visit at the bank from Marcus, Abe and Sarah's boy. He seemed quite upset. I don't know what happened, but he told me that he wants to graduate early and join the military." He decided to stay as close to the truth as he could. Mrs. Burton was leaning in to catch every word. He thought about adding more, but left her with, "Do you suppose the boy has done something and needs to get away? Or could it be money trouble, and Abe wants him out of the house? I just don't know. What do you think?"

"I haven't heard a thing about this, but I'm not surprised. In fact, I've expected it for years. Those two took him in when he was very young, but it was before they had a child of their own. That's the root of the problem right there. It takes a lot of time to raise a child properly, but some people just aren't up to the task, if you know what I mean. Some people can't manage to take care of more than one child, and that may be the case here. Children need lots of attention, and if it's a choice of giving what little you have to your own child or another who just happens to be in your care, well, you know what parents of limited means will do."

"So, do you think it is the time needed, or is it a financial problem?"

"Now, that's hard to say, but I'll bet that they are just overwhelmed, the poor couple. After all, some people just aren't cut out to be parents. But they're a church family. We'll rally around them. There will be no finding fault or pointing the finger of blame."

"How can we best help them?" Newport posed, reeling her in.

"Oh, now you leave that to me. I know about these things. I'll handle it all. Yes, I can take care of this. I just need some more information."

You'll make up what you need, he thought. "I'm sorry, I don't know enough to paint any kind of picture, but I knew just talking to you would make me feel better. You have a reputation for wisdom and discretion."

Mrs. Burton beamed at him. "Don't you worry. I will be very discreet."

"I know you will." With that, George Newport excused himself and went home to have a few celebratory drinks.

June 2019

"So, this is the famous Big Mike's auction house," said Mr. Williams.

"Most folks just call it the sale barn," I told him. I was very pleased that he wanted to come, or at least, said that he did. "Mostly, Big Mike sells livestock and ag-related products. But once a month, usually on a Saturday, he has a big auction where anyone can bring something they want to sell. Big Mike auctions it off and takes a cut of the sale price. You'd be surprised at the stuff you see on sale here."

"I already know a man can buy a big popcorn maker on a wagon and stage lights."

"Yeah, I take a lot of grief for some of my purchases," I admitted.

A man I recognized, but whose name I could not recall, walked up to us. "Hi, Bob. Hi, professor," he said, looking at us each in turn. "I just wanted to tell you how much my wife and kids enjoyed your star talk the other night."

"Well, thank you very much," said Mr. Williams.

"All my boy keeps talking about is getting a telescope. I told him if one goes on sale here tonight, I'll bid on it for him."

"Bob tells me that there are all kinds of strange and wonderful things for sale here."

"Yep, though I think the chances of a telescope going up for auction tonight might be a little bit on the slim side."

"Do you have binoculars?"

"I think I've got an old, beat-up pair somewhere. Why?"

"Before you invest in a telescope, and I by no means want to discourage you from doing that, you might take your boy out to a dark spot in the country, like Bob's place, where there isn't a lot of light, and see what you can see with a good pair of binoculars. You can see craters on the moon with most good binoculars, and they are a whole lot less expensive than a good starter telescope."

"I would have never thought of that. Thanks, professor. Good to see you again," the man said and moved on to the next group of people he wanted to talk to. This was a perfect example of what I liked best about Mr. Williams: he was obviously a very smart man, but he didn't talk down to anyone. He imparted information that he thought might be interesting, helpful, or useful in some way without trying to sound like a big shot. The result was that people looked up to him even more.

"If a telescope does go up for auction tonight, I know at least three people in the crowd who will have a good laugh," I said. I had hoped to see Big Mike so I could say hi, but he was probably busy getting ready for tonight's auction. I saw another familiar face and called out, "Hey, Albert, what was the hot sale item so far today?" Albert haunted the sale barn. He was an old, retired farmer who couldn't do the work anymore. Sadly, none of his kids wanted to take over the farm, so he leased the land to another farmer. Now, he stops in at the sale barn nearly every day to talk with the farmers and ranchers, as well as Big Mike and Lottie.

"A couple young fellas had cut some real good-looking hedge posts. Nice length on them. Anyhow, they hauled them in the back of a pickup, and that truck's back bumper was close to dragging the ground. Heavy and stout they were. Must've stuck out a good three or four feet past the tailgate. Anyhow, Big Mike had just finished auctioning a truckload of firewood, and he turned and asked the boys what they had to sell. They told him they had cut these hedge posts. Big Mike asked if they would deliver them or wanted the buyer to take them here. They said take them here. That was their mistake. I could've told them that there wouldn't be many people there who could haul those posts away. A lot of the guys there had trucks, of course, but probably took one look at the back end of the boy's truck and decided they didn't want their back end destroyed, too.

Anyhow, Big Mike, he starts the auction. He asks $50, which was a fair price, actually probably a good deal for the buyer, but no one said anything. Then he asks $40. Nothing. Not a peep from anyone. Then, he just tries to get an opening bid, so he asks for $25. For those posts, that would be one heck of a deal, now. Not one man went for it. So, Big Mike, he drops it to $10. One man offered the ten. No one raised him. The guy got those posts for ten bucks. Shoot, there were more than ten posts. He got them for less than a dollar a post. I couldn't help but feel sorry for those boys, you can't even afford to cut them for that price, but that's the way it goes, I guess. Fella that bought those posts had brought his cattle trailer with him. Pretty smart if you ask me. You never know what kind of a deal you might come across. Oh boy, I forgot, Big Mike would have taken his cut out of that, too. I think that's what they mean about adding insult to injury. Anyhow, that was probably the best deal of the day. Oh, there's Tom. I'd better say hello. See you fellas."

I explained to Mr. Williams that this sale went on pretty much all day and into the night. The day auction was stuff people hauled in to sell that day, while the night auction was stuff people brought in all month, or stuff Big Mike stumbled across during his travels.

"What's in those paper bags?" Mr. Williams asked.

"That's the kids-only auction," I explained." Big Mike wants to have something for the kids to do, so he sets up a table with those paper bags all stapled shut. He lets the kids bid on them."

"Even though they don't know what's in the bag?"

"Yep. I guess the kids think it's fun. Big Mike caps the bidding at one dollar. Usually, the winning bid is a quarter or fifty cents, or something like that. Then the kid gets to open it up."

"What kind of stuff is in there?"

"Oh, all kinds of different stuff. Last month, Mary got a bag with a yo-yo and a pencil. The time before, little Katie got an old metal top; you push a lever on the top, and it spins. Probably, it's stuff that comes in old boxes from an estate sale. It isn't worth much, so he bags it up for the kids to bid on."

"And a life-long auction goer is born."

"Yeah, something like that," I laughed. Until he had pointed them out, I had forgotten about the kids' auction bags. Now I wished that I had been more encouraging about the children coming, but Sue had wanted our kids to get to bed early tonight. Mrs. Stevens wanted the same for Abbie, and Mr. Williams told me that his wife was very tired. I thought about calling him a braggart, but I'd had one close call today, so I kept my mouth shut.

We walked around and looked at the things to be auctioned off. A couple of them caught my eye. A box of old picture frames, all shapes and sizes, called out to me. I thought about a picture of each of our foster children on the mantel. We have group shots, but not all that many pictures of just one individual child. Also, wouldn't it make a great Christmas gift to send a family who had stayed with us a picture of them standing beside their kids on ponies in an old rustic frame? The other item was a large, stainless steel, triple kitchen sink. I told Mr. Williams that I might have a go at that, but didn't tell him about the frames.

"Are you remodeling your kitchen?"

"No. What I want to do is put a small kitchen into that small side room in the dairy barn dance hall movie studio ice cream parlor."

"I didn't know you were planning on doing more work on the place. I thought you had just finished the remodeling."

"I doubt I'll ever finish adding on to the place. I keep thinking of improvements I could make and other events I could host if I had better facilities. I just do little things as I get the money; I don't borrow to do it. I can do a lot of the work myself, but I've worked with some good contractors on jobs around the area. When they don't have enough work to keep them busy, I'll ask for their help. Sometimes I pay them outright, while other times I trade work. I always try to make sure they feel like they got a good deal, and I work more hours for them than they do for me. A good plumber or electrician is worth his weight in gold when you're doing some complex building or remodeling. My design ideas aren't always up to code."

As the auction got underway, the picture frames went for way more money than I was willing to spend. Maybe they were antiques or something. Maybe someone just overpaid. But a few minutes later, I bought the sink for $17. I was a very happy man when I paid Lottie and carried the sink out to my truck. I thought Mr. Williams was behind me, but as I didn't see him, I went back inside to look for him. He was still standing over by where we had been sitting when I had made my triumphant winning bid. I walked over and asked him if he was ready to go. He asked me if we could stay a while longer. I was certainly happy to do it because I enjoyed being here, but we had ridden in together and I needed to take him back to the farm and then turn around and head for work at the interstate motel. I didn't need to be there until 11:00, so I didn't need to leave my place until 10:30, although I preferred to leave a few minutes earlier than I needed to.

"I saw something I'd like to bid on," he said. "I think Peg would like it. It reminds me of Vermont, and a time I'd almost forgotten about until today. Peg and I were walking from the restaurant back to our hotel when it started raining buckets. In just the two blocks we had to walk back, we were soaked to the skin. Much like today," he added with a smile. "There was this little secondhand shop we looked around in the next day. I bought this old umbrella with a carved wooden elephant head handle. Peg said it was the ugliest thing she'd ever seen. I said that we needed an umbrella."

"When was this?" I asked.

"It will be fifteen years ago next month."

"This was on your honeymoon, wasn't it?"

"Yes."

"And now you've found another umbrella with an elephant head handle."

"No. I found Peg's revenge."

"You lost me, professor."

"I kept that umbrella for years until it turned inside out in the wind, but on our first anniversary, Peg bought an equally ugly elephant foot umbrella stand. It wasn't a real elephant foot, just a wooden umbrella stand painted to look like one of those ugly things. She said if I was keeping that old umbrella, I needed a place to put it."

"Big Mike has an imitation elephant foot umbrella stand for auction?"

"Yes, he does, and it's going home with me."

"Why do you want two of them?"

"The original was damaged in the move to Lincoln. The joke was over, so we threw it away." He smiled a wistful smile. "My wife and

I are serious people. Getting older and having three children has made us that way, I guess. Sometimes, I just want to have a moment where we are silly and fun, again. The way we were all those years ago. When I give this stand to Peg, I think it will make her laugh."

"Sounds like a good reason to me."

SUMMER 1980

George Jr. worked at his father's bank over the summer vacation. He had worked there in the past, but this time his father was pushing him to learn more about the business. George Jr. was a poor student, and like all poor students, he blamed his teacher, Gladys. George Newport had tried to show his son the ropes, but was frustrated by his son's inability to understand the simplest things. Also, although he would never admit it, he was a very bad teacher. He knew the banking business but couldn't explain it very well.

Gladys was pressed into service. She taught all the first-time tellers anyway, so this seemed appropriate. Gladys was patient and kind, but George Jr. thought he knew it all and, consequently, made a wreck of everything he touched. His cash drawer was always off at the end of the day. Gladys was left to try to find the mistakes and fix them. George Jr. insulted long-time customers and displayed other bad judgments. Gladys tried to smooth over hurt feelings and correct the problems that George Jr. caused, but it was difficult. She couldn't think of a way to tell Mr. Newport that his son would never be a very good banker. She hoped he would see it and recognize it for himself, but he had too much pride in both himself and his son to see any problem.

Every day, Newport would take his son to lunch, usually at Norma's café, but sometimes they would drive to the county seat for lunch with other bankers and assorted businessmen. Newport liked showing off his son, the heir apparent to his banking empire. Today, they would have a quick lunch at Norma's. Newport had two appointments this afternoon, so today's lunch would have to be a short one, less than two hours. Norma served alcohol, but usually not until Buck came in around four o'clock to set up the bar for the after-work crowd. George Newport was one of the few customers who drank with his lunch. This noon, he limited himself to four scotch and sodas. He wanted to tell his son what was going to happen.

"You'll finish college next year. Then you'll start at the bank full-time. I want you to come on as head teller right from the start. I'll move you into loans pretty quickly, and you can work with me making deals all over the county."

George Jr. considered telling his father the truth: he wasn't anywhere close to graduating. He started each semester off with a full class load, but in a few weeks, he had fallen behind or was struggling generally. Then, he would drop two or three classes. At this rate, he would be lucky to graduate in another five years. How could he tell his father that he thought it would take him at least eight years to graduate from college? He wasn't sure he could get a business degree at all because he had to keep dropping accounting. Perhaps, he could get an associate's degree instead of a bachelor's. After all, a degree is a degree. It's all about what you do with it.

"I figure five years, maybe ten, at the outside, and you'll take over the bank. I'll stick around as president emeritus to help out as long as you need. Then your mother and I will do some traveling. I would like to see the world while I'm still young enough. Remember that Georgie—don't work your life away."

"Actually, Dad, I was thinking I'd like to take some time to travel myself."

"Well, sure, you can take whatever vacation time you want, but you need to get up and running first. The bank is our bread and butter; we have to take care of it."

"So, where will that Gladys fit in all of this?" George Jr. asked, changing the subject. He had nothing but contempt for the woman.

"Her role won't change," said Newport. He knew Gladys was important to the bank and did necessary work there, although he wouldn't acknowledge that she essentially ran the bank. His ego wouldn't allow him to recognize that without her, the bank would simply dissolve into chaos. She oversaw the tellers, negotiated most of the loans, and stomped out fires. Her efforts allowed George Newport to have long lunches and take meetings where he spent most of his time bragging and drinking.

"When I run the bank, she may have to go," said George Jr. He knew that she spent all her time running from one thing to another. Maybe if she concentrated on one thing at a time, she could work more efficiently. She certainly didn't listen to his ideas to make things work better. The bank would be better off without her, he thought.

"Gladys is useful. She worked for your grandfather, she works for me, and someday, she'll work for you. She knows lots of people in the area. I wouldn't be too quick to get rid of her if I were you." George Newport held up his glass to signal that he was ready for another drink.

"But I'll run the bank the way I see fit."

"Once I'm gone, you'll be the boss, and you can do what you want. Although by then, Gladys will probably be ready to retire anyway. No sense in rushing things. These things often work themselves out. She is a loyal employee, and I'm sure she'll work hard for you."

"If you say so." George Jr. let it drop. He just couldn't take the idea of Gladys looking over his shoulder and correcting him all the time. How would that look, having the boss answering to an employee? Moments ago, he was concerned about telling his father that it would take him much longer to graduate, and now, he had moved on to how he would run things when he was in charge. George Jr. wasn't especially stupid. Neither was he smart. He was, however, arrogant, ignorant, mean, entitled, and lazy. That is a very bad combination, no matter what your situation is or what is handed to you on a silver platter.

George Newport finished his fourth scotch and soda. He thought about getting another, but decided against it. He could offer a drink in his office for his next appointment, who was it now?

June 2019

I got back home a little before nine. The auction went smoothly and quickly. It was all over by 8:30. Mr. Williams offered to help carry the kitchen sink into the side room of the dairy barn dance hall movie studio ice cream parlor. It wasn't all that heavy, so I thanked him, pulled it out of the back of the truck, and carried it in myself. "We got back sooner than I expected. What are you going to do tonight?" I asked Mr. Williams.

"Same thing I've been doing all week. I'm off to set up the telescope as soon as I hide the umbrella stand in my car. Would your kids like another look?"

"I'm sure of it, but I'd better check with Sue. She wanted them in bed early tonight."

"If they want to have a look, send them out. You know where I'll be set up."

"Thanks," I said, and then walked to the house. To my surprise, everyone was inside playing board games. I wasn't sure how many different games were going on, and it appeared some of the players were involved in more than one game at a time. "We're back," I announced to the room.

"What did you bring me?" asked Katie.

"You have to share with the whole family. It's big and silver and shiny. I bet you'll never guess."

"It's your bedtime. Guessing will have to wait until tomorrow," said Sue.

"It is time for bed, isn't it?" said Jackie to Abbie. Both Katie and Abbie whined at the idea of leaving before the mystery was revealed.

"Well, I don't want you to lose any sleep over it. It's a kitchen sink," I said.

Charlie whispered something into Sasha's ear. Sasha said, "Now you really have bought everything at the sale barn." Mrs. Williams spat out the tea she had just sipped. She tried to stifle her laughter, which, of course, made it worse.

"Don't worry," Sue said, "It's funnier than you know."

"Why is that funny, Mommy?" asked Leah.

Mrs. Williams, now fully recovered, answered her daughter. "There is an old saying that ends with everything but the kitchen sink. In this case, Bob has bought everything but the kitchen sink from the sale barn and now, he has bought that, too." She looked at Sasha and said, "Let's go say hi to your father before we have to go to bed."

"Can I go look at the telescope?" Mary asked Sue.

"Mr. Williams told me just a minute ago that the kids were welcome to come out and have a look through the telescope," I told Sue.

"Mary, you may go out for a few minutes, but as soon as you have your turn, come back in, it's bedtime." Turning to Isabella, she asked, "Would you like to go out for a few minutes?"

"Uh, no thank you," was her quiet reply.

"I will wish you all good night, now. Mary, you heard Sue. Come right back in after you've had your look."

"I know," said Mary as she darted out of the house.

"She seems like a good girl," said Jackie.

"She can be. Then there are other times."

"Sounds like there's a story behind that."

"When we first got Katie, we put her into the room with Mary and Isabella for her first night with us. We figured she'd be a little scared and nervous, and we didn't want her to be alone. We told the girls to be especially nice to her. Mary's idea of being nice was to tell her a bedtime story. A ghost story. I had to work that night, so poor Sue had to sit up all night until Katie calmed down enough to go to sleep."

"I feel like one child is a full-time job. I can't imagine five," said Jackie.

"They're good kids, for the most part. Actually, great kids considering the cards life has dealt them," I said. "Anyway, I've got to get ready to go to work. I've got the night shift, tonight."

"When do you sleep, Bob?" asked Jackie.

"Oh, I catch forty winks every day or two," I said as I headed up the stairs to take a quick shower and change into my interstate motel clothes. When I came back downstairs, the party had moved outside. The three mothers had taken the littlest kids off to bed, and except for Isabella, all the other kids were out by the telescope. I drove away without saying goodbye.

The 30-minute drive to work gives me time to think. Of course, it also gives me time to fret about things. A friend of Mary's from school is going to Disney World for a family vacation this summer. So, Mary has been campaigning for us to take a trip to Disney, Universal, and Sea World. How do you explain to a ten-year-old that the cost of seven round trip-airline tickets, lodging, meals, park admissions, and souvenirs would be several thousand dollars more than we could afford? I don't feel bad about being unable to afford a trip to Florida theme parks. I do, however, feel bad that our big trip this summer will be to watch the fireworks display at the county seat. These kids deserve so much more than I can give them. I try not to think about it, but I do. I try not to feel inadequate, but I do. Then I decided it was far too lovely a night to have a dark night of the soul.

I pulled into the motel parking lot and pulled myself together. As I walked in, I was surprised to see Gene still there. "Thought you'd be home asleep by now."

"Oh, no. I manage a crappy motel on the highway. I can't think of anyplace I'd rather be on a Saturday night than right here," he said with what I guessed was irony.

"What happened?"

"Afternoon help called in sick, again." He stressed the word again. "I finally get Becky to go out with me, and I get the call. It wasn't going to be anything fancy — I'd just planned for dinner and a movie, you know. If she had an OK time, maybe she'd go out with me again. Breaking my date with her at the last minute probably won't endear me to her. I didn't want to call you because you work overnight, and this was Shelly's first day off in a week. So, here I am.

Becky was a cute girl in town that Gene had mentioned on more than one occasion. He must really be smitten because I'd never heard him talk about another girl before. "That's the joy of management," I said, hoping to lighten the mood.

"I tell you, Bob, I'm starting to think I'm in the wrong business. Whenever anything goes wrong, I have to be here to deal with it. I work nights, weekends, and holidays with no promise of a consistent day off or regular schedule. I'm really getting frustrated."

"The hotel business is tough. We're open 365 days a year, 24 hours a day. That's not going to change. You should remember this is your starter motel. Prove that you can manage this one and make money for the chain, and you'll move up to a bigger place with a bigger budget and staff. You'll always be on call, of course, but you'll have assistants to fill in for sick employees or when it gets unexpectedly busy."

"The bigger the hotel, the bigger the problems," he said dejectedly.

"Don't forget, the bigger the staff, the more personal problems you get to deal with, as well."

He laughed a little. "Funny, you're not making me feel better."

"You could be like one of the two families that have been staying in our motel for over a month. Their homes were flooded out, and they had nowhere to go. Count your blessings — it could be worse."

"You sound like my dad."

"He must be a very wise man," I said humbly.

"Yeah, yeah, alright. I'm going home. Full house here tonight, so I'll be back early to help with checkout. Just a couple of notes on the desk. See you in a few hours," he started for the door.

"Goodnight, boss," I said as he walked out. Maybe there was something in the air. We were all feeling sorry for ourselves tonight. I tried to keep busy, or I'd fall asleep. I checked the pool area. We close it at ten o'clock. There were a few towels and pop cans, but it wasn't much of a mess. I started a load of laundry and checked the desk notes. There was nothing important that needed to be done until I started breakfast preparations, just a lot of little tasks that were more annoying than anything else. I thought about the advice I had just given my boss. Did I really tell him to count his blessings?

The next few hours went by at the speed of a three-legged turtle. But when I started breakfast, things started to go a little faster. The first wave of early bird checkouts managed to space themselves out so I couldn't get breakfast to come together. No sooner had I started on the eggs than another family was ready to check out and I ran back to the front desk. I had, however, gotten the coffee going, so there wasn't a lot of grumbling about the slim pickings in the dining nook. Most travelers want a hot breakfast but will settle for cold cereal if there is coffee to go with it. Sue called and asked me to pick up a dozen eggs on the way home. Our hens couldn't keep up with all our guests. Gene arrived a little after seven, and we soon caught up with the second wave of Sunday morning checkouts. I stayed on a couple hours longer than normal because there was still no sign of the day desk guy. Our maids showed up on time and began work on the rooms that had just been vacated. About ten o'clock, the last wave of checkouts hit. Only a few guests remained in the hotel, those who were staying multiple days and a few who had obviously overslept. Our checkout time is eleven. I started to clean up the dining area, but Gene told me to head home.

"You don't have to tell me twice."

"Thanks for staying late, Bob."

I waved as I walked out, got in my car, and drove home. It's only a 30-minute drive to Crossroads, but this morning it seemed much longer. I needed sleep.

I have a good life, really. I'm married to a wonderful woman. Our current crop of kids is a good bunch. They get along with each other, mostly, and help out around the place. They help run the farm, host the events, and take care of the guests in the cabins. They keep up the grounds, take care of the animals, and help with the cooking and cleaning. It's not like some of the folks in town think, though. We don't foster kids just to have a cheap workforce. We do try to provide a good life for the kids, and we could run the farm without them. I've got an old spindle. I can drive the center piece into the ground, drop the top part on and hitch all four ponies to it. Just throw the birthday party kids on each pony and away they go, round and round. But we think it's important for our foster kids to have chores to do. Collecting eggs, taking care of the animals, mowing, and helping with meals, these tasks teach them responsibility. That's important work.

So, why is it, on mornings like this, I just want to keep driving? I crossed the county line to get to the motel. What would be so bad about crossing another and then another? What would I find if I just kept on driving? I can't imagine I'd find a better life, just a different one. Perhaps I'd find something to call my own. A place I belonged. The farm is Sue's. Her father left it to her in his will. The locals put up with me because I married into the community, but I've never really felt a part of it. I've tried to make improvements to the farm. I've shifted the focus from agriculture to hospitality. I don't know much about farming, but I studied hotel management in college. I'm not so much putting my mark on the farm as trying to keep it going the only way I know how.

The kids aren't mine, either. They're just on loan from the state. Sue and I tried to adopt foster children on two different occasions, early on. We spent a lot of money on lawyers but ended up broke and broken-hearted. Parents will not give up their rights to their children, no matter how screwed up and bad for the kids they may be. Courts always want to leave the door open for parents to get their kids back when they straighten themselves out. So, we stopped trying to adopt and tried to make the best home for them that we could. Sue is great at that. I do my best for them, but most of the time, it isn't good enough. I let them all down in so many little ways. Then, there was Allan. He still haunts me. What I could have — should have done differently. These kids deserve their parents back, shiny and new and unbroken. I know it's not a perfect world, but it should be better. I should be better. I should be so much more than I am.

This is my life. I have chosen this. But I keep thinking about my plans back in college. I was going to get a job with a large, upscale hotel chain. I was going to work all over the world. Whenever I got bored or tired of one exotic location, I'd transfer to a different one. I was young and strong, and the only thing I could do was anything whatsoever. You need me in France? I'll learn the language. London? I already know that language. Japan, Australia, or Tahiti? I'm ready. My bag is packed. Let's go.

I have no business feeling sorry for myself. In farm country, two bad harvests in two consecutive years mean ruin for the average family farm. The flooding this year certainly didn't help things. I'm better off than a lot of folks. Sometimes things just get to me. I know nothing about psychoanalysis, but maybe it's the responsibility that I feel like running from. That would be funny, wouldn't it? I think I'm teaching the kids responsibility, and here I am wanting to run from it myself. Maybe it's because 50 is now in my rearview mirror and I'm running out of time to do something with my life. Maybe it's because I sometimes feel Sue and the kids would be better off without me. Maybe I need a good night's sleep instead of going to work.

This line of thinking drops on me from time to time, and I don't know why. Strangely enough, it usually happens when things are going well. I'll work through it. I always do. I have to. Ringling Brothers no longer tour, so I can't run away and join the circus.

I stopped at the store to get eggs and asked to use the phone. My cell had died. I called Sue to ask if there was anything else she needed while I was in town. She couldn't think of anything, so I went to the back of the store to get the eggs. Mrs. Higgs was in the store but pretended not to see me. That was OK with me. I heard the store phone ring, and the checker answered. "Did anyone see where Bob got off to?"

"He's probably out baptizing babies," Mrs. Higgs muttered.

"I'm right here," I said, ignoring Mrs. Higgs' crack. Sue called back because we needed bread. So, I left the store with bread and eggs, and headed home. When I finally arrived the kids were playing in the yard, but I didn't see any of the adult guests. I couldn't believe my luck. Just a few steps into the house, up the stairs, and into bed, that was my plan. Inside the house, I was stopped by Katie. She had a blanket and a book. "Read me a story."

Some things in life cannot be ignored. A little girl and a story book are at the top of the list, even if you've been awake for 30 hours. We settled onto the couch, and she sat on my lap. She had only recently started to do that. Maybe she finally felt comfortable enough, or finally trusted me enough, I don't know. I was going to read a quick story and then go to bed. I put my head back and closed my eyes, just for a minute. I must have fallen asleep. The next thing I knew, Sue had her hand on my shoulder. "Go to bed," she said. "I'll take it from here."

"You don't have to tell me twice."

April 1980

Mrs. Burton did her work well. She asked everyone she met if they knew about the trouble Abe and Sarah were having with Marcus. No one had heard of any trouble, so they thought up some possibilities. One story concerned Marcus getting in trouble at school so often that Abe would no longer cover for him. This was impossible to believe as Marcus had only had one fight back during his freshman year; two sophomore boys tried to give Marcus a rude welcome to high school, and Marcus administered a beating that the two would not soon forget. Marcus didn't go looking for fights, and now the word was out all through the school that you probably shouldn't mess with him. So, anyone who had children in high school knew there was nothing to that story. There were more versions of trouble in Abe's household. Abe and Sarah were having problems with their marriage, and getting rid of Marcus would relieve one source of stress. This story got a little more traction than the first, but anyone who knew Abe and Sarah knew this was a ridiculous tale.

Yet another account held that little Sue didn't like Marcus and just couldn't get along with him. What choice did the family have but to get rid of their foster child to please their actual child? More people seemed to see this as plausible. Sue had been such a bright, outgoing little girl, but in recent years had become quiet and remote.

Other stories floated around, too. Not one story gained consensus, but everyone knew that there was some kind of trouble on the farm.

When Marcus talked with the Navy recruiter, the conversation started one way, the Navy man trying to sign up a dumb, young, kid. After a couple of minutes, the recruiter realized what he had: a very bright young man who was driven to succeed in life. This kid might be able to get into the academy. His grades were excellent. He was a hard worker both in and outside of the classroom. He wasn't playing sports; that could be a problem, but he was working after school and on the farm. Surely, a senator from the great state of Nebraska would write a letter of recommendation. Now the recruiter had to slow down and remember that he was there to sell Marcus on the Navy. "Your education is free. That would help your family, wouldn't it? With a degree from the Naval Academy, you could be an engineer, pilot, scientist, astronaut, or doctor. How about computers? That's the big thing now, and the Navy is all in on that. Oh, by the way, the President of the United States is a graduate of the Naval academy. You want to start early, and as long as you're 17 by the summer before classes start, you're good to go. Talk it over with your parents." Marcus didn't need to talk it over. A real future, room and board, no tuition, and over a thousand miles away from here. Check, check, check, and check.

The next day, Marcus informed his family about his plans: he would graduate from high school a year early and apply to the Naval Academy. Abe began to ask if Marcus had thought this all through. Marcus pulled an envelope from his pocket. He had written on the back. "Mr. Clarke says that I should be able to graduate at the end of my junior year without any problem. I'll have enough credits. The Navy recruiter said he'd get me a checklist of things I need to do this year and next year, in what order, and all the deadlines. First step: get your permission."

"Are you sure this is what you want?" asked Sarah.

"I am."

"Then you have our permission and our full support," said Abe. "I couldn't be prouder. Now, what's the second step?"

"I'll need letters of recommendation. The recruiter says from a senator."

"How do we contact a senator?" Abe asked.

"Write a letter. Say what you want to do and provide references for the senator's staff to check with," said Sarah. "I'll bet Jeff would be willing."

"Having a sheriff as a reference would probably be a good thing," agreed Abe. "Big Mike, or, for that matter, anyone you've ever worked with would say that you're a hard worker. How about the school counselor?"

"He already said he would help in any way he could," said Marcus.

"Then let's get this ball rolling," said Abe. "I'll call Jeff and Big Mike." He got up from the table and went into the den. He sat behind the desk his father had made. He called Jeff and grabbed a piece of paper in case he needed to make a note, and waited. Jeff was out on a call, so Abe left a message to call back when he could. Then he called Big Mike. An answering machine picked up. "Zero for two," Abe mumbled to himself. Here he was ready to spring into action, and all he was doing was sitting.

A thought occurred to him. This seemed sudden. Marcus wasn't even through his sophomore year and here he was planning the next ten years of his life, maybe longer than that. How long do you have to serve to pay off the Navy for that academy training? Was it four years? Was it six, or more? Abe would have to find out. What brought this on all of a sudden? He didn't recall Marcus even talking about the military before. He couldn't remember Marcus ever planning past short-term goals, like a part-time job after school or in the summer. All he had thought about at Marcus's age were girls and football, and probably not in that order. He laughed at himself, got up, and walked back into the kitchen. "After you do your four years of school at Annapolis, how long do you have to serve?" he asked Marcus. Before he got an answer, the phone rang. Instead of going to the den, Abe picked up the kitchen wall phone and said, "Hello."

Their Methodist Minister was on the other end of the line. "Hi, Abe. How are you and Sarah doing?"

"We're fine."

"And Marcus and Sue?"

"They couldn't be better."

"Good to hear. I was wondering if I could get together with you and Sarah sometime this week. I know it's difficult for you to get away from the farm, so I was thinking I'd stop by, if that's OK with you."

"We're always glad to see you, Reverend." Sarah shot Abe a questioning glance. Abe shrugged his shoulders in response. "Any day is fine. Stop by about lunch time, and we'll kill the fatted calf."

"How about tomorrow, then?" the Minister asked.

Abe put his hand over the receiver and asked Sarah, "You doing anything tomorrow?"

"No, tomorrow is fine," said Sarah.

Abe spoke into the phone again, "Tomorrow is fine, Reverend."

"Great. See you then." He hung up.

"I wonder what that was about?" said Abe.

"I have no idea. Reverend Street hasn't been out here in a couple years, and that was when he first got here and tried to visit as many of us in the congregation as he could," said Sarah. The Reverend Street had replaced the young Reverend Jones more than two years ago.

The phone rang again, and Abe said, "Hello."

"I heard you called," said Jeff over the phone.

"Now that's what I call service. I don't know why people complain about the sheriff department's slow response time," joked Abe.

"We can't all be farmers with nothing to do but wait by the phone," Jeff gave it right back to him.

"What do you know about the Naval Academy?"

"Now, that's not the last question I thought I'd be asked today, but I'd have to say that it's near the bottom of the list."

"Marcus is thinking about applying."

"Wait a minute. He's nowhere near old enough, is he?"

"I had questions, too, but the boy has been looking into it. He figures that he can graduate after his junior year and start at the academy that summer."

"Good heavens, how old are we getting?" Jeff paused for a moment. "Give me a second. I'm trying to piece something together in my head."

"I don't know if I have that long."

Abe could hear the smile in Jeff's voice as he asked, "By the way, were you aware that you and Sarah are having marital problems?"

"We are?"

"Yep, everyone says so."

"I had no idea."

"The husband is always the last to know."

"Do you mind telling me what you're talking about?" asked Abe.

"I've been hearing from two or three people that you and Sarah are having problems and that you may kick Marcus out of the house."

"How in the world did anyone get that idea?"

"Hard to say where or how these things start, but I can sure tell you that they're hard to kill. I told everyone who asked about you that everything is OK with you and Sarah. But you know how rumors are."

After they spoke for a few more minutes, Abe hung up and said to Sarah, "I think I know why Reverend Street is coming for a visit."

June 2019

I woke up with that strange, groggy feeling of a person who wants another few hours of sleep. I couldn't get my eyes to focus on the clock. What time is it? What day is it? Finally, I picked up the clock and brought it up to my face: four o'clock. Is it four in the morning or the afternoon? I lifted the corner of the window shade. It was light outside, so it was afternoon. It was probably Sunday, but I wasn't sure. I flopped over onto my back and tried to gather my senses. After a couple of minutes, I rolled out of bed, shaved, and then took a shower. I got dressed and walked downstairs. Sue, Charlie, and Isabella were working in the kitchen. "Good morning," I said.

"Good afternoon," Sue answered.

"This is Sunday, right?"

"We're getting the big Sunday supper ready, Bob," said Charlie.

"I can see that," I said. I was about to ask if they needed any help, but decided to sit down instead. I thought about things for another minute, and Sue put a cup of coffee in front of me. I kissed her hand. "Bless you and your good works."

"You should taste it before you bless me. That's instant coffee," Sue said.

"Any port in a storm," I said as I took a sip and then a gulp.

"George Grant is fishing back at the pond," Charlie said.

"He said that he'd like to talk with you when you wake up," Sue added.

"What time did he get here?"

"Couple hours ago," Charlie answered.

"Well, I'm not especially awake, but maybe by the time I walk back there, I'll be coherent."

"It's not that long a walk," said Sue.

"Ha ha," was my witty comeback. Sue didn't joke around often, but I enjoyed it when she did. I left and walked back to the pond. I found George Grant sitting on a small camp stool, watching his bobber playing in the water. "I figured a plumber would be sick and tired of water and would avoid it on his day off."

"Nah, I'm not trying to control this water."

"Catch anything?"

"Couple little ones. Threw 'em back."

"I hope you don't hold that against me. I'm still looking forward to working with you next week."

"That's what I wanted to talk to you about."

"Uh-huh," I said nervously.

"The job is getting bigger. I was hoping you could work a few more days, maybe another week."

"Are you kidding? That's great news. You had me scared for a minute. Yes, whatever you need, George. I'll be there with bells on."

SUMMER 1983

After six years of college, George Newport Jr. graduated with a general studies degree. He never finished a single accounting class. As for his GPA, he earned what was euphemistically referred to as a gentleman's C after seeking out and taking the easiest classes on campus. His father never asked what his degree was in, as he just assumed it was business-related. Now it was finally time for George Jr. to join the family banking business. This was great news for George Newport, who by now was getting drunk every day instead of just most days. George Jr. was less excited about it, as he had enjoyed his college experience and knew that he now would be expected to work eight hours a day, five days a week. Gladys was the least excited about it of all. She had been working more hours as Mr. Newport's drinking had increased, and now was working even more to correct all the mistakes the new head teller was making. She had given up hope that Mr. Newport would see how unsuited his son was for banking. George Jr. was now her boss and direct supervisor. She was officially in charge on Saturday when neither of the Newports bothered coming in. Now, she simply tried to keep the bank running while answering to a drunk and an incompetent.

Marcus was in his second year at Annapolis. Both Sarah and Sue wrote letters to him faithfully. Marcus wrote back every week or so. His letters were often funny, but he couldn't completely hide the fact that he didn't enjoy the Naval Academy. In one of his letters, he wrote, "As I sit here writing this, I heard someone yell out their window, 'The Naval Academy sucks!' I don't know why he felt the need to shout this. Everyone here already knows it."

He didn't hate everything about the academy, only most things. The honor code was good, but his fellow midshipmen, or at least many of them, looked for the smallest infraction. Anything that could be reported would be reported as a violation. A shoe scuff, being a few seconds late, even helping one of your classmates with homework was a violation and was sure to be reported; everyone was expected to do their own work with no outside help or tutoring. In the plus column, Marcus was surprised to learn that he enjoyed sailing, his summer training program. He also enjoyed the physical training, even when it was grueling. Perhaps, especially when it was grueling. He was used to being watched closely. Although it bothered him, he was well-equipped to deal with it. His grades were good; he worked well with others on teams and in drills. But, as in high school, he made no close friends.

June 2019

"While you're here, George, I'd like to get your opinion on something," I said as he put his fishing tackle into the back of his truck.

"What can I help you with?"

"Let's take a ride in your truck up to the dairy barn. I want you to tell me what you think it would take to put a kitchen in there."

On the ride, George said, "Hey, I heard this one at the barber shop. A guy is very self-conscious about his wooden eye. He had been rejected by girls his whole life. He figured it was because his false eye was made of wood instead of glass. Anyhow, he is so lonely he goes to the big dance. He is leaning against the wall when he sees a girl with a huge nose. He thinks she has probably been made fun of her whole life, too. He gets his courage up and asks her if she would like to dance. She jumps to her feet and enthusiastically says "Oh, would I, would I." He says, "Oh yeah? Well, big nose, big nose."

"That is both funny and a little sad," I said while chuckling. As George pulled his truck alongside the dairy barn, I said, "Come see if I've got enough space in here to put a kitchen."

We walked in and looked around. "It isn't very big. Just how much of a kitchen do you want?"

"I want something that professional caterers could work in."

"Bob, most of the caterers around here cook the food at their own place and then bring it to the event in those, what-do-you-call-ems, silver serving things with the top that slides off and the candle under it to keep the food warm. Usually, they just need tables to put it on, and if you don't have that, then they bring their own tables."

"Don't use those big technical terms. You'll confuse me. But do you think I've got enough room to put a big stove, fridge, and sink in here? Maybe a microwave, too?"

"Oh, sure. That shouldn't be any trouble."

"Excellent. Now, over by where I've got my porta-potties..."

"I didn't keep any of the fish I caught, you know."

"I'm paying for your advice by listening to your jokes," I said with a straight face.

"Then I probably owe you a whole lot more advice."

"I was thinking of replacing the porta-potties with a permanent bathroom over about the same place."

"That could be a little trickier. You may have to do an awful lot of digging with a backhoe to tie it into your septic system. Or, you might want to have an independent line to its own septic tank. I'd have to think about which would be best, cheapest, and easiest."

"What I'd like to do is set that up like one of those nice highway rest areas with a big concrete shelter and, at least, four toilets and sinks."

"Of course, that shouldn't be a problem for a man with all your money."

"That much, huh?"

"The concrete work alone would be way over ten thousand, and we haven't even started on the plumbing yet," he said. I felt he was being way too practical with the money I didn't have yet.

"Oh, before I forget, how much to add a couple toilets in the dairy barn?"

"You win the lottery or something?"

"Always planning ahead, George. Someday, I may be able to do some of it."

SUMMER 1983

"You've had a couple of good months at the bank," George Newport said to his son. "I want you to move from the head teller position to loans. You'll need to pass the state insurance exam. We make some great money with insurance."

"I don't want to be an insurance salesman," George Jr. whined.

"Now, son, finance is the right hand and insurance is the left. Loaning money is the king, but insurance is the queen. In a small town, running an independent bank, you need multiple streams of income. Have Gladys help you study for the test."

George Jr. didn't argue. It was just after ten o'clock in the morning, and his father already had a couple of drinks in him. He left his father's office and walked to his own office. As he passed through the lobby, he noticed that Gladys had left her desk and was helping the teller with a customer. There were three people waiting in line, but he didn't feel the need to open another teller window. Gladys and the teller could handle it; after all, it was what they were paid to do. In his office, he looked in the phone book to find out about the insurance exam. He would call the Nebraska State Department of Insurance, or some similarly titled state agency, to get the details. There was no need to ask Gladys anything. In fact, it galled him that his father would suggest that he get Gladys to help him prepare. He would find out when the test was, show up, and take it. How hard could it be?

Besides, he had other things on his mind. His parents were fighting again. Every evening was the same: his father was so drunk as to be worthless, and his mother talked nonstop about going to Denver or Kansas City to shop for a few days. Each wanted the other to change, and each knew that it would never happen. He wondered if they would get a divorce. It would probably be good for both of them.

Then he had a thought: who owns the bank? His grandfather had. Did he leave it to his daughter, George Jr.'s mother? Or had he signed it over to his father, George Sr? He would have to find out exactly who owned what and what effect a divorce would have on the business. At the rate they were going, a divorce seemed more likely than not. After moving back home after college, he had only stayed with them for a month and three weeks. By then, he had his first few paychecks and got his own place. Before long, he would move out of this one-horse town and live somewhere that had some action. He could drive to work every day. One of the perks of the job was his brand-new Trans Am. He bragged that it was the fastest and coolest car in the county. His father said that the bank provided a car for the bank officers. As far as he could tell, he and his father were the only two bank officers. Was his mom's car paid for by the bank, too? Well, one way or another, it was.

George Jr. walked back to his father's office. He thought he'd better ask now rather than later in the day; his father would likely be drunk by lunchtime. "I want to know what your plan is for me at the bank. Long term, I mean."

"Short term, you are moving to loans."

"Yes, I know that. We just talked about that.

"So we did."

"What do you have planned for me next year? In five years?"

"I've told you all this before, haven't I?"

"Things change. I want to know what I can expect."

"I expect you to take on more and more responsibility over the next year. I want you to do every job in the bank. I want you to know how everything works and fits together. When you've done it all, I will name you Vice President of the bank," George Newport said proudly.

"That sounds good, but you've talked about retiring. Are you still thinking about that? What's your timeline?"

"I haven't given it a lot of thought. I wanted to see how you were coming along. But I guess it won't do any harm to tell you that I thought that somewhere between five and ten years from now I'd turn the whole thing over to you."

"Will I have any ownership?"

"My, you are ambitious. Just like I was at your age."

"Who owns the bank, Dad?"

"That's not an easy, clear-cut thing. I control the bank, but, for all intents and purposes, your mother owns half, and I own half. Of course, it's not that simple, but I guess it's close enough."

"So, if you and Mom get a divorce, what happens?"

"I don't think that's going to happen," said George Newport, even though he had been thinking about that possibility quite often lately. "What's brought on all these questions?"

"I've been thinking about my responsibilities and my future. I need to have a foundation that's certain. I need to know where my place is. Am I going to be an owner, or just another employee?"

"You're being handed a bank on a silver platter. There's no way you're just another employee."

"But, without ownership, I am," said George Jr. Now is the time to push, he thought. He watched as his father finished his drink and poured another. "Why not give me a small percentage, say five percent?"

"I couldn't do that. Then your mother would own more than me, uh, I mean, the balance..."

George Jr. cut him off before he could collect his thoughts. "The five percent doesn't have to come from you, does it?" George Jr. smiled a wicked little smile as his father began to catch up. "I've seen you tell Mom to sign papers all the time. She never reads them. So, if my five or ten percent came out of her part, you'd have the controlling interest, wouldn't you?"

"What do you want, really?"

"You see family businesses that fall apart all the time, don't you? I just want to ensure that this one survives. If I inherit when each of you pass on, the bank that grandfather started — the bank that you built — will stay in the family."

"I'd have to review our wills, but I think that your mother gets my half if I go first, and I get her half if she goes first."

"That's easy to change. Just leave your half to me. I'll be doing the work anyway. That would be better than leaving it to Mom, wouldn't it? Remember, I don't want your share until you're not using it anymore. You can ask Mom to leave her share to me, too."

"But then we'd be equal partners."

"Only if Mom goes first. And, you know how it is, we guys always die first."

George Newport sipped his drink. The boy made a lot of sense. If he could get majority control of the bank by giving his son some of his wife's share, that could only be good for him. There was a lot to unpack here. Eventually, his son would get it all. Why the hurry? OK, he'd been the same when he first started: ambitious, driven, and always wanting more. A man with a plan. He'd married the boss's daughter to get what he wanted; although, in those days, he really had wanted her, too. He pushed his father-in-law to leave half of the bank to him, instead of leaving everything to his daughter. But it wasn't like his son thought. He didn't just stick papers under his wife's nose, and she signed them. She made sure she understood what she was signing. She was a banker's daughter, after all. Finally, he said, "I'm not sure how to talk your mother into giving up any of her share of the bank."

"Oh, Dad. She's not giving it up; she's giving it to me."

"Perhaps, you should talk to her."

George Jr. thought about this. Yes, perhaps he should talk to his mother. He could make sure her interests were protected. What else could he tell her? What did she most want to hear? To his father, he said, "I think you're right. Working on a problem from two sides is best, isn't it? Every son wants to work with his father, after all. I'll think about how best to approach Mother." He left his father's office for the second time that morning and walked back to his office. He passed Gladys, who was back at her desk, talking about loan options on the phone.

When he sat down at his desk, George Jr. picked up the phone and dialed his mother. "Hello, Mom. I was just thinking that I don't get to see you much now that I've moved out." He paused while she spoke. Then he launched in, "I know your birthday's coming up....What, it's past? I can't believe I missed it. Well, I know just how to make it up to you. When can I take you shopping?"

June 2019

Marcus pulled up to the house. His arrival brought joy not only to Slobber, but also to the children. He greeted each child in turn and then petted the dog. I was sitting on the porch with Mr. Williams.

"Hi, Henry. How's it going, Bob?" he asked.

"Glad I get the chance to see you again," Henry Williams said to Marcus.

"You can thank Bob for that." Turning to me, "So you've got some complicated carpentry to do, huh?"

"I sure do, and I knew you'd be just the man for the job."

"Did you think of me because of my extraordinary skill, intelligence, or good looks?"

"Because you work cheap," I answered him.

"Can I tag along to your shop?" asked Mr. Williams. "I haven't had a chance to see inside it."

"You're more than welcome, but don't get your expectations too high. It really is a pretty basic shop," I said. We walked across the barnyard to Sue's grandpa's old shop.

I showed the two men the drawings of the combination work bench and storage cabinet that George Grant had given me. "My problem is to figure out how to make this section strong enough to hold up the whole piece without being too bulky to move around. I was hoping we'd be able to screw it into the wall, but they don't want this to be a permanent placement."

"Well, first I'd say you might want to put this on wheels. If they want to move it around, that should make it a whole lot easier. Next, remember that in design, triangles are your friend. Triangles are naturally strong and don't need as much reinforcing," said Marcus. "I'd recommend cross pieces here in the back."

Mr. Williams looked over the drawing and made a couple of good suggestions. He and Marcus began talking, and I must admit, the conversation went over my head a time or two. Both men were well-educated, and Mr. Williams had a voice that was so well-modulated I felt smarter just listening to him.

"Let's make some cuts," said Marcus. "What wood does Mr. Grant want you to use?"

"He didn't specify, but I was thinking of three-quarter-inch plywood for the back," I told him.

"That will be strong, but also quite heavy. If moving this thing around is a priority, you may want to use something lighter," Mr. Williams suggested.

"What are you thinking?" asked Marcus. For the next several minutes, we happily exchanged ideas.

"By the way, Bob, you wouldn't know why my cruiser is getting exceptional gas mileage all of a sudden, would you?"

I turned away. "How would I know? Ask Tim, he's the mechanic."

Mr. Williams was trying not to laugh, but with his hand over his mouth and his shoulders shaking, he gave away my secret. OK, so he didn't give it away. Marcus guessed it, but I had to blame someone.

"I'm a little slow sometimes," Marcus said to Mr. Williams. "My gas mileage soared on three different occasions. Each time, after I was out here. I should have put it together sooner."

"Perhaps you could get the county to spring for a locking gas cap," I said.

"You see how my brother-in-law mistreats me?"

"I mistreat you?" I turned to appeal to Mr. Williams. "Last summer, I spent a whole day chasing down a man who I thought was a location scout for a movie studio." I turned back to face Marcus. "You wouldn't happen to know how I got that idea, would you?"

"How would I know where you get your crazy ideas?" said Marcus, grinning broadly.

"Who was he?" asked Mr. Williams.

"Turns out he was a salesman. He sold industrial water pumps. I found that out after I followed him all the way into Lowe."

"How did you get the idea he was a location scout?"

"No less a man than the sheriff's deputy told me he was a movie scout."

"Pity. Just think what a boon for business if someone shot a movie out here," said Marcus.

We went back to work on my project for George Grant. After a few minutes, Mr. Williams asked Marcus, "What happened with those three boys from the other night?"

"I talked with their parents. Got mixed results, but things went about like I thought they would."

"How so?"

"I know all the parents. I took a different tack with each set. The first visit went well. The parents were appalled at their boy's behavior. They promised to ground him as a punishment and to keep him away from the other two boys' bad influence. The second visit was a little more difficult. They couldn't imagine their little darling doing anything wrong. When I went into great detail about the fight, they backed off. That's the kid I'm most worried about out of the three. He could go either way. I hope his parents get him in line. Then the last home visit was to a family I've had dealings with before. They're the most openly racist family in the county."

"As a Black sheriff, how do you talk to them?"

"I didn't even bring race into the discussion. I knew that it was a nonstarter. What I did was try to shame the father by pointing out that his boy needed two friends to beat up one smaller boy."

"Did it work?"

"It probably didn't do much good, but I thought pointing out that he wasn't fighting his own battles would get their attention.

Out here, that's one of the biggest sins for a boy. If you pick a fight, you'd better be man enough to finish it yourself, without any help from your friends. Rightly or wrongly, boys are supposed to stand on their own two feet, whereas girls, well, you protect girls."

"I know what you're saying," said the professor. "It's tricky with girls. You want to raise your daughters to be self-reliant, but the parenting instinct to protect is very strong. I'm not sure if it's the same with boys, because I don't have a son."

"It is and it isn't, I suppose," I said. "I want to protect all these kids, but the sad thing is that, often, I'm protecting them from their own parents. I just wish I could do more for them. Give them more."

"You and Sue give them what they need. If you don't think so, then just imagine where they'd be without you," said Marcus.

"I've only been here a few days, but I can attest to that," said Mr. Williams.

"That's kind of you to say, but I see how you and your wife take care of your girls. They're strong, happy, and healthy. They have everything they need and probably quite a lot of what they want. I wish I could provide that for my kids."

"Don't get hung up on stuff," said Mr. Williams. "I'm not at all sure we're teaching the girls the right financial lessons. In fact, I know we aren't. Peg is a good woman, but she is much too concerned with appearances. We have a new car with all the gadgets. We live in a nice house, in a nice neighborhood. Not just a nice neighborhood, but the correct neighborhood for a university professor. You gentlemen may not believe this, but university professors don't make all that much money."

"Broke?" asked Marcus.

"Oh, no. I'd have to look up to see broke."

"When I worked part-time for Big Mike, way back when, he had a saying, 'My credit is great. I owe everybody,'" said Marcus.

"I'm right there," said Mr. Williams. "Peg wanted to take our vacation in Paris, but that would have sunk our financial boat. So, we came here. No offense, Bob," he quickly added.

"No. None at all. We are more than pleased you're here. Besides, you probably couldn't get pony rides in Paris. I know that would make Malia sad."

"It's Leah, not Malia."

"I'm sorry, I thought Leah was short for Malia."

"Most people think that. I understand. When Sasha was born, Peg wanted to name her Malia. I have never cared for that name, so we compromised and named her Sasha, which I think is a cool name. When Leah was born," Mr. Williams paused for a moment. "Now, I wonder, did Peg think Leah was short for Malia. Maybe she got her way, and I didn't even realize it."

"Big fans of the Obamas?" asked Marcus.

"Really now, how could we not be?"

I could think of a whole lot of people in the area who would be more than willing to provide a long list of reasons why not, but I kept that thought to myself. Whenever I'm around a political conversation, I tend to run the other way. When cornered, I'll tell people that I have my own stupid, uninformed political opinions, so I don't need to hear theirs. As for racism, I've never understood it. If you are bound and determined to dislike someone, just get to know them. We all have so many faults that you can find two or three excellent reasons to hate anyone you want. What they look like should be the least of it.

"Damn," said Marcus. He had torn his shirt on a rough part of my project. "I better see if I can mend this."

"Why do you always wear your uniform when you come to the farm to work?"

"If you saw the closet in my apartment, you'd see I have few other options."

"I can just picture it. A whole closet full of khaki sheriff-department uniforms."

"Don't you have regular clothes for when you're off duty?" asked Mr. Williams.

"Not really. Whenever I leave my apartment, I'm on duty. Why buy more clothes? I attend church, go grocery shopping, and do everything else in my uniform. It's a big county. I could be called to any part of it at a moment's notice. Any time I travel outside of the county, it's for official business: prisoner transport, testimony, or a meeting with other law enforcement. What would I need jeans or a suit for?"

"Also, you're campaigning for reelection nonstop," I said.

"There's more to that than you know," he said to me. Marcus turned to Mr. Williams. "When I got out of the Navy, the sheriff, a family friend, hired me as his deputy. He had just lost his deputy to the state patrol. Anyway, the sheriff's department consisted of the sheriff and me. We spent almost all our time out and about because the sheriff believed that it was important for people to see us on the job. The sheriff would usually have me out in this part of the county while he patrolled the eastern half. We didn't spend much time together, so he asked me to meet him every Sunday morning at the Catholic church in Lowe.

"Jeff, the sheriff, was a religious man. He never missed a Sunday if he could help it. Originally, the idea was to touch base and, since I was still green, give me a chance to ask any questions that I might have. We sat side by side in uniform there in church. I felt self-conscious at first, but after a while it seemed natural. After Jeff retired, I thought it would be a good idea to continue the practice, but instead of picking one church, I went to them all in turn. People were quite welcoming for the most part. Although I will admit, a few congregations let me know I wasn't welcome. Prejudice isn't always about race. Sometimes it's about the uniform you wear and what it represents to each person. Overall, I'd say going to church every Sunday has been good for me as a person. And, yes, Bob, it has almost certainly helped me at election time."

"I knew it," I said.

"I need to take care of this rip. I've got a needle and thread in my car. I'll be right back."

"Just trying to get out of work, again," I cracked.

"Always run to a problem, not away. Take care of little tears before they become bigger ones." Marcus walked out of the shop.

"The man has a sewing kit in his patrol car. Talk about being prepared. Is he really the Boy Scout he seems?"

"Marcus is the best man I know." Then I added quickly, "But If you tell him I said anything good about him, I'll deny it."

"Your secret is safe with me. You two are more like brothers than brothers-in-law."

"Yeah, he's the big brother I never wanted. Seriously, when I first moved here, Marcus was the only person, besides Sue, I was absolutely sure I could count on. Abe, Sue's Dad, was in the final stage of cancer. Sue and I got married much sooner than we otherwise would have, because she wanted her dad to be there on her wedding day."

"Were you a farm kid?"

"Far from it. I majored in hotel management. I also worked a lot of construction jobs. As a somewhat innocent young man back in the 1980s, I found working construction to be quite the vocabulary-building experience. Some of those guys could use any four-letter word as a noun, verb, adjective, or adverb, often all in the same sentence. Anyway, I knew nothing about farms."

"Well, then, I've got to ask you the same question I asked Marcus the other night. Why do you live here?"

"Doesn't seem like I belong here, does it?"

"No, I didn't mean that at all. It seems like this is exactly where you belong."

"Thanks for that, but some days I'm still not sure. I got a job right out of school with the Hyatt Hotel chain. I thought I'd work my way up through the management ranks and work at different exotic hotels all over the world. That was my dream anyway."

"Why didn't you?"

"After I started with Hyatt, I wrote and called Sue for months. We met in college. She was still in school. I was afraid we'd drift apart. Long-distance relationships are pretty tough. One day, one of the other employees at my hotel invited me to go to a party with her. She was the kind of woman we used to call a bombshell. All the guys at work were constantly hitting on her. Maybe she was interested in me because I was the only male employee who wasn't aggressively pursuing her. I can't think of any other reason she'd be interested in me. Anyhow, I told her I had a girlfriend. I don't think she'd been turned down before, because she leaned in and planted a kiss on me. It was a good one. My first thought after that kiss surprised me. I was a healthy young man. I should have been persuaded. But, as it turned out, that was the moment I knew that Sue was the only woman I would ever want."

"A short time later, Sue dropped out of college to take care of her dad. I knew she could never leave her father while he was sick. I was a young man in love for the first and only time. I knew I was a goner. We were married right here on the farm by the county judge, a friend of Jeff's. I thought after Abe died that we'd get back to my dream, but this is where Sue wanted to be, and I wanted to be where she was."

"I know that feeling."

"For my bachelor party, Marcus took me snipe hunting. That started us down the road we're still on all these years later."

"What's snipe hunting?"

"If you ever find yourself standing in the middle of the back field holding a burlap bag and after more than two hours finally realizing that no one is coming and you make the long walk back through the woods, around the pond, across another field, through the pasture and barnyard to see Marcus, Abe, Jeff and a few other yahoos sitting on the front porch laughing at you, well, then you'll know that you have been the guest of honor at a snipe hunt."

"I assume that also causes a man to surreptitiously add gasoline to the tank of his brother's vehicle."

"You assume correctly, sir."

"So, how did you learn to farm?"

"I never did. I mean, not really. Abe was too sick to help me, and Marcus was the new man at the sheriff's department, so he couldn't spare much time. He did help out as much as he could, though. I visited the county ag extension agent and asked what I should plant on the farm. He suggested a for sale sign. About all I do is plant pumpkins in the field and, of course, our vegetable garden. We have a few apple and pear trees, and I'm trying to grow some Christmas trees, but that's about it."

"So, you saved the farm by doing what you know best: turning it into a hotel."

"First, I didn't save anything. The farm was Abe's, free and clear. No mortgage. Second, yes, I did the only thing I know how to do: keep working and adapting to the situation at hand. I decided to go with the cruise ship model: all-inclusive, for anyone staying overnight. I figured we'd attract more people with a one-price-up-front style. After Abe passed, Marcus saw that I intended to stick it out. Abe had willed half the farm to Marcus and half to Sue. A few weeks later, Marcus handed me an envelope and told me it was a late wedding present. He had signed over his half of the farm to Sue and me. He really is the best man I know."

Marcus walked back into the shop. "Look at that," he said, pointing to the now mended rip on his shirt. "My time in the Navy wasn't a total loss. I learned how to sew."

Sue came into the shop and told us that supper was ready.

"Bob, you and Sue need to do something about your bees. I got dive-bombed when I went to my car. You either need to train them or I'll have to get one of those white beekeeper suits," Marcus joked.

"Beekeeper," I said, more to myself than anyone else. "That would be perfect. The bees do all the work. I wonder what I'd need to start and what it would cost?"

"Oh, no," said Sue.

"What?" I looked at Sue. She was frowning at Marcus.

"This is not my fault," said Marcus.

My wife sighed, turned, and left the workshop.

Marcus and Mr. Williams began to laugh. I didn't get the joke.

FALL 1983

Everyone who ever met Abe knew him to be one of the strongest men they had ever met. Not just physical strength, but mentally tough as well. It seemed that there was no bad news that Abe didn't take in stride, thinking carefully about what was best to do and then deliberately moving ahead. Nothing rattled him until Sarah died. The doctor said it was a stroke. Abe couldn't believe it; she was only in her mid-fifties. The doctor told him that strokes were more dangerous for younger people. At least that's what Abe thought he said. He couldn't seem to process what he was told or what had happened. Sue was shocked by her mother's death, which had come quickly and without warning. She was trying to be strong for her father who she could see was struggling. She contacted Marcus at the naval academy. A Navy chaplain made emergency arrangements so Marcus could travel back to Nebraska. She called the sheriff, and Jeff dropped everything to come and be with his old friend. She called Reverend Street.

The Reverend hadn't been to Abe and Sarah's house since he had gone three years ago to counsel them on what he had heard was a troubled marriage. When he first broached the subject, he thought they were trying to hide the problem. He pushed harder and quickly found that they didn't have a problem, he did — an information problem. Mrs. Burton, for all her faults, was often a reliable source of information. Still, he wouldn't have acted if it had just been Mrs. Burton who said there were problems with their marriage. No, several people had said so. When he found out that there was nothing to it, the Reverend felt foolish. The next Sunday, he preached an extraordinarily strong sermon on the evils of bearing false witness.

Sue planned the funeral. She went with Abe to the funeral parlor, but Abe couldn't pull himself together. The big man had taken the one blow that he couldn't stand up to. Sue answered the funeral director's questions and then turned to her father, asking, "Is that OK?" Abe just nodded; he was unable to speak.

Marcus had a hard day travelling. He took a plane to Omaha. From there, he took a bus to the county seat. The bus ride, with multiple stops, took almost twice as long as his plane trip. Jeff picked him up at the depot in Lowe to take him the rest of the way. Marcus had known that the sheriff was a good friend of Abe's, but he hadn't realized until this car trip that Jeff was close to Sarah, as well. Every time Jeff told Marcus how sorry he was, Marcus thought he should be saying that to the sheriff.

Jeff stopped in Crossroads at the general store. "I'm sorry for the stop, but Sue asked me to pick up a loaf of bread. I won't be a minute."

Marcus got out of the car to stretch his legs. It had been a long day. Sitting on the bench in front of the store was Paul Foster. Foster looked at Marcus in his uniform and said, "I heard you was a Navy man, but I didn't believe it. Now you and me have got something in common." Foster lifted the sleeve of his shirt to show Marcus an old, crudely done tattoo of an anchor. "I had this done at the end of WW II. I was in the Navy back then. Did my bit and then reupped. Didn't make a career of it, though. Maybe I should have. What do you have planned?"

Before Marcus could answer, a voice from down the sidewalk interrupted them. "Well, now, don't you look pretty in your uniform? Did you finally find someplace that would take you?" George Jr. said with a sneer.

Marcus was tired, and George Jr. was the last person on earth he wanted to talk to, now or ever. He turned back to Paul Foster and said, "I haven't really thought about long term. I'll already owe five years to the Navy for the academy training once I graduate."

George Jr. pushed Marcus. "Hey, I'm talking to you," he said as he pushed him again. "Don't they teach you manners at that fancy sailor school?"

"That's the last free one you get," said Marcus.

George Jr. stepped towards him with the intent of shoving him again. This time, Marcus blocked with his left arm and threw a straight right. Marcus's fist hit George Jr. squarely on the nose, which made a popping sound followed instantly by a crunch. Blood gushed down George Jr.'s face as he brought his hands up to his nose. "You broke my nose," he shrieked, "You stupid son of a..."

Marcus launched another right into George Jr.'s stomach. The punch knocked the wind out of him. George Jr. dropped to his knees, trying to catch his breath. "No, they don't teach manners, but they do teach boxing," said Marcus as he patted George Jr. on the shoulder.

Jeff came out of the store. "What's going on here?"

"That's what happens when you mess with a Navy man," cackled Paul Foster.

"Marcus?" The sheriff looked at him.

"He pushed me. I explained that I didn't care for that sort of treatment," explained Marcus.

"I want him arrested," George Jr. managed to say, his breath beginning to return.

"I seen the whole thing, sheriff. That piece of trash on the ground there came up and pushed the Navy man. He was backed up against the car with nowhere to go, and that sorry excuse for a man went to push him again. It was self-defense, pure and simple. I'd swear to it in court."

"Get into the car," Jeff said to Marcus. "And you," he said to George Jr., "stop bleeding on the ground, or I'll arrest you for littering and being a public nuisance."

"I'm telling my father," George Jr. spat out.

"I'm sure you will," said the sheriff.

Marcus said, "Thank you, sir," to Paul Foster as he did as he was told and got into the car.

"My pleasure, young fella."

When they got to the farm, Sue ran to Marcus and threw her arms around his neck. She had done her best to stay strong for her father, but now the floodgates opened, and she began to sob.

Jeff gave the two some privacy and walked into the farmhouse. "Hey, Abe. Sue had me stop and pick up some bread..." The sheriff stopped speaking as he turned into the kitchen and saw that huge table covered from one end to the other with food. "It's good to live in or around a small town. Your friends and neighbors take care of you, don't they?" Jeff said.

Abe nodded. It was all he could manage.

Jeff sat down beside his friend and said, "Marcus is here. He's outside with Sue." The sheriff paused and waited for Abe to say something. After a moment, he could tell that Abe couldn't make conversation. He filled the silence: "We stopped on our way here and picked up a loaf of bread." Looking at the table, "I guess we didn't really need to. Looks like you'll be eating on this for a month."

Abe offered a weak smile that quickly vanished.

"Marcus got into it with George Newport Jr. I didn't see what happened, but the only witness said that Junior shoved Marcus. When I walked out of the store, Junior was on his knees with blood all over his face and shirt. I probably should have taken the time to check him out and make sure that he wasn't badly hurt, but I just didn't want to."

Marcus walked into the house with Sue. As they stepped into the kitchen, Sue wiped her eyes and said to her father, "Look who's here."

Abe stood and shared an awkward moment with Marcus. They started to shake hands, then moved to hug each other in an odd greeting that was part handshake, part hug. Abe started to say something, then stopped. Marcus nodded.

They all ate a little, but not much, mostly picking at their food. Sue began to put things into the refrigerator. Marcus took his bag — he only brought one — upstairs to his room. When he came back down, he heard Jeff say, "I was thinking that I might stay the night, if that's OK with you folks."

"I'm glad you are," said Sue. "I'll get your room ready."

"Oh, good heavens, you don't need to do that. I can sack out on the couch."

"Can you imagine what Mom would say to that?" Sue said with a smile. Then the smile dissolved.

"I'll help you," said Marcus. The two went back upstairs to make up the guest room.

"Looks like I'll be sleeping in the lap of luxury," said Jeff.

Abe managed to move from the kitchen into the living room. When Sue and Marcus came back down, the four of them sat.

"You now have a properly made-up bed," Sue told Jeff.

"If I have learned nothing else at the Naval Academy, I now know how to make a bed," said Marcus.

"You'll be happy to know that I remembered to pick up a loaf of bread," said Jeff.

Sue laughed, "I guess we didn't really need it, did we?"

"You have lots of friends around here. Just try to remember that over the next few days. It's OK to lean on others when you need to," Jeff said. He turned to Abe. "You want to try to get some sleep, or would you rather stay up for a while?"

Abe didn't answer. He sat back in his chair and barely managed a shrug. Then he stood and said, "I'm going to try to sleep." He turned and walked up the stairs.

Jeff shouted after him, "If you want to talk, you know which room I'm in." Then he said to Sue and Marcus, "I guess I'll try to get some sleep, too." He said goodnight and went up to bed.

When Jeff was upstairs, Sue said, "I wonder why he wanted to stay the night?"

"He's probably worried about Abe. I am too, to tell the truth." Marcus looked around the room. "Do you mind if I sit out on the porch?" Marcus asked.

"Not if I can come too. I need someone to talk to." They moved out to the front porch, and each sat down in a rocking chair. The night was quiet and still. They sat silently for a little while until Sue said, "I'm so glad to have you home. I just wish it wasn't...." Her voice trailed off.

"I know what you mean. You don't know how many times I've thought about being right here on this porch. Just sitting and rocking. But, yeah, I wish it was under different circumstances." He paused for a moment. "So, how are you holding up?"

"I'm not sure it's sunk in yet. Mom died yesterday, just like that, no warning, no nothing. Dad seems to have shut down. He's only said a couple dozen words since, well," she left the thought unfinished. "He did say that he wants the funeral as soon as possible. Maybe he thinks that will make it easier for those of us left behind. I don't know."

"Maybe he's right. I don't know, either." He sat still for a minute. A cool breeze rustled the trees. "I want to thank you for writing to me. It means a great deal to me."

"Of course. I wanted to and I enjoyed your letters."

"I'll miss Sarah's letters."

"Maybe I can get Dad to write."

Marcus smiled but didn't laugh. "I'd be very surprised if you managed to do that. Sarah could talk about her feelings and pour her love out on the page. I don't see Abe doing that."

"You might be surprised. Maybe, once he gets started, he'd be able to express himself."

"I'm not saying he's emotionless; he just doesn't let his emotions out. He's not any different from most of the men around here. It isn't bad, it's just the way he is. Sarah always made me feel cared for and loved. I suppose Abe did too, in his own way. "

"He does love you, you know."

"I've never been sure of that."

"You can be sure. He does. I know he does."

"Whether he does or doesn't, I understand how much I owe him. I'll spend the rest of my life in his debt. Without Sarah and Abe, without Jeff, and without you, I don't know where I'd be."

"Everyone needs someone. Especially a kid. You're no different from anyone else, as far as that goes. Don't you ever forget that you have family here." Sue thought for a moment. "They wanted to adopt you, you know."

"I know."

"But you didn't let them. I never understood that."

"I couldn't explain it when I was a kid. I'm sure I hurt their feelings. I just thought that someday, somehow, a long-lost relative would come looking for me. I kept holding out hope that I belonged somewhere."

"You belong here."

"I'm glad you think so, but you saw how people were around me, in church, in school, in town. I still don't understand why it was so hard for them to accept me for who I am. Still, there it is. I'm an outsider. Anyway, I wish I could have explained that to your parents. I wasn't rejecting them; I was holding out hope of finding where I belonged."

They sat and talked for another hour. They realized how much they had missed each other, but they were exhausted and finally had to turn in.

The funeral was on Saturday morning. The Methodist church was full to overflowing. Abe, Sue, and Marcus sat in the first pew. Abe had asked Jeff to sit with them in the family section. Abe and Jeff both wore suits and ties. Neither Jeff nor Abe was used to wearing a tie, which added to their discomfort. Marcus wore a dress uniform. Sue wore a simple dress. Reverend Street said nice things about Sarah, as one might expect, but, as Sarah had been a genuinely good person, the praise didn't seem at all excessive. As the service ended, Abe began to cry. Quietly, at first. Then, violent, wracking sobs. It was the very last thing he wanted to do — showing his grief in public — but, probably, just what he needed to do.

June 2019

"Katie, have you been in my bathroom?" I asked the girl who was standing outside my bedroom door, wearing Sue's shower cap.

She very solemnly shook her head, *no*.

"You know you are not allowed in our bedroom and private bathroom, don't you?"

She managed a simple, "Yes."

Sue and I have almost no privacy as it is, what with five foster kids, and guests both paid and unpaid. Our bedroom and attached bathroom are our only oasis from the rest of our lives, so we strenuously protect them. This was an important teachable moment, but Katie looked so adorable that it was all I could do to keep from laughing. "How did Sue's shower cap get on your head?"

Her eyes got big, and then she said, "It fell on my head."

I thought I might do myself serious internal damage by holding in my laugh. But I managed to say, "Let's have it fall back where it goes."

I had heard the phone ring a minute before, but was dealing with boundary issues, so I hadn't tried to answer it. Apparently, Sue had. She called up the stairs for me. When you've been married a long time, you recognize when something is wrong simply by the tone of your wife's voice. She hadn't shouted. She did, however, sound urgent. I went downstairs to find her collecting her purse and car keys.

"Marcus has been shot. They're taking him to the hospital now. That's all I know," she said.

"Wait, I'll go with you."

"No. I don't know how long I'll be. You need to watch the kids and take care of things here. I'll call as soon as I know any more."

I was stunned. I wanted to tell her to stop and ask her again what happened, but she was out the door and gone. It took me a bit to process. My quiet wife was so very strong at that moment. It shouldn't have surprised me. Someone she loved needed her, and nothing would prevent her from doing everything she could to help. I tried to gather myself, but my thoughts kept bouncing off one another. What do I tell the kids? What do I tell the guests? I looked at the clock, but the time didn't register. I looked again: 10:30. I'd need to start making lunch soon. What were we going to have? I didn't know what hospital they were taking Marcus to. The small one about 50 miles away? The larger regional hospital that was 100 miles away? Was Marcus so bad that they would life-flight him to Lincoln or Omaha?

Jake must have come in at some point. I hadn't seen him or noticed him until he asked, "What's wrong, Bob?"

"Katie is wearing Sue's shower cap," I said distractedly.

"What?" he said with a questioning smile.

"Who is supposed to help with lunch today?"

"Not me," Jake said quickly. "I think it's Charlie and Isabella's turn."

"Where are they?"

"Charlie and Sasha are watering the ponies. I'm not sure where Isabella is. My guess is, she's probably reading. Is everything OK? You look kind of funny."

"I thought by now you'd be used to how I looked," I said, recovering a bit.

"Want me to get Charlie?"

"No. We don't need to start lunch yet," I said. My thoughts were still confused, but I began to make mental lists and flowcharts. I wouldn't tell anyone about Marcus until I got a call from Sue with more information. As far as everyone knew, Sue just had to go into town. I'd keep it that way for now. If anyone asked where she was, I'd simply say that I didn't know. Sadly, everyone would believe that. I'm sure she'll call before any of the children become worried; at least, I hope so. At any rate, I'd deal with that when I must, and not a moment before. Now, what do you suppose we have around here to feed thirteen people for lunch?

FALL 1983

When George Newport died, just a few weeks after Sarah, the people of Crossroads and the surrounding area felt that their world was changing. Some talked of these things happening in threes and waited to see who was next. Others wondered why two people, both in their fifties, would die within so close a time. Perhaps the coffee loafers at Norma's café had the most interesting conversation on the topic.

"I heard it was liver failure."

"Nah, it was a heart attack."

"Much as he drank, could be anything."

"Richest man in town, and he couldn't buy himself another day." Heads nodded in agreement all around the table.

"Was it true that he was dead in his car for a day and a half before anyone noticed?"

"It wasn't a whole day, but it was overnight."

"But he parked in front of the bank."

"Yep."

George Newport had left the bank at about 11 on a Wednesday morning. He was going to lunch alone. He got into his car and closed the door. That was the last thing he ever did. All day long, people walked past his car to enter and exit the bank. Although most noticed him sitting in his car, not one person stopped to say hello. As the two tellers left the bank that evening, they saw their boss sitting in his car, but they just kept walking. They were off the clock, and that meant they didn't have to deal with him anymore that day. George Jr. was in Lincoln taking the insurance exam, again. When Gladys left the bank after doing the books and closing up, she saw him sitting in the car but decided not to bother him. She thought he was drunk again.

When she came to work on Thursday morning, Gladys saw that the car was in the same spot, and George Newport was in the same clothes as the day before. But, as Gladys later admitted to herself, the first thing to strike her as terribly wrong was that George Newport was never at the bank that early.

At his funeral, the church pews were half empty. He had been a regular at the Methodist church, so most of the congregation's members turned out for the service. The rest of the town and the surrounding area did not. Unlike Sarah's funeral, where the church was overflowing with people seeking comfort in the service, the attendees of the Newport funeral spent the service looking at their watches and fingering their car keys.

June 2019

"Could I have a word with you, please?" I asked Mr. and Mrs. Williams. I looked around to see that none of the children were in earshot and said, "Marcus has been shot. Sue is on her way to the hospital now."

"What?"

"What happened?"

"That's all I know. Sue will call later with more details. I wanted you to know, but I don't want to tell the children until I know more."

"I understand," said Mr. Williams.

"Excuse me. I want to find Mrs. Stevens." I left and found her pushing Abbie on the swings. We moved a few steps away from Abbie, and I quietly gave her the same two sentence message I had given to the Williams.

I rounded up Charlie and Isabella. "What are we making for lunch?" I asked.

"I don't know. Where's Sue? She knows," said Charlie.

"Sue had to go into town, so I'm helping you two make lunch."

"Sue makes sure we have vegetables," said Isabella.

"That's very helpful," I said. "Let's check what's in the fridge."

It seemed everyone came piling into the kitchen at the same time: Jackie Stevens and Abbie, all five members of the Williams family, and my other three kids. "We thought that you'd done so much to take care of us that it was our turn. Today we're making you lunch," said Jackie Stevens.

"That's so nice of you, but, really, I can manage," I said.

"We have been here almost a week. We know where everything is. Now just sit down over there out of the way," commanded Mrs. Williams.

I did as I was told and Katie came over and crawled into my lap. "I'm sorry I went into your bathroom," she said. I hugged her to me. I felt as though I could sit here for hours.

The phone rang.

SPRING 1984

As the months passed, Abe kept going to church. Reverend Street had encouraged him not to withdraw from his friends and neighbors and to keep to his routine as much as possible. Abe knew that he was just going through the motions, but he got up every morning and did what he had always done on the farm.

Sue, on the other hand, did not. The teenage girl who had helped her mother cook some meals, kept her room clean, and did an occasional load of laundry now took care of the house. She did all the cooking. She did all the laundry. She cleaned every room in the house. She didn't stay connected with friends, perhaps because death isn't something teenagers understand. Her friends felt awkward around her. They didn't know what to say, so, for the most part, they didn't say anything to her. Sue didn't know how to deal with her new normal. The adults in her life all treated her with extra kindness, and that seemed strange to her.

Even though she was too young to drive legally, her parents had given her a car for her birthday. It was an old beater, but it got her back and forth to school. This wasn't unusual. Most farm kids learned to drive many kinds of vehicles — tractors, combines, large grain trucks, and cars — at an early age. After all, the only cop she was likely to run into in this part of the county was a family friend. Now, however, instead of going for a soda pop with friends after school, she went to the grocery store to buy what they needed for the household. When she got home, she would check on her father and help wrap up the milking for the day or do other farm chores. Then she would start on supper. After they had eaten, Abe would go out to finish whatever chores needed to be done, and then he would sit on the porch and relax.

Meanwhile, Sue would do the dishes, a load of laundry, and start on her schoolwork. Sometimes, when she had a lot of homework, she would take a break and clean the living room or the den before she finished her math or an essay.

Abe didn't want to burden his daughter with his pain, so he didn't talk to her as much as he always had. He thought he was protecting her. What he did was add to her isolation. Sue had always been able to discuss anything with her mother. She could talk with her father, but only about a few things. She looked up to and admired her father. She wouldn't let him see her as weak, fragile, or emotional. She could be herself with her mother, even when she was scared or uncertain. With her father, she wanted to be the person who made him proud.

Sue had always written to Marcus, but now her letters grew longer. She wrote about her concerns and the way life was now, without her mother. Marcus did his best to make her feel better. He tried to write funny stories about plebes falling off an obstacle into the mud, but Marcus didn't think his letters helped much.

Sue was touched when she realized that Marcus was watching out for the younger kids at the academy. He would write about the need to learn how to take it. He understood that. He understood the purpose of it. What he didn't get was the attitude of some of his fellow upperclassmen, who seemed to enjoy being cruel. What kind of person actually enjoys dishing it out? Sue had always known that Marcus was a good person. Now she knew that he would be a great officer who would take care of his sailors. Anyone under his command, if they did their job, would be fortunate indeed.

One Sunday, Sue and Abe rode to church in Abe's old truck. Normally they'd take a car, but Abe had bought some equipment at the sale barn on Saturday and couldn't get it all in one load. So after church, Abe had planned on getting the rest of the load. Sue was not happy about this. The truck was dirty and dusty. Not only would they have to dust themselves off before going into church, but she'd have to wash everything when they got home.

The Stuart baby was being baptized, so the whole clan and all their friends would be in church. The church had no parking lot, and cars were already lined up on both sides of the street for blocks in each direction. Abe parked in front of the Newport house, well down the street from the church.

"If George Newport was alive, seeing this old junker in front of his house would probably kill him. Hey, you know, that's almost enough to make me wish he was alive again. Almost."

"Dad! You shouldn't talk like that."

"Are you saying that it's wrong for me to be happy at the thought of my old, beat-up truck giving George Newport another heart attack?"

"We're only a couple of blocks away from the church. Try to behave yourself."

Abe didn't say more, but he wore a smile all the way through the church service. Afterwards, he congratulated the members of the Stuart family and then took a leisurely walk back to his truck. When he climbed into the cab and turned the key, nothing happened. He tried again and got a clicking sound.

"What's wrong?" asked Sue.

"With this old beast, it could be anything," Abe said. He got out of the truck and opened the hood. Sue joined him in front of the truck. "Could be the starter motor. Looks like we've got a good connection on the battery." He fiddled around with other wires, got back in the driver's seat, and turned the key again. The truck still wouldn't start. "I swear, for little or nothing I'd take the license plates off this thing and leave it here." He slammed the hood down.

They walked back to the church, but most of the cars were gone. "Probably a big party at the Stuart house," Abe said. Fortunately, they saw old Mr. Bass. "My vehicle broke down," Abe explained.

"Well, it would be a pretty good hike back to your place in your church clothes, wouldn't it? How about I give you two a ride?"

"We would be much obliged," said Abe.

Mr. Bass dropped Abe and Sue off at home. He turned down the offer of lunch and drove away. Abe picked up the phone and called the local mechanic. He got the answering machine. "Hey, Carl, this is Abe. My truck is about three blocks south of the Methodist church. I think the starter is shot. Could you take care of it for me? Oh, and call me if it's anything more than the starter, will you? I don't want to sink a lot of money into that old thing. Thanks." Abe hung up. Turning to Sue, he said, "I guess I'll have to pick up the rest of my sale barn stuff when my truck gets fixed." Sue didn't answer. She continued getting lunch ready.

That evening, Mrs. Burton returned home from her sister's house over in Oakville. She hadn't been to church because her sister had been sick, and Mrs. Burton had spent all day caring for her. She walked from her car to her door, but before entering, she scanned the neighborhood. She saw Abe's truck on the street. She wondered what Abe was doing in town at this hour of the evening. Then she realized that the truck was parked in front of the Newport house. Mrs. Burton sucked in a big breath of air. Could it be? The widow and the widower? She quickly went to her phone.

The next morning, Mrs. Burton was nearly overcome when she saw that the truck was still out front of the Newport house. She didn't see Carl, a few minutes later, hook up the tow bar and drive off, pulling Abe's truck over to the garage. She had been far too busy talking on the phone.

June 2019

"He is in surgery now. I don't know the whole story, but the deputy said Marcus was shot twice, once in the hand and once in the side. Oh, Bob, it took more than an hour from the time he was shot to get him from the Callahan place to the hospital," Sue told me over the phone.

"What does the doctor say?" I asked.

"I haven't talked with a doctor. The woman at reception said that the doctor will come talk to us after the operation. I just don't know."

"How are you?"

"I'm fine. I'm not the one who was shot."

"No, but your brother was," I said. I could hear her begin to cry. "I wish I was there with you now."

"You have to take care of the kids."

"I know. Still, I'd like to be with you."

"I think the doctor is coming. I'll call you right back."

"Don't hang up! Let me listen." She didn't hang up, but I couldn't really hear much of the conversation. After a moment, Sue came back on the line.

"Did you hear that?" she said.

"No. Tell me."

"His injuries are serious, but not life-threating," she said, sounding like she was repeating the doctor's words verbatim.

"That's great news, honey."

"I'm going to stay here until Marcus wakes up."

"When can you see him?"

"The doctor said I can look in on him when they move him to the ICU, but only for a minute. He probably won't wake up until tomorrow."

"Maybe you should come home and get some sleep, and then go back tomorrow."

"I'm staying until he wakes up," she said in a way that let me know the subject was closed.

"I could bring you something. What do you need?"

"I don't need a thing. I've got everything I could ever want or need."

I knew just what she meant. We talked for a few more minutes, and then I hung up the landline, got up from my chair, and opened the door. I thought I'd have to walk back into the kitchen to make my announcement, but everyone seemed to be in the living room waiting for me. "Kids, your uncle Marcus was hurt at work today, but he is going to be OK." The adults breathed a sigh of relief, but the kids seemed startled.

"What happened?" Charlie asked.

"I don't know very much about it yet," I said truthfully. "The important thing is that he will be OK, and that Sue is there with him."

"Come on. Let's finish lunch," said Mrs. Williams.

The group moved back to the kitchen. Mr. Williams stayed behind, and I asked him, "How did the kids all know to come out here and wait for me to finish my phone call?"

"We certainly didn't say anything, but Mrs. Stevens, my wife, and I all gravitated out here when you went to take the call in private. I guess the children just followed us."

"Kids do seem to be able to tell when something is wrong, don't they?" I said.

"I've never been able to hide anything from my girls, that's for sure," said Mr. Williams.

SPRING 1984

A fter church the following Sunday, Mrs. Burton took it upon herself to explain to Sue that adults need companionship. "It isn't that your father loves you any less, he just needs to be around someone his own age, that's all."

"I'm not sure I understand," said Sue.

"Your father and Mrs. Newport have been seeing a lot of each other, haven't they?"

"We see her after church, when she comes," said Sue.

"Oh, no, dear. I mean outside of church."

"I don't know what you mean."

"Oh, my. I've said too much. Excuse me, dear," and Mrs. Burton went off in search of Abe. She found him drinking coffee in the church basement. "Everyone in town knows about it except your daughter. You really should consider how your relationship affects her, you know. Sarah and George not even gone a year and you two taking up with one another. Well, the younger generation just doesn't follow the rules of decorum, I suppose."

Abe took a sip of coffee. He thought he knew what she was talking about but wasn't entirely sure. She rattled on for a few more minutes until Abe zeroed in on the main point: apparently, he and the widow Newport — who Abe still thought of as Miss Hagar — were having an affair. He considered denying it. After all, there was nothing to it. However, denying it would somehow make the story more credible. He chose a different path. When Mrs. Burton paused for a breath, he asked, "Do you know what makes your stories fascinating?"

"What?"

"Nothing," Abe replied flatly.

That evening, Jeff stopped by the farm after supper and sat on the porch with Abe. The two old friends talked for a while, and then Abe asked, "Jeff, did you know that I was carrying on an affair with Miss Hagar?"

"I heard about it from no less than three different people this week," came Jeff's reply.

"Why didn't you tell me? I'd have liked to know about a thing like that. I just heard about it in church this morning."

"You're kidding."

"No. Mrs. Burton told me. Needless to say, I was surprised. I figured I'd be the first to know if I had an affair. Here I find out that everyone in town knows about it but me.

"That is shocking. Don't you know that your love has been smoldering for what, over 40 years now?"

Abe snorted. He paused for a second, and then he said, "Seriously, though, Sue seems pretty upset."

"That's not surprising. It's been a horrible year for her all the way around without this stupid gossip. That's got to be hard for a teenage girl to take."

"She didn't say a word on the ride home from church, and all she said at supper was, 'I'm not going to church anymore.'"

"Maybe your Reverend Street could help."

"If you mean with Sue, I'm not sure she would listen to him right now. And if you mean with the congregation, I'm not sure how many more 'bearing false witness' sermons the man has in him."

June 2019

I took Sue a change of clothes in an overnight bag. She had slept in a chair in the waiting room of the small hospital. The other chairs were filled with sheriffs and deputies from six counties, police from the county seat, and members of the state patrol. While Sue changed clothes in the bathroom, one of the cops told me the story as it had been pieced together, so far. Marcus had been called to the Callahan farm, where Callahan had gotten drunk and beaten his wife. When Marcus got there, Callahan opened up on him with a handgun. Marcus was hit twice and tumbled into the rosebushes. His head was cut by the thorns. Callahan took off. Mrs. Callahan called for help, and they got Marcus to the hospital as fast as they could, but it took several minutes for his deputy to get to the farm after the shooting, and then even longer to get to the hospital, even with lights and sirens. When you live out where the roads aren't paved, it can take a while to get help. Anyhow, they caught Callahan in York and marched him into the station past a gauntlet of cops. I heard he wet his pants. I hoped much worse would happen to him.

Sue had peeked into Marcus's room. It wasn't technically visiting hours yet, but the nurses only seemed to mind if more than one person went in.

"He's awake," Sue said in a stage whisper. Everyone in the waiting room moved toward his room.

The duty nurse took charge immediately, "I'm going in to check him out. Then I'll update the doctor. Then and only then, can one family member see him for one minute. We are not going to wear the man out with visitors." She closed the door behind her as she disappeared into Marcus's room. Several minutes later, she came out and said to Sue, "You can see him now, but just for a minute. Don't wear him out. He needs rest." She went to the nurse's station to call the doctor.

One of the officers said to Sue, "Let him know that we're all out here."

"I'll tell him, but I'm sure he already knows," Sue said.

She went into the room but left the door ajar. I stood just outside. I could hear most of what Sue said, but I couldn't hear Marcus. His voice was too soft and weak.

"You have a lobby full of people out there... When it's time for you to leave the hospital, you'll come stay with us on the farm... How could you be any trouble? You're family... Don't you argue with me."

At this juncture, I poked my head into the room and said to Marcus, "I wouldn't argue with her if I were you," and then to Sue, "You should let him rest."

Sue had been holding his hand. She gently laid it back onto the bed and patted it. "I'll be back later."

"Do you need anything else right now?" I asked Sue when she stepped from the room.

"No."

"I need to get back. Mrs. Stevens and Abbie are leaving today."

Spring 1988

G ladys did her best to keep the bank running, but her best efforts weren't enough to offset the arrogance and incompetence of George Jr. She had a series of difficult conversations with him that all ended the same way: he would insult her and tell her to get out of his office.

"We have to do this in order to comply with FSLIC rules," Gladys would say.

"I say we don't. We are a privately held savings and loan. That means I can do whatever I want," George Jr. would counter.

The conversations were on various topics, but always with Gladys earnestly trying to get her boss to see that the bank was careening towards default. Then, one day, finally, the conversation ended differently.

"If we do that, we will trigger a bank examination," Gladys tried to explain.

George Jr. thought that he had been more than patient and fair with this worrywart. His grandfather had hired her. His father thought she was useful, but George Jr. couldn't see it. Now she was threatening him with a bank audit. He had had enough. "Listen, you stupid cow, my father kept you on because he felt sorry for you. Do you think you're necessary to this bank? Well, let me tell you right now, you're not! You're fired. Now get out and don't come back."

Gladys didn't respond. She couldn't believe it had come to this. After working at the bank for her entire adult life, over 40 years now, she was being thrown away. "I need to finish a few things before I go," she finally said. Even though she had just been fired, she wanted to leave things in order.

"No, you don't," George Jr. said. "We don't need you to destroy files or plant some bomb on your way out." This was the first thing that came to his mind, because, of course, it is exactly the kind of sabotage he would engage in if he were the one being fired.

Thoughts of revenge or destruction never occurred to Gladys. In fact, on her way out, she picked up the outgoing mail. She considered taking the awards and certificates from her desk, which she had earned over the years. But even though they had her name on them, she thought that they belonged to the bank. She left with her purse, coat, and the mail. She walked to the post office and was about to go in, but didn't want to face anyone, so she dropped the mail into the mailbox in front of the post office. Just then, Jeff pulled into the parking place in front of the post office and got out of his sheriff's department vehicle.

"Hi, Gladys."

"Hello, Jeff," Gladys said. She still didn't want to talk with anyone.

It didn't take law enforcement training to tell that something was wrong. "Are you feeling OK?" Jeff asked out of genuine concern.

She wasn't going to say anything. Gladys wasn't the kind of person to complain or seek sympathy, but Jeff had been one of the very few boys in high school who had been kind to her. All these years later, that made a difference. She told him everything.

"Well, that little..." Jeff stopped himself from finishing the sentence. Mad as he was, he had much practice in holding his tongue, because as a sheriff, public servant, and elected official, that was usually the best course. "Come with me." They got into his car and took the extremely short drive over to Norma's café.

The coffee loafers were going strong. It was just after ten o'clock in the morning; this was their time, the sweet spot between breakfast and lunch. "What brings an important man like you in here, sheriff?" asked one.

"You can't fill up your ticket book by sitting around here, you know," said another.

Normally, the sheriff would good-naturedly give it right back to them, but this morning, he was a man on a mission. Ignoring them, he said to Norma, "I need to make a long-distance call. I will reimburse you. Can I use your office? And could you bring some hot tea for Gladys?"

Norma was about to ask what was up, but instead, silently opened her office door and held out her hand to offer up the empty chairs. Then she went to get the tea. When she returned, Jeff was on the phone.

"No, that's not good enough. She has 40 years of banking experience, and she could bring in a hundred new clients." He paused to listen to the voice on the other end of the line. "Ray, I thought of you first, but there are other banks that will snap her right up." He paused again. "I think that would be OK. Now, how about a title?" Yet another pause, and then, "No, you come on. How about 'manager in charge of new accounts?'"

Norma was not in the habit of eavesdropping. With the stupid conversations that went on out front, she usually tried very hard not to overhear. She did have normal curiosity, however. She asked Gladys in a soft voice so as not to interrupt Jeff, "What's going on?"

"I think I just got a new job," Gladys replied. She was carried away by the events of the morning. Had she stopped to think about it, she might have retired then and there. She had continued to live with her parents after graduating from high school. She got her job at the bank and lived close enough to walk to work every day. She cared for her parents as they grew older, and she inherited the house, car, and the rest of the estate when they passed. She had never made very much money at the bank, but she still lived on much less than she earned. She invested the balance in indexed mutual funds with a company called Vanguard, which her first boss, Mr. Hagar, had suggested to her as a good place to put money for retirement. While she didn't have a million dollars in her retirement account, what she did have seemed like a fabulous sum to her and would have surprised everyone in her small town had they known.

When Jeff hung up, Norma said, "Who were you talking to?"

"That was the regional vice president of the First National Bank."

"I didn't know you knew the vice president of a big bank."

"I should. He's my brother. And don't be impressed by the title, that bank's lousy with vice presidents. They're slopping over with vice presidents. They have more vice presidents than we've got squirrels."

Norma laughed, left her office, and closed the door behind her. She would miss the convenience of taking the day's receipts down the street to the bank, but she would not trust her money to that idiot, George Jr. Now, with Gladys gone, there was no one left who knew what they were doing. She was certain the bank would fail.

Jeff wrote something on a piece of paper and passed it across the desk to Gladys. "What's this?" she asked.

"It's the starting salary I've negotiated for you. Sorry, it isn't much, but it's the best I could get out of the tightwad. After you show them what you can do, I'm sure you'll make more."

Gladys looked at the number written on the paper and put her hand to her lips. "This is more than twice as much as I make now," she said softly.

In the office, Jeff made another call. This one was to the state department of banking and finance. He identified himself as the county sheriff and formally requested an investigation into the local bank.

"I wish you hadn't done that," said Gladys.

"From what you have told me, as a law enforcement officer, I have no choice. I believe banking law is being violated, and the public good is at risk." With that, the sheriff got up and walked out of the office into the café. Gladys followed him.

"I never liked that Junior," said one coffee loafer.

"He ain't a patch to his grandpa," said another.

Jeff shot a glance at Norma and smiled. Addressing the crowd, he said, "I see that you're all up to date. Now, as a public official, it would be improper of me to recommend one bank over another. I will, however, tell you that Gladys is the new accounts manager at the First National Bank over at the county seat starting on Monday."

"Well then, that's where I'm moving my money," said yet another of the coffee loafers, followed by a chorus of like-minded comments.

One of the favorite jokes among the coffee loafers was 'What are the three fastest means of communication? Telephone, telegraph, and tell a woman.' It is, however, doubtful that any group of women anywhere could spread the word more effectively than this group of old guys. By the end of the day, almost everyone in the western half of the county was planning on changing banks the following week.

JUNE 2019

I got back to the farm as Jackie was loading her car. Without being asked, Charlie and Jake had helped her carry her bags from the cabin. When I walked up to her, she asked, "How is Marcus?"

"He seems pretty good, all things considered."

"I don't know him at all, but it still seems wrong that we're leaving. It's almost like we're abandoning him. Isn't that silly?"

"Not at all. I know just what you mean. There's something about this place that just sucks you in and makes you feel like you want to be part of it."

"It's the people. That's what it is," she said with that great smile of hers. "My brother was right about this place. Abbie and I have enjoyed our time here. Now, the hard part," she said as she looked over at the swing set where Abbie was playing with Alisha and Katie. We walked over to the girls. "Time to go, Abbie."

"No," said Abbie, simply.

"We talked about this last night, remember. We said goodbye to the ponies, and now it is time to say goodbye to your friends."

"But I don't want to go. I want to stay here," Abbie said while trying to work herself up into an emotional fit. Alisha and Katie began to cry. Mrs. Stevens picked up Abbie. Mrs. Williams came over, kneeled, and hugged Alisha. I put my hand on Katie's shoulder. She was used to people coming and going, but she was carried away with the moment.

"I know it's sad when our friends have to go home," said Mrs. Williams.

Alisha snuggled into her mother's shoulder and agreed by saying, "Uh-huh."

Mrs. Stevens began carrying Abbie toward the car when Abbie shouted, "I didn't say goodbye to Slobber." I don't know where the dog was, but he heard his name and came running. At the car, Mrs. Stevens set Abbie down, and she hugged Slobber around the neck. "Goodbye, Slobber."

"Now it is time to go," said Mrs. Stevens as she picked Abbie up and buckled her into her car seat.

Everyone waved as they drove off down the long driveway.

"Let me see. Whose turn is it?" I looked around. "Jake and Mary, come with me."

We went into the just vacated cabin and began cleaning. Jake stripped the beds, and I cleaned the bathroom while Mary dusted. Jake began to put fresh sheets on the beds as I caught a glimpse of Mary sneaking up behind him and touching the duster to the top of his head. Jake reached up and scratched his head with his left hand as Mary tried not to laugh. Then she did it again. This time when he reached up to scratch, he touched the duster. He turned, shouted, and chased a giggling Mary around the room.

"If you two want to run around, run these dirty sheets to the laundry and have Charlie start a load of laundry."

"I know how to do the washer," said Mary.

"Have Charlie do it," I reiterated, the vision of a laundry room full of suds going through my head.

The two bundled up the dirty sheets and took off for the house. In a little over half an hour, I had the cabin in good shape and ready for the next guest. I walked to the house and into the laundry room. The sheets were still in the washer, so I went to the kitchen and got a glass of lemonade. I called to check in with Sue. Marcus was resting; she was fine, and nothing had really changed. It was a nice day, so once the washer finished, I took the sheets out the back door and hung them on the line. When I went back around the house, I saw Mr. Williams sitting in the big rocking chair on the front porch.

"I can't believe this is the last day I get to do this," he said. "I feel a little like that little girl, Abbie, when I think about checking out tomorrow."

"Don't start crying or you'll get me started," I said. He chuckled.

"I'm serious, though, when I say that I've had a really great time here. I know the girls have had fun, and even though she probably won't admit it, I think Peg has enjoyed herself, too."

"That makes me happier than you'll ever know," I said. "So, what would you like to do on your last day here?"

"There is not a thing in the world wrong with doing this," he said.

"I think I can make it better." I left him rocking on the porch as I went into the kitchen and poured a tall glass of lemonade. I walked back out onto the porch and handed it to him. "There," I said. "Now, isn't that better?"

"Perfect."

SPRING 1988

When the man from the state department of banking and finance came to town, he interviewed George Jr, Gladys, and two of the bank tellers. He also checked in with the sheriff. First, he interviewed George Jr. at the bank. As one might expect, George Jr. tried to blame everything on his disgruntled, former employee, Gladys. The more he spoke and tried to obfuscate, the clearer the picture became for the bank examiner. When he interviewed Gladys in her home, he came away with the surprising thought that this high school graduate might be one of the smartest, most capable bankers he had ever interviewed. After speaking with the tellers one at a time, he gained a sense of the working atmosphere in the bank. The next day, a team of four auditors arrived with an order authorizing them to review all the bank's records for the past seven years. The day after that, the bank was closed, but only for one day. When it reopened, it was a government-controlled bank. The auditors took more than a month to review all the transactions. On the first day, they found enough evidence of fraud and misappropriation to suggest a criminal investigation. After a full month, the case moved from county to state and then finally to federal jurisdiction.

Jeff met with the county attorney. Both men were unhappy that the federal authorities had taken over. The county attorney had wanted to try an interesting case for a change. As for Jeff, his chief regret was that he didn't get to put handcuffs on George Jr. He was consoled by being present when George Jr's car was taken from him. It was bank property.

George Jr. was tried in federal court in Lincoln. He was found guilty and sentenced to a white-collar prison. The people of the county thought he got off easy.

After much legal wrangling, Mrs. Newport was allowed to keep her house. There had been much speculation that it was bank property, but Mr. Newport had a deed in his name that passed to his wife upon his death. Within a year, she sold the house and moved away. The rumor was that she remarried in Denver to a real estate agent. No one in town was sure of this, though, except for Mrs. Burton.

JUNE 2019

When Sue came home that evening, the kids fell all over themselves trying to be the first to hug her. I managed to get in a glancing kiss as she said hello to everyone. After she had given an update on Marcus' condition, she said that she needed to go upstairs for a minute but would be right back down to start supper. I went up to check on her a few minutes later to find her lying across the bed, asleep. I took off her shoes, put a blanket over her, and pulled the door shut as quietly as I could. I went back downstairs and outside. I had Charlie and Jake pull the picnic tables around to the front of the house. "In honor of the Williamses last night with us, we are grilling out," I announced. The real reason, of course, was that I didn't want all the commotion in the kitchen to wake Sue. I was sure she hadn't gotten much sleep in the last couple of days.

As I grilled steaks, I asked my guests what they would most like to do on their last evening with us.

"Pony ride," said Leah enthusiastically.

"You have had a hundred pony rides this week, girl," said Mrs. Williams.

"I want a hundred and one," she answered back with a big smile.

"I know a young man who would be thrilled to make that happen for you," I said.

Charlie rolled his eyes but said nothing. Sasha said to him, "I'll help."

"How about you, Alisha. What would you most like to do?"

An interesting thing happened. She didn't hide from my question by burying her face on her mother's side. She looked back at me and said, "Put my feet in the water."

I wasn't sure what she meant at first. "Oh, you want to go fishing," I said.

"No. Just put my feet in the water."

"You liked sitting on the dock beside your father and putting your feet in the pond, didn't you?" asked Mrs. Williams. Alisha nodded her head to confirm it. "Then how about after supper we walk back to the pond with your father and soak our feet?" She turned to me and said, "Before you ask me what I want, I'll save you the time. I want the same thing as my baby girl."

I turned to Mr. Williams and said, "I don't have to ask you, sir. But just so you know, I can't make it get dark any sooner."

"It's only been a week, but you already know me so well."

FALL 1990

It was nice for Abe to have the family back together, if only for a couple of days. Marcus was home on leave. Sue was home from college. Abe had invited Jeff to come out and catch up with the kids. They had eaten a big meal and were now sitting on the porch.

"Where all have you been?" Jeff asked Marcus.

"I have set foot on Guam, the Philippines, Japan, South Korea, Australia, and New Zealand," Marcus said. "Though I have to admit, I've seen a lot more water than land."

"It must be something to see so much of the world," said Abe. "I've only been out of the state a couple times in my whole life."

"It does give me stories to tell, that's for sure. But—." He paused for a long time. No one jumped in to fill the void. They let him take his time to say what he needed to. Finally, he finished his sentence. "I have never felt more at home at any time or at any place than I do right here, right now. Isn't that crazy?"

"Why would that be crazy?"

"I just couldn't wait to get out of here. I always knew I was an outsider. It didn't matter where — at school, in church, in town — I didn't belong anywhere. Except, maybe here."

"This little farm isn't such a bad place. I was born here. I've lived my whole life here. I plan to grow old and die here." As Abe said this, Jeff shot him a glance.

"My, aren't you two uplifting speakers," joked Sue.

"I didn't mean to bring everything down. What I really wanted to say is, well, that I love you three. I'm proud to call you my family and my friends." Marcus looked down. He was embarrassed by what he'd said, but at the same time, he wasn't. "I never said that to Sarah. That will probably end up being the greatest regret of my life." When he looked back up, his eyes were shining.

"I'm proud of you, son. You know that don't you?" Abe just managed to say.

Sue hugged Marcus around the neck, and Jeff reached over and put his hand on Marcus's shoulder. He didn't say a word, but he didn't have to.

"Well now, little Miss Uplifting, what about you? How's college?" asked Jeff.

Sue released Marcus from her python-like hug and sat back in her chair. "Well," she started uncertainly, "Classes are going all right." Now it was her turn to pause. She blurted out, "I met the most wonderful boy."

"You?" Marcus said in mock shock.

Abe looked on with that strange emotional mix that only comes with parenthood. His daughter was beaming a smile that could light up the whole barnyard at midnight. He hadn't seen her this happy since she was a very little girl, and he felt, for a moment, the joy that parents feel when they know that their children are happy. At the same time, he felt the dread of the inevitable: his daughter growing up and moving away from him. She was already gone most of the time at the university. Now she was home to tell him of her great love for some guy Abe had not yet met.

"So, tell us about him," commanded Jeff.

"His name is Bob. He's majoring in hospitality."

"What's that?" asked Abe.

"Running hotels and restaurants and such," said Jeff. "Now, quiet, let her tell it."

"We met at a party. I wasn't even going to go, but I wanted to dance. I hadn't danced in so long. He asked me to dance, and I think I surprised him by saying 'Yes' so fast." Sue laughed and then continued. "He was a terrible dancer, but he was so sweet. He kept apologizing for stepping on my feet. He asked me to teach him to dance better. I knew it wasn't because he cared about dancing. He wanted to be a better dancer for me. Because he could tell that dancing was important to me. We talked the rest of the evening and met the next day for his dance lesson. We went out to eat and just talked for hours. It was so easy to talk to him, and he listened to me. Really listened. I've never met a boy like him before." Sue knew she was gushing, but she didn't care. She expected the three men to make fun of her, but they were looking at her with big smiles.

Not the kind of smirk that is the precursor of an insult, but the warm smile of someone who loves you and is happy for you.

"When do we get to meet Prince Charming?" asked Marcus. Brothers are duty-bound to give their sisters a hard time.

"I'm not sure," Sue said seriously. "I invited him for this weekend," she looked at her father, "I know I should have asked you first, Dad, but I want you all to meet him. He had to work. He works the night shift on weekends at a local hotel doing the books. He picks up construction jobs sometimes for extra money." She began warming to the subject again, "He wants to work in the great hotels all over the world. He has a plan for his life for the next fifty years. He wants to travel and see the world. Not just see the world, but live all over and really experience..." She looked around. "I guess I sound a little foolish, don't I?"

"Not at all, honey," said Jeff. "You sound just exactly like what you are: a young woman in love."

Sue's face reddened. "I guess I am."

"What is Bob's full name?" asked Jeff.

"Robert Ansley Comstock."

"You know his middle name?" her father asked.

"His middle name is Ansley?" asked Marcus.

"Why are you writing that down?" Sue asked Jeff. Jeff had written Robert Ansley Comstock on a small notebook and then returned it to his breast pocket.

"My guess, your boyfriend is about to get a background check by the sheriff's department of Arnold County," said Marcus.

"Jeff, you wouldn't," said Sue.

"I would," came the reply.

"Maybe we should talk about something else for a minute," suggested Marcus.

Jeff looked over at Abe. "Maybe it's about time we did." Abe just shook his head *no*, in reply.

"I've lost track, Marcus. How much longer do you have to serve?" asked Sue.

"To pay for the four years of my naval academy training I owe the United States Navy five years. I've done over four, so I've got less than a year to go. So, I need to think about what I'm going to do next."

"What are your thoughts?" asked Abe.

"I'm not sure, to tell you the truth. I haven't felt the pressure to think about my future until now. That's the problem when you know about what your life is going to be for nearly a decade. I could make choices within the framework, of course, like what to study, and what specialty I wanted to pursue, but all in all, everything was laid out for me."

"Are you thinking about re-upping?" asked Jeff.

"I've thought about it, but I don't think I will. The Navy is a rigid place. Everything is seen in absolute terms: right and wrong with no grey areas. I don't mean to talk it down; I like the structure. I think everyone can benefit from discipline, but it can get a little tight, sometimes."

"I know you didn't like the academy," said Sue. "But I saw a change in your letters when you got the ship you wanted. You sounded happy."

"Happier," said Marcus. "It's hard work, every day, but at least I'm not in the academy anymore."

"Sounds to me like you didn't care for the academy," said Jeff.

"Oh, he hated the naval academy," said Sue.

"There were times I did, yes," said Marcus, "But most of the time I only disliked it." Everyone laughed. "Oh, don't laugh. I had my reasons. I had excellent room inspections until one time, I was written up because the shirts on hangers in my closet weren't spaced exactly two inches apart. The guy brought a ruler. He was looking to find any reason to write me up, and I got the feeling he wouldn't have left the room until he found one."

"There's a ringing endorsement," said Abe.

"That's just the way the Navy is. You sit down to eat your soup with a spoon, and someone of a higher rank tells you to use a fork. You'd better not argue. You'd better do it, even though you know it won't work. It won't matter, though, because someone of an even higher rank will then tell you to use your knife."

"It does sound like maybe it's time to consider life outside of the Navy," said Abe.

"Yes. I think so too. It's just that the thought of life outside of that rigid structure is scary."

"You? Scared?" said Sue.

"Maybe scared is the wrong word. More like uncertain."

"I'm trying to remember an old song, goes something like 'looking back and longing for the freedom of my chains,'" mused Jeff.

"Olivia Newton-John, I think," said Sue. "I don't remember the title of the song."

"I can't remember either. I must be getting old. All I have is one line of a song floating through my head, and I can't dredge up the rest," said Jeff.

"Still, you should be thankful for that uncertainty. It means you've got choices. In your case, lots of them. Naval academy graduate and veteran will open a lot of doors for you," Abe said, steering the conversation back around.

"I hate to say it, because I've had such a good time catching up with you kids, but I've got to get up early in the morning," said Jeff.

"Me, too, sheriff," said Abe. "I'll walk you to your car."

"Don't go. It's still early," said Sue.

"Yeah. I haven't seen you for a year," said Marcus.

"In case you two have forgotten, this is a dairy farm. I've still got to get up at 4am," said Abe.

"I'll be sure to see you before you have to leave, Marcus," said Jeff. "And Sue, I'm sure I'll see you again whenever you can get away from college for another quick weekend visit."

"More like whenever she can tear herself away from her boyfriend," said Marcus. Sue punched him in the arm. As Abe and Jeff walked from the porch to the car, Marcus called after them, "And let me know the results of Ansley's background check." Without turning around, Jeff waved over his head in acknowledgement. Sue punched Marcus in the arm again, a little harder this time.

When they got to the car and out of earshot, Jeff asked, "I thought you were going to tell them tonight?"

"I was."

"Well then, why didn't you?"

"You heard why. My daughter's in love. My son said he was home. I've waited 20 years to hear him say that."

"There was a time I didn't think you cared one way or another about that boy."

"Yeah, well, I was young and dumb. Now, I'm older and wiser."

"You're older, anyway."

Abe tried to laugh, but he turned serious. "I just want them to have one last happy night at home before I tell them."

JUNE 2019

I shook hands with Mr. Williams. "I've enjoyed having your family here. Just so you know, I don't say that to everyone."

He smiled and said, "Bob, you'll never know how much I've enjoyed it here. Your family is wonderful, and your sky is — " he paused. "I don't have the words to do it justice."

"I was surprised that you didn't have your telescope out last night."

"The things you can see out here with the naked eye are quite impressive. To have my last night out here be so cloudless and clear was a real blessing."

"Yes, well, I arranged that special for you," I joked.

"When I walked back from the pond last night, I saw you on top of a long ladder unscrewing that barnyard light, so I know you arranged that."

"It's on a sensor. It comes on automatically when it gets dark. I figured you'd be able to see better without it." I rubbed the back of my neck. I didn't want our last conversation to get too serious. "Just one more thing. Around here, when a man stands out in the middle of a field at night all by himself for more than two hours, well, people are apt to think that he's crazy."

"My wife already thinks that. She knows me better than everyone else in the world, so that's probably the proper assessment."

"Well, crazy — or that he was tricked into holding a snipe bag."

We started a slow walk to his SUV. Mrs. Williams was talking with Sue. They were holding hands. I couldn't hear the conversation, but I heard each of them say something about Marcus. In the tangle of kids saying goodbye to one another, Sasha and Charlie stood facing each other but not looking at each other. Finally, Sasha leaned in and gave Charlie a quick kiss on the cheek. Then she turned and bolted for the car. I marveled that there was still innocence in the world.

"We were going to stop off at the hospital to see Marcus on our way home, but Sue said they still won't let anyone but family see him," said Mrs. Williams.

"I'm afraid that will be for a few more days yet," Sue confirmed.

Looking at me, Mrs. Williams said, "When we first got here, I knew I would hate it, but it wasn't that bad."

"So, did you put 'exceeded expectations' on your comment card?" I asked.

"You have comment cards?" Mrs. Williams asked. Swing and a miss, I thought. Mr. Williams was trying to hide a smile behind his hand. As Mrs. Williams put Alisha into her car seat, we walked to the driver's side.

"Do we hug now, or what?" Mr. Williams asked me.

"Not around here, we don't."

He laughed that great laugh of his, reached over, and wrapped me in a big hug. "Safe travels," I said as he released me and got into his car.

He rolled down the driver's side window. "Goodbye, Ansley," he said and then drove away.

"I swear, I'm going to put Jell-O into Marcus's IV," I shouted after him.

FALL 1990

At breakfast the next morning, Abe sat down at the huge kitchen table with his children. He looked at them and realized that not only were they fine adults, but that he and Sarah had a hand in getting them there. Mostly Sarah, though, he thought.

"What are you smiling at, Dad?" Sue asked.

He decided to come out and say it. "At the fine adults that you two have grown up to be."

Sue and Marcus smiled proudly but said nothing.

"There are some other things I need to tell you while you're both here."

"That sounds ominous," said Marcus.

Abe started easy. "I've sold off about 200 acres. I'll probably sell quite a bit more. My hope is that there will be something to leave to you two when I'm gone."

His audience was confused. Sue said, "But, you're not old. Why are you doing this?"

"I'm 67."

"That's no answer."

Marcus jumped in, "Why are you doing this, really? If you want to slow down or retire, you can do that without selling the place off. What's going on?"

"I've got medical bills." He stopped and composed himself.

"You're sick?"

He didn't feel sorry for himself; he felt sorry that what he had to say would cause his children pain. "A few months ago, I thought I had the flu. It hung on for so long that I finally went to see the doctor. He ran a bunch of tests, and when the results came back, well, that's when he gave me the long face."

"What is it?" asked Marcus.

"Cancer, same thing that took Pop."

"But that's not a death sentence, they cure that all the time now, Dad," said Sue, the desperation rising in her voice.

"It's all through me. Not one thing to cut out, hundreds. Radiation won't work because they can't target one area. The way the doctor explained it, they try to zap one place with that poison to kill the cancer without the poison killing you. It's all over me, so there is no one spot. Doc said, if it was him, he wouldn't even start with that stuff. I'd be sick for all of whatever time I have left."

"There must be something they can do," said Sue.

"I could get another opinion, maybe find someone who would hook me up to that poison, but I might never leave the hospital. Right now, I feel pretty good. Doc says I could have a lot more good days."

"I've got a little money. You can have it all. You don't have to sell the place," said Marcus.

"The bills are all paid in full. I just want to do this while I feel up to it. Big Mike is sending his boys out next week to take the cows for auction. Usually, the seller has to haul them in, but Big Mike is doing me the favor. Then the milking machines, and most of the farm equipment will go."

"We could borrow money. You don't have to — "

"Your mother and I learned a difficult lesson about debt years ago." Marcus swallowed hard. Abe continued, "We worked and saved and did without to get out of debt, and then we stayed there. I kept that old combine running for ten years past what it should have. When it died for good, we didn't replace it. There was no way to save the money for a new one, so instead of planting our usual crops, I put everything into hay. I fed the cows and sold the extra bales. Your mother and I didn't make as much money as we could have, but we never went into debt again."

"If all the bills are paid, then why are you selling?"

"I'm selling all the livestock because in a few months, I may not be able to take care of them anymore. I'm selling the land—I'm hoping to keep 80 acres—because I want to be sitting on a pile of cash when the bills for the last few months of my life come in. I may have to spend my last days in a hospital or one of those what-do-you-call-ems."

"Hospice."

"Yeah. One of those."

"I always knew you were a brave man, but I never knew how brave until this very minute," said Marcus.

"What's brave? I'm doing what I need to so I can pay my own way, no matter what comes at me. I don't want you two to have to worry about anything. Well, I am going to keep a few chickens. I love having fresh eggs in the morning."

"What can I do?" asked Sue.

"You can finish college. I've got the money part of that covered. You just need to do the studying, graduate, and live your life. One last thing. Tell that fella of yours to take a weekend off. Bring him out here. I'd like to meet him."

JUNE 2019

"I 'm sure the kids will be OK on their own for a few hours. Charlie is very responsible, and Jake is a lot of help as well."

"What about Mary?"

I thought that one over for a minute. "Perhaps they could duct tape her to a chair," I suggested.

"Would you be serious?"

"Just trying to be helpful."

"Look, you stay here and do the birthday party. I'll go visit Marcus by myself."

"I want to see Marcus, too. It's silly for us to take two cars just so you can visit for a few hours longer. You drive down, I do the birthday party, then drive down in another car, and then we both drive back. That's just a waste."

The phone rang before we could escalate our disagreement into a major fight. I answered it. My boss Gene needed me to cover the night shift. Shelly was sick.

"OK. I just want you to remember that I gave in on this one. Our next argument, it's your turn," I said to Sue after I hung up the phone.

"Your boss wants you to come in tonight, doesn't he?"

"Yes, he does."

Sue walked triumphantly out to the car and drove off. A few minutes later, I walked outside as the Milburn birthday party came up the drive in four vehicles, and kids tumbled out in every direction. Slobber was on hand to greet them.

"Slobber! Slobber, don't eat those children."

The birthday party went on longer than I had hoped. By the time they left, I knew I didn't have time for a nap. I changed into my interstate motel clothes, then told the kids to behave and do as Charlie says. I avoided eye contact with Mary and drove away. This would be yet another long day. My home was in one county, Marcus' hospital was in a second county, and my motel job was in a third.

When I got to the hospital, the nurse was nowhere in sight, so I snuck into Marcus' room, breaking the one visitor rule, as Sue was already there. Marcus was dozing, but roused when I came in.

"Ansley!" I said loudly, in mock anger, but not loud enough to bother anyone in another room.

A smile slowly spread over Marcus' face. "Don't make me laugh," he said weakly. "I'll pull my stitches out."

"You felt the need to tell Mr. Williams my middle name?"

"Henry seems like a nice guy. I thought he should know."

"He said he wanted to stop by and see you on his way back home, but your sister wouldn't let him." I was feeling playful and lobbed this one at Sue.

"I just told him — ." Sue stopped in mid-sentence, probably remembering the old country adage, "Never wrestle with a pig in mud. You won't accomplish anything but getting dirty, and the pig enjoys it."

"What's wrong?" I asked her, smiling.

"You're an idiot," she answered.

"I'm calling security," said Marcus.

I dropped the act. "Mr. Williams really did want to stop and see you."

"Wish I had more time to talk to him. He seems like a good guy."

"That's one of the real downsides to the hotel business. The people you take a liking to are gone too soon, and the ones you don't like seem like they will never leave."

"I was surprised that Henry spent so much time with you and me. I thought he'd want all the time he could get with his family, this being their vacation," Marcus said.

"Oh, he spent most of his time with his wife and daughters. It's obvious that he loves his family. Living with four women, I think he just needed a little guy time," I said.

"Speaking of family," Marcus turned to Sue. "You've been here for hours every day. Go home. Spend some time with those kids."

Sue stood up and turned to me. "Oh, Bob, before I forget, I wanted to tell you I'm taking the kids to church on Sunday," she said.

"What did you do, promise God if Marcus was OK, you'd go back to church?" It came out of my mouth as a joke, but I realized right away that it was exactly what happened. I had spent the same number of hours not knowing if Marcus would live or die, but I had spent them at home. Sue had been sitting in a hospital waiting room, not exactly alone because of all the cops that were there, but without the support I'd had. It was no wonder she had bargained with God.

"Over the last couple of days, almost every preacher from Arnold County has stopped by to visit Marcus. Each of them spent time talking with me while Marcus slept. I already knew, by that time, that Marcus would be all right, but still, they offered comfort when I needed it."

"Still, you don't need to — " I started to say before she cut me off. I knew her family had always gone to church and that something had happened to sour her on the experience. I just didn't know what.

"I do, and I owe it to the children to offer them the same experience I had growing up. I was foolish. I just seemed to forget the kindness shown to me by most of the congregation. I let the bad behavior of a few people drive me away. I thought that people in church should be better than people who didn't go. Going to church doesn't make you any better than anyone else, but it certainly doesn't make you worse."

I didn't know what all was contained in those few sentences, but I would have plenty of time to figure it out. More importantly, I would do what I could to help Sue struggle with it and figure it out for herself. "I work this Saturday night, but I should be home in plenty of time to go with you and the kids."

"Church can provide structure for the kids," said Marcus. "Structure is good."

"Structure is good. I think I got that in a fortune cookie once," I said.

"It's the best I can do with all the pain meds they're pouring into me."

Sue squeezed his hand and kissed him on the forehead. "I'll be back tomorrow. Call if you need anything at all."

"I will," he said as Sue took the first few steps of her long journey home. She touched my arm with her hand and smiled at me as she walked past. When she had left the room, he said, "I can't help but notice that she didn't kiss you goodbye."

"She likes you more than she does me."

"That goes without saying, doesn't it?"

"Are they letting you eat anything yet?"

"Just from this plastic bag," he pointed to his IV.

"Good. I'm bringing in a big ole greasy cheeseburger and eating it all in front of you."

"Eat it slowly, so I can enjoy it, too.

"Really, now. What can I bring you?"

"Don't need a thing. I'm lucky to be here, you know?"

"All right, then. What do you want to do when you get out of this dump?"

"I've been thinking a lot about that. I think it's time for me to go to Colorado and see those mountains. I'm only running 50 years behind."

"From what I hear, they're still there."

The duty nurse walked into the room. "Visiting hours are over. You have to go."

"This is my brother-in-law," Marcus said.

"I don't care if he's the Prince of Wales. Visiting hours are over."

"I'll drop by tomorrow."

"You do that. And don't forget the cheeseburger."

"You will do no such thing. This man has severe internal injuries. Solid food is absolutely forbidden."

"How about if I put it in a blender?" I inquired.

"Out."

"Tomorrow," I said as I waved and started out the door.

"Later, man," Marcus said after me.

As I drove to work, I thought about Marcus. The guy was facing a long recovery and yet he seemed happy. How does he do that? It occurred to me that Sue seemed happy as well. While the thought pleased me, it also baffled me. I've given her so little over the years. Perhaps true happiness comes from being grateful for what you have and not caring about all the things you don't have. Is that the secret? Could it really be that simple? Or, maybe, it's just being in the right place and knowing it.

Both Sue and Marcus are of the farm. Even Slobber is of the farm. He protects the children. He protects the garden from the deer and rabbits. He protects the chickens from coyotes and foxes and is happy doing all of it. Then it occurred to me that Mr. Claws was not what I thought of as of the farm, but he was useful. Even with all our buildings surrounded by fields, we very rarely see a mouse. Sure, he is bad-tempered and no good with people, but he belongs. He just showed up one day and never left. Kind of like me.

I don't have much, but viewed another way, what I've got is quite a lot. Sue said she had been foolish. I suspect that describes me more than it does her. For years, I've felt like an outsider because a few people haven't accepted me. So what? Most people have. Slowly at first, to be sure, but over the years I've tried to be a worthy part of the community, and the folks in the area have responded in kind. How could I be so foolish as to let the opinions of a few color the way I feel about this little part of the world and my place in it? I resolved to be happy if I could.

When I got out of the car in the motel parking lot, I looked up at the sky. I could see the moon and a couple of stars, but that was about it. The parking lot was bright, and the only thing louder than the buzzing of those lights was the traffic noise of the interstate. I don't belong at a big fancy corporate hotel like the ones I dreamed of in my youth. It doesn't matter that the luxury resorts of the world are infinitely more posh than the little farm. I'm also well aware that the population base in the area isn't big enough to support my family business, at least not as a full-time job. I'll probably have to work here or at some other motel part-time, as well as at construction jobs, for years to come. It doesn't matter. I have a place to go home to. A place where I belong. A place with a million-dollar view of the stars.

ACKNOWLEDGEMENTS

When I finished the first draft of this book in the fall of 2020, I was very proud of myself. Then I looked back over what I had written. I wasn't going to show it to anyone, but I finally asked my daughter, Elizabeth, to read it and tell me what she thought. She said, "You've got the bones of a good story here." That simple statement, brilliant in its own way, encouraged me to keep working on it. If she'd told me it was great I'd have known she was trying to spare my feelings, and I would have put the book into a dark drawer, never to be seen again. Thanks, honey, I owe you one.

As I continued rewriting, I asked several others to read it and offer their feedback. I am greatly in the debt of Mary Jane McPherson, Jan Deeds, Jennifer Morgan, and Kim Klescewski. Your comments and suggestions helped me improve the manuscript and turn it into an actual novel.

Finally, I need to thank the person who set up a space in the corner of the basement where I could block out the chaos and write for a couple of hours every night after work. Perhaps that doesn't sound like much, but it made all the difference. I also need to thank my editor, tech support, accountant, and entire office staff. Fortunately for me, all those job titles belong to the same person: my wife Barb. Thank you; I couldn't have done it without you.

ABOUT THE AUTHOR

Howard Sanford is an old man, newly retired, and the author of one book. He is severely technologically impaired, has no social media presence of any kind, doesn't understand websites, but is quite proud of the fact that he has a Gmail address. He lives the good life in Nebraska with his wife and daughter.